FLOWERS FOR ALGERNON made its first appearance in print as a short story which was widely anthologized and translated internationally. It received further acclaim as a memorable television drama, and was rapidly purchased for film production. Then, enlarged and richly peopled, Daniel Keyes' haunting story became an award-winning novel—recipient of the Nebula Award for the Best Novel of the Year by the Science Fiction Writers of America.

This fascinating tale of a daring human experiment has been described as "a love triangle between two people," "a suspenseful, gripping story," and "a brilliant fantasy." It is all these things. It is one of the most strikingly original and engrossing novels of our time!

FLOWERS FOR ALGERNON

FLOWERS FOR ALGERNON
By Daniel Keyes

BANTAM BOOKS
TORONTO · NEW YORK · LONDON · SYDNEY · AUCKLAND

*This low-priced Bantam Book
has been completely reset in a type face
designed for easy reading, and was printed
from new plates. It contains the complete
text of the original hard-cover edition.*
NOT ONE WORD HAS BEEN OMITTED.

RL 7, IL age 13 and up

FLOWERS FOR ALGERNON

*A Bantam Book / published by arrangement with
Harcourt Brace Jovanovich, Inc.*

PRINTING HISTORY

Harcourt edition published March 1966
2nd printing .... April 1966

*Bantam edition / October 1967
30 printings through July 1972
Bantam Pathfinder edition / October 1972*

32nd printing	..November 1972	35th printing	....January 1974
33rd printing	.......May 1973	36th printing	......June 1974
34th printing	........July 1973	37th printing	......April 1975

Bantam edition / July 1975

39th printing	......June 1976	47th printing	.......July 1980
40th printing	....October 1976	48th printing	...February 1981
41st printing	....February 1977	49th printing	...September 1981
42nd printing	......June 1977	50th printing	....January 1982
43rd printing	....October 1977	51st printing	......April 1983
44th printing	...September 1978	52nd printing	....March 1984
45th printing	......June 1979	53rd printing	...December 1984
46th printing	....October 1979	54th printing	...September 1985

*All rights reserved.
Copyright © 1959, 1966 by Daniel Keyes.
This book may not be reproduced in whole or in part, by
mimeograph or any other means, without permission.
For information address: Harcourt Brace Jovanovich, Inc.,
1250 Sixth Ave., San Diego, CA 92101.*

ISBN 0-553-25665-3

Published simultaneously in the United States and Canada

PRINTED IN THE UNITED STATES OF AMERICA

H   62 61 60 59 58 57 56

For my mother
And in memory of my father

Any one who has common sense will remember that the bewilderments of the eyes are of two kinds, and arise from two causes, either from coming out of the light or from going into the light, which is true of the mind's eye, quite as much as of the bodily eye; and he who remembers this when he sees any one whose vision is perplexed and weak, will not be too ready to laugh; he will first ask whether that soul of man has come out of the brighter life, and is unable to see because unaccustomed to the dark, or having turned from darkness to the day is dazzled by excess of light. And he will count the one happy in his condition and state of being, and he will pity the other; or, if he have a mind to laugh at the soul which comes from below into the light, there will be more reason in this than in the laugh which greets him who returns from above out of the light into the den.

Plato, *The Republic*

progris riport 1 march 3

Dr Strauss says I shoud rite down what I think and remembir and evrey thing that happins to me from now on.
I dont no why but he says its importint so they will see if
they can use me. I hope they use me becaus Miss Kinnian
says mabye they can make me smart. I want to be smart.
My name is Charlie Gordon I werk in Donners bakery
where Mr Donner gives me 11 dollers a week and bred or
cake if I want. I am 32 yeres old and next munth is my
brithday. I tolld dr Strauss and perfesser Nemur I cant
rite good but he says it dont matter he says I shud rite
just like I talk and like I rite compushishens in Miss Kinnians class at the beekmin collidge center for retarted
adults where I go to lern 3 times a week on my time off. Dr.
Strauss says to rite a lot evrything I think and evrything
that happins to me but I cant think anymor because I
have nothing to rite so I will close for today . . . yrs
truly Charlie Gordon.

progris riport 2—march 4

I had a test today. I think I faled it and I think mabye
now they wont use me. What happind is I went to Prof
Nemurs office on my lunch time like they said and his se-
cretery took me to a place that said psych dept on the
door with a long hall and alot of littel rooms with onley a
desk and chares. And a nice man was in one of the rooms
and he had some wite cards with ink spilld all over them.
He sed sit down Charlie and make yourself cunfortible
and rilax. He had a wite coat like a docter but I dont
think he was no docter because he dint tell me to opin my

mouth and say ah. All he had was those wite cards. His name is Burt. I fergot his last name because I dont remembir so good.

I dint know what he was gonna do and I was holding on tite to the chair like sometimes when I go to a dentist onley Burt aint no dentist neither but he kept telling me to rilax and that gets me skared because it always means its gonna hert.

So Burt sed Charlie what do you see on this card. I saw the spilld ink and I was very skared even tho I got my rabits foot in my pockit because when I was a kid I always faled tests in school and I spilld ink to.

I tolld Burt I saw ink spilld on a wite card. Burt said yes and he smild and that maid me feel good. He kept terning all the cards and I tolld him somebody spilld ink on all of them red and black. I thot that was a easy test but when I got up to go Burt stoppd me and said now sit down Charlie we are not thru yet. Theres more we got to do with these cards. I dint understand about it but I remembir Dr Strauss said do anything the testor telld me even if it dont make no sense because thats testing.

I dont remembir so good what Burt said but I remembir he wantid me to say what was in the ink. I dint see nothing in the ink but Burt sed there was picturs there. I coudnt see no picturs. I reely tryed to see. I holded the card up close and then far away. Then I said if I had my eye glassis I coud probaly see better I usully only ware my eyeglassis in the movies or to watch TV but I sed maybe they will help me see the picturs in the ink. I put them on and I said now let me see the card agan I bet I find it now.

I tryed hard but I still coudnt find the picturs I only saw the ink. I tolld Burt mabey I need new glassis. He rote somthing down on a paper and I got skared of faling the test. So I tolld him it was a very nice pictur of ink with pritty points all around the eges but he shaked his head so that wasnt it neither. I asked him if other pepul saw things in the ink and he sed yes they imagen picturs in the inkblot. He tolld me the ink on the card was calld inkblot.

Burt is very nice and he talks slow like Miss Kinnian dose in her class where I go to lern reeding for slow adults. He explained me it was a *raw shok test*. He sed pepul see things in the ink. I said show me where. He dint show me he just kept saying *think* imagen theres something on the card. I tolld him I imaggen a inkblot. He shaked his head so that wasnt rite eather. He said what does it remind you of pretend its something. I closd my eyes for a long time to pretend and then I said I pretend a bottel of ink spilld all over a wite card. And thats when the point on his pencel broke and then we got up and went out.

I dont think I passd the *raw shok test.*

3d progris riport

martch 5—Dr Strauss and prof Nemur say it dont matter about the ink on the cards. I tolld them I dint spill the ink on them and I coudnt see anything in the ink. They said maybe they will still use me. I tolld Dr Strauss that Miss Kinnian never gave me tests like that only riting and reeding. He said Miss Kinnian tolld him I was her bestist pupil in the Beekman School for retarted adults and I tryed the hardist becaus I reely wantd to lern I wantid it more even then pepul who are smarter even then me.

Dr Strauss askd me how come you went to the Beekman School all by yourself Charlie. How did you find out about it. I said I dont remembir.

Prof Nemur said but why did you want to lern to reed and spell in the frist place. I tolld him because all my life I wantid to be smart and not dumb and my mom always tolld me to try and lern just like Miss Kinnian tells me but its very hard to be smart and even when I lern something in Miss Kinnians class at the school I ferget alot.

Dr Strauss rote some things on a peice of paper and prof Nemur talkd to me very sereus. He said you know Charlie we are not shure how this experamint will werk on pepul because we onley tried it up to now on animils. I said thats what Miss Kinnian tolld me but I dont even care if it herts or anything because Im strong and I will werk hard.

I want to get smart if they will let me. They said they got to get permissen from my familie but my uncle Herman who use to take care of me is ded and I dont rimember about my familie. I dint see my mother or father or my littel sister Norma for a long long long time. Mabye their ded to. Dr. Strauss askd me where they use to live. I think in brooklin. He sed they will see if mabye they can find them.

I hope I dont have to rite to much of these progris riports because it takes along time and I get to sleep very late and Im tired at werk in the morning. Gimpy hollered at me because I droppd a tray full of rolles I was carrying over to the oven. They got derty and he had to wipe them off before he put them in to bake. Gimpy hollers at me all the time when I do something rong, but he reely likes me because hes my frend. Boy if I get smart wont he be serprised.

progris riport 4

mar 6—I had more crazy tests today in case they use me. That same place but a differnt littel testing room. The nice lady who give it to me tolld me the name and I askd her how do you spell it so I can put it down rite in my progis riport. THEMATIC APPERCEPTON TEST. I dont know the frist 2 werds but I know what test means. You got to pass it or you get bad marks.

This test lookd easy because I coud see the picturs. Only this time she dint want me to tell what I saw in the picturs. That mixd me up. I tolld her yesterday Burt said I shoud tell what I saw in the ink. She said that dont make a difrence because this test is something else. Now you got to make up storys about the pepul in the picturs.

I said how can I tell storys about pepul I dont know. She said make beleeve but I tolld her thats lies. I never tell lies any more because when I was a kid I made lies and I always got hit. I got a pictur in my walet of me and Norma with Uncle Herman who got me the job to be janiter at Donners bakery before he dyed.

I said I coud make storys about them because I livd with Uncle Herman along time but the lady dint want to hear about them. She said this test and the other one the *raw shok* was for getting persinality. I laffd. I tolld her how can you get that thing from cards that sombody spilld ink on and fotos of pepul you dont even no. She lookd angrey and took the picturs away. I dont care.

I gess I faled that test too.

Then I drawed some picturs for her but I dont drawer so good. Later the other testor Burt in the wite coat came back his name is Burt Selden and he took me to a diferent place on the same 4th floor in the Beekman University that said PSYCHOLOGY LABORATORY on the door. Burt said PSYCHOLOGY means minds and LABORATORY meens a place where they make spearamints. I thot he ment like where they made the chooing gum but now I think its puzzels and games because thats what we did.

I coudnt werk the puzzels so good because it was all broke and the peices coudnt fit in the holes. One game was a paper with lines in all derections and lots of boxs. On one side it said START and on the other end it said FINISH. He tolld me that game was *amazed* and I shoud take the pencil and go from where it said START to where it said FINISH withowt crossing over any of the lines.

I dint understand the amazed and we used up a lot of papers. Then Burt said look Ill show you something lets go to the sperimental lab mabye youll get the idea. We went up to the 5th floor to another room with lots of cages and animils they had monkys and some mouses. It had a funny smel like old garbidge. And there was other pepul in wite coats playing with the animils so I thot it was like a pet store but their wasnt no customers. Burt took a wite mouse out of the cage and showd him to me. Burt said thats Algernon and he can do this amazed very good. I tolld him you show me how he does that.

Well do you know he put Algernon in a box like a big tabel with alot of twists and terns like all kinds of walls and a START and a FINISH like the paper had. Only their was a skreen over the big tabel. And Burt took out his clock and lifted up a slidding door and said lets go Algernon and the mouse sniffd 2 or 3 times and startid to run. First he ran down one long row and then when he saw he coudnt go no more he came back where he startid from and he just stood there a minit wiggeling his wiskers. Then he went off in the other derection and startid to run again.

It was just like he was doing the same thing Burt

wanted me to do with the lines on the paper. I was laffing because I thot it was going to be a hard thing for a mouse to do. But then Algernon kept going all the way threw that thing all the rite ways till he came out where it said FINISH and he made a squeek. Burt says that means he was happy because he did the thing rite.

Boy I said thats a smart mouse. Burt said woud you like to race against Algernon. I said sure and he said he had a differnt kind of amaze made of wood with rows skratched in it and an electrik stick like a pencil. And he coud fix up Algernons amaze to be the same like that one so we coud both be doing the same kind.

He moved all the bords around on Algernons tabel because they come apart and he could put them together in differnt ways. And then he put the skreen back on top so Algernon woudnt jump over any rows to get to the FINISH. Then he gave me the electrik stick and showd me how to put it in between the rows and Im not suppose to lift it off the bord just follow the little skratches until the pencil cant move any more or I get a little shock.

He took out his clock and he was trying to hide it. So I tryed not to look at him and that made me very nervus.

When he said go I tryed to go but I dint know where to go. I didnt know the way to take. Then I herd Algernon squeeking from the box on the tabel and his feet skratching like he was runing alredy. I startid to go but I went in the rong way and got stuck and a littel shock in my fingers so I went back to the START but evertime I went a differnt way I got stuck and a shock. It didnt hert or anything just made me jump a littel and Burt said it was to show me I did the wrong thing. I was haffway on the bord when I herd Algernon squeak like he was happy again and that means he won the race.

And the other ten times we did it over Algernon won evry time because I coudnt find the right rows to get to where it says FINISH. I dint feel bad because I watched Algernon and I lernd how to finish the amaze even if it takes me along time.

I dint know mice were so smart.

progris riport 5   mar 6

They found my sister Norma who lives with my mother
in Brooklin and she gave permissen for the operashun. So
their going to use me. Im so exited I can hardley rite it
down. But then Prof Nemur and Dr Strauss had a arga-
ment about it frist. I was sitting in Prof Nemurs office
when Dr Strauss and Burt Selden came in. Prof Nemur
was worryed about using me but Dr Strauss tolld him I
looked like the best one they testid so far. Burt tolld him
Miss Kinnian rekemmended me the best from all the people who she was teaching at the center for retarted adults.
Where I go.

Dr Strauss said I had something that was very good.
He said I had a good motor-vation. I never even knowed
I had that. I felt good when he said not everbody with an
eye-Q of 68 had that thing like I had it. I dont know
what it is or where I got it but he said Algernon had it
too. Algernons motor-vation is the chees they put in his
box. But it cant be only that because I dint have no chees
this week.

Prof Nemur was worryd about my eye-Q getting too
high from mine that was too low and I woud get sick
from it. And Dr Strauss tolld Prof Nemur somthing I dint
understand so wile they was talking I rote down some of
the words in my notebook for keeping my progris riports.

He said Harold thats Prof Nemurs frist name I know
Charlie is not what you had in mind as the frist of your
new breed of intelek** coudnt get the word *** super-
man. But most people of his low ment** are host** and
uncoop** they are usally dull and apathet** and hard to
reach. Charlie has a good natcher and hes intristed and
eeger to pleese.

Then prof Nemur said remembir he will be the first
human beeing ever to have his intelijence increesd by sergery. Dr Strauss said thats exakly what I ment. Where
will we find another retarted adult with this tremendus
motor-vation to lern. Look how well he has lerned to
reed and rite for his low mentel age. A tremen** achev**

I dint get all the werds and they were talking to fast but it sounded like Dr Strauss and Burt was on my side and Prof Nemur wasnt.

Burt kept saying Alice Kinnian feels he has an over-whelm** desir to lern. He aktually beggd to be used. And thats true because I wantid to be smart. Dr Strauss got up and walkd around and said I say we use Charlie. And Burt noded. Prof Nemur skratchd his head and rubbd his nose with his thum and said mabye your rite. We will use Charlie. But weve got to make him under-stand that a lot of things can go wrong with the expera-mint.

When he said that I got so happy and exited I jumpd up and shaked his hand for being so good to me. I think he got skared when I did that.

He said Charlie we werked on this for a long time but only on animils like Algernon. We are sure thers no fisi-cal danger for you but there are other things we cant tell untill we try it. I want you to understand this mite fale and then nothing woud happen at all. Or it mite even suc-seed temperary and leeve you werse off then you are now. Do you understand what that meens. If that happins we will have to send you bak to the Warren state home to live.

I said I dint care because I aint afraid of nothing. Im very strong and I always do good and beside I got my luky rabits foot and I never breakd a mirrir in my life. I droppd some dishis once but that dont count for bad luk.

Then Dr Strauss said Charlie even if this fales your making a grate contribyushun to sience. This experimint has been successful on lots of animils but its never bin tride on a humen beeing. You will be the first.

I told him thanks doc you wont be sorry for giving me my 2nd chanse like Miss Kinnian says. And I meen it like I tolld them. After the operashun Im gonna try to be smart. Im gonna try awful hard.

progris riport 6th   Mar 8

Im skared. Lots of pepul who werk at the collidge and the pepul at the medicil school came to wish me luk. Burt the tester brot me some flowers he said they were from the pepul at the psych departmint. He wished me luk. I hope I have luk. I got my rabits foot and my luky penny and my horshoe. Dr Strauss said dont be so superstishus Charlie. This is sience. I dont no what sience is but they all keep saying it so mabye its something that helps you have good luk. Anyway Im keeping my rabits foot in one hand and my luky penny in the other hand with the hole in it. The penny I meen. I wish I coud take the horshoe with me to but its hevy so Ill just leeve it in my jaket.

Joe Carp from the bakery brot me a chokilat cake from Mr Donner and the folks at the bakery and they hope I get better soon. At the bakery they think Im sick becaus thats what Prof Nemur said I shoud tell them and nothing about an operashun for getting smart. Thats a secrit until after in case it dont werk or something goes wrong.

Then Miss Kinnian came to see me and she brout me some magizenes to reed, and she lookd kind of nervus and skared. She fixd up the flowres on my tabel and put evrything nice and neet not messd up like I made it. And she fixd the pilow under my hed. She likes me alot becaus I try very hard to lern evrything not like some of the pepul at the adult center who dont reely care. She wants me to get smart. I know.

Then Prof Nemur said I cant have any more visiters becaus I got to rest. I askd Prof Nemur if I coud beet Algernon in the race after the operashun and he sayd mabye. If the operashun werks good Ill show that mouse I can be as smart as he is even smarter. Then Ill be abel to reed better and spell the werds good and know lots of things and be like other pepul. Boy that woud serprise everyone. If the operashun werks and I get smart mabye Ill be abel to find my mom and dad and sister and show them. Boy woud they be serprised to see me smart just like them and my sister.

Prof Nemur says if it werks good and its perminent they will make other pepul like me smart also. Mabye pepul all over the werld. And he said that meens Im doing somthing grate for sience and Ill be famus and my name will go down in the books. I dont care so much about beeing famus. I just want to be smart like other pepul so I can have lots of frends who like me.

They dint give me anything to eat today. I dont know what eating got to do with geting smart and Im hungry. Prof Nemur took away my choklate cake. That Prof Nemur is a growch. Dr. Strauss says I can have it back after the operashun. You cant eat before a operashun. Not even cheese.

PROGRESS REPORT 7 MARCH 11

The operashun dint hert. Dr. Strauss did it while I was sleeping. I dont know how because I dint see but there was bandiges on my eyes and my head for 3 days so I couldnt make no PROGRESS REPORT till today. The skinny nerse who wached me riting says I spelld PROGRESS rong and she tolld me how to spell it and REPORT to and MARCH. I got to remembir that. I have a very bad memary for speling. Anyway they took off the bandiges from my eyes today so I can make a PROGRESS REPORT now. But there is still some bandigis on my head.

I was skared when they came in and tolld me it was time to go for the operashun. They maid me get out of the bed and on another bed that has weels on it and they rolld me out of the room and down the hall to the door that says sergery. Boy was I serprised that it was a big room with green walls and lots of docters sitting around up high all around the room waching the operashun. I dint no it was going to be like a show.

A man came up to the tabel all in wite and with a wite cloth on his face like in TV shows and rubber glovs and he said rilax Charlie its me Dr Strauss. I said hi doc Im skared. He said theres nothing to be skared about Charlie he said youll just go to sleep. I said thats what Im skared about. He patted my head and then 2 other men waring wite masks too came and straped my arms and legs down so I coudnt move them and that maid me very skared and my stomack feeled tite like I was gone to make all over but I dint only wet a littel and I was gone to cry but they put a rubber thing on my face for me to breeth in and it smelld funny. All the time I herd Dr Strauss talking out loud about the operashun telling evrybody what he was gonna do. But I dint understand anything about it and I was thinking mabye after the operashun Ill be smart and Ill understand all the things hes talking about. So I breethed deep and then I gess I was very tired becase I went to sleep.

When I waked up I was back in my bed and it was very dark. I coudnt see nothing but I herd some talking. It was the nerse and Burt and I said whats the matter why dont you put on the lites and when are they gonna operate. And they laffed and Burt said Charlie its all over. And its dark because you got bandijis over your eyes.

Its a funny thing. They did it while I was sleeping.

Burt comes in to see me evry day to rite down all the things like my tempertur and my blud preshur and the other things about me. He says its on acount of the sientific methid. They got to keep reckerds about what happins so they can do it agen when they want to. Not to me but to the other pepul like me who aint smart.

Thats why I got to do these ~~progis~~ progress reports. Burt says its part of the esperimint and they will make fotastats of the ~~rip~~ reports to study them so they will know what is going on in my mind. I dont see how they will know what is going on in my mind by looking at these reports. I read them over and over a lot of times to see what I rote and I dont no whats going on in my mind so how are they going to.

But anyway thats sience and I got to try to be smart like other pepul. Then when I am smart they will talk to me and I can sit with them and listen like Joe Carp and Frank and Gimpy do when they talk and have a discushen about importent things. While their werking they start talking about things like about god or about the truble with all the mony the presedint is spending or about the ripublicans and demicrats. And they get all excited like their gonna have a fite so Mr Donner got to come in and tell them to get back to baking or theyll all get canned union or no union. I want to talk about things like that.

If your smart you can have lots of frends to talk to and you never get lonley by yourself all the time.

Prof Nemur says its ok to tell about all the things that happin to me in the progress reports but he says I shoud rite more about what I feel and what I think and remembir about the past. I tolld him I dont know how to think or remembir and he said just try.

All the time the bandiges were on my eyes I tryed to think and remembir but nothing happined. I dont know what to think or remembir about. Maybe if I ask him he will tell me how I can think now that Im suppose to get smart. What do smart pepul think about or remembir. Fancy things I bet. I wish I new some fancy things alredy.

March 12—I dont have to rite PROGRESS REPORT on top evry day just when I start a new batch after Prof Nemur takes the old ones away. I just have to put the date on top. That saves time. Its a good idea. I can sit up in bed and look out the window at the gras and trees outside. The skinney nerses name is Hilda and she is very good to me. She brings me things to eat and she fixes my bed and she says I was a very brave man to let them do things to my hed. She says she woud never let them do things to her branes for all the tea in china. I tolld her it wasnt for tea in china. It was to make me smart. And she said mabey they got no rite to make me smart because if god wantid me to be smart he would have made me born that way. And what about Adem and Eev and the sin with the tree of nowlege and eating the appel and the fall. And mabey Prof Nemur and Dr Strauss was tampiring with things they got no rite to tampir with.

She's very skinney and when she talks her face gets all red. She says mabey I better prey to god to ask him to forgiv what they done to me. I dint eat no appels or do nothing sinful. And now Im skared. Mabey I shoudnt of let them oparate on my branes like she said if its agenst god. I dont want to make god angrey.

March 13—They changed my nerse today. This one is pritty. Her name is Lucille she showd me how to spell it for my progress report and she got yellow hair and blew eyes. I askd her where was Hilda and she said Hilda wasnt werking in that part of the hospitil no more. Only in the matirnity ward by the babys where it dont matter if she talks too much.

When I askd her about what was matirnity she said its

about having babys but when I askd her how they have them she got red in the face just the same like Hilda and she said she got to take sombodys temperchure. Nobody ever tells me about the babys. Mabye if this thing werks and I get smart Ill find out.

Miss Kinnian came to see me today and she said Charlie you look wonderful. I tolld her I feel fine but I dont feel smart yet. I thot that when the operashun was over and they took the bandijis off my eyes Id be smart and no a lot of things so I coud read and talk about importent things like evryebody else.

She said thats not the way it werks Charlie. It comes slowley and you have to werk very hard to get smart.

I dint no that. If I got to werk hard anyway what did I have to have the operashun for. She said she wasnt sure but the operashun was to make it so that when I did werk hard to get smart it woud stick with me and not be like it was before when it dint stick so good.

Well I tolld her that made me kind of feel bad because I thot I was going to be smart rite away and I coud go back to show the guys at the bakery how smart I am and talk with them about things and mabye even get to be an assistint baker. Then I was gone to try and find my mom and dad. They woud be serprised to see how smart I got because my mom always wanted me too be smart to. Mabey they woudnt send me away no more if they see how smart I am. I tolld Miss Kinnian I would try hard to be smart as hard as I can. She pattid my hand and said I no you will. I have fayth in you Charlie.

PROGRESS REPORT 8

March 15—Im out of the hospitil but not back at werk yet. Nothing is happining. I had lots of tests and differint kinds of races with Algernon. I hate that mouse. He always beets me. Prof Nemur says I got to play those games and I got to take those tests over and over agen.

Those amazes are stoopid. And those picturs are stoopid to. I like to drawer the picturs of a man and woman but I wont make up lies about pepul.

13

And I cant do the puzzels good.

I get headakes from trying to think and remembir so much. Dr Strauss promised he was going to help me but he dont. He dont tell me what to think or when Ill get smart. He just makes me lay down on a couch and talk.

Miss Kinnian comes to see me at the collidge too. I tolld her nothing was happining. When am I going to get smart. She said you got to be pashent Charlie these things take time. It will happin so slowley you wont know its happening. She said Burt tolld her I was comming along fine.

I still think those races and those tests are stoopid and I think riting these progress reports are stoopid to.

March 16—I ate lunch with Burt at the collidge resterant. They got all kinds of good food and I dont have to pay for it neither. I like to sit and wach the collidge boys and girls. They fool around somtimes but mostly they talk about all kinds of things just like the bakers do at Donners bakery. Burt says its about art and polatics and riligon. I dont know what those things are about but I know riligon is god. Mom use to tell me all about him and the things he done to make the werld. She said I shoud always love god and prey to him. I dont remembir how to prey to him but I think mom use to make me prey to him a lot when I was a kid that he shoud make me get better and not be sick. I dont rimember how I was sick. I think it was about me not being smart.

Anyway Burt says if the experimint werks Ill be able to understand all those things the studints are talking about and I said do you think Ill be smart like them and he laffed and said those kids arent so smart youll pass them as if their standing still.

He interduced me to alot of the studints and some of them look at me funny like I dont belong in a collidge. I almost forgot and started to tell them I was going to be very smart soon like them but Burt intiruppted and he tolld them I was cleaning the psych department lab. Later he explaned to me their mussent be any publisity. That meens its a seecrit.

I dont reely understand why I got to keep it a seecrit. Burt says its in case theirs a faleure Prof Nemur dont want everybody to laff espeshully the pepul from the Welberg foundashun who gave him the mony for the projekt. I said I dont care if pepul laff at me. Lots of pepul laff at me and their my frends and we have fun. Burt put his arm on my sholder and said its not you Nemurs worryd about. He dont want pepul to laff at him.

I dint think pepul would laff at Prof Nemur because hes a sientist in a collidge but Bert said no sientist is a grate man to his colleegs and his gradulate studints. Burt is a gradulate studint and he is a majer in *psychology* like the name on the door to the lab. I dint know they had majers in collidge. I thot it was onley in the army.

Anyway I hope I get smart soon because I want to lern everything there is in the werld like the collidge boys know. All about art and politiks and god.

March 17—When I waked up this morning rite away I thot I was gone to be smart but Im not. Evry morning I think Im gone to be smart but nothing happins. Mabye the experimint dint werk. Maby I wont get smart and Ill have to go live at the Warren home. I hate the tests and I hate the amazeds and I hate Algernon.

I never new before that I was dumber than a mouse. I dont feel like riting any more progress reports. I forget things and even when I rite them in my notbook sometimes I cant reed my own riting and its very hard. Miss Kinnian says have pashents but I feel sick and tired. And I get headakes all the time. I want to go back to werk in the bakery and not rite ~~progris~~ *progress* reports any more.

March 20—Im going back to werk at the bakery. Dr Strauss told Prof Nemur it was better I shoud go back to werk but I still cant tell anyone what the operashun was for and I have to come to the lab for 2 hrs evry nite after werk for my tests and keep riting these dumb reports. They are going to pay me evry week like for a part time job because that was part of the arraingment when they got the mony from the Welberg foundashun. I still dont know what that Welberg thing is. Miss Kinnian explaned me but I still dont get it. So if I dint get smart why are they paying me to rite these dumb things. If their gonna pay me Ill do it. But its very hard to rite.

Im glad Im going back to werk because I miss my job at the bakery and all my frends and all the fun we have.

Dr. Strauss says I shoud keep a notbook in my pockit for things I remembir. And I dont have to do the progress reports every day just when I think of somthing or somthing speshul happins. I told him nothing speshul ever happins to me and it dont look like this speshul experimint is going to happin neither. He says dont get discouriged Charlie because it takes a long time and it happins slow and you cant notise it rite away. He explained how it took a long time with Algernon before he got 3 times smarter then he was before.

Thats why Algernon beats me all the time in that amaze race because he had that operashun too. Hes a speshul mouse the 1st animil to stay smart so long after the operashun. I dint know he was a speshul mouse. That makes it diffrint. I coud probaly do that amazed faster then a reglar mouse. Maybe some day Ill beat Algernon. Boy woud that be somthing. Dr Strauss says that so far Algernon looks like he mite be smart permanint and he says thats a good sine becaus we both had the same kind of operashun.

March 21—We had a lot of fun at the bakery today. Joe Carp said hey look where Charlie had his operashun what did they do Charlie put some brains in. I was going to tell him about me getting smart but I remembered Prof Nemur said no. Then Frank Reilly said what did you do Charlie open a door the hard way. That made me laff. Their my frends and they really like me.

Their is a lot of werk to catch up. They dint have anyone to clean out the place because that was my job but they got a new boy Ernie to do the diliveries that I always done. Mr. Donner said he decided not to fire him for a while to give me a chanse to rest up and not werk so hard. I told him I was alright and I can make my diliveries and clean up like I always done but Mr. Donner says we will keep the boy.

I said so what am I gonna do. And Mr. Donner patted me on the shoulder and says Charlie how old are you. I told him 32 years going on 33 my next brithday. And how long you been here he said. I told him I dint know. He said you came here seventeen years ago. Your Uncle Herman god rest his sole was my best frend. He brout you in here and he askd me to let you werk here and look after you as best I coud. And when he died 2 years later and your mother had you comited to the Warren home I got them to releese you on outside werk placmint. Seventeen years its been Charlie and I want you to know that the bakery bisness is not so good but like I always said you got a job here for the rest of your life. So dont worry about me bringing in somebody to take your place. Youll never have to go back to that Warren home.

I aint worryd only what does he need Ernie for to diliver and werk around here when I was always deliviring the packiges good. He says the boy needs the mony Charlie so Im going to keep him on as an aprentise to lern him to be a baker. You can be his asistent and help him out on diliverys when he needs it.

I never was a asistent before. Ernie is very smart but the other pepul in the bakery dont like him so much. Their all my good frends and we have lots of jokes and laffs here.

Some times somebody will say hey lookit Frank, or Joe or even Gimpy. He really pulled a Charlie Gordon that time. I dont know why they say it but they always laff and I laff too. This morning Gimpy hes the head baker and he has a bad foot and he limps he used my name when he shouted at Ernie because Ernie losst a birthday cake. He said Ernie for godsake you trying to be a Charlie Gordon. I dont know why he said that. I never lost any packiges.

I askd Mr Donner if I coud lern to be an aprentise baker like Ernie. I told him I coud lern it if he gave me a chanse.

Mr Donner looked at me for a long time funny because I gess I dont talk so much most of the time. And Frank herd me and he laffed and laffed until Mr Donner told him to shut up and go tend to his oven. Then Mr Donner said to me theirs lots of time for that Charlie. A bakers werk is very importint and very complikated and you shoudnt worry about things like that.

I wish I coud tell him and all the other people about my real operashun. I wish it woud reely work alredy so I coud get smart like evrybody else.

March 24—Prof Nemur and Dr Strauss came to my room tonight to see why I dont come in to the lab like I am suppose to. I told them I dont want to race with Algernon no more. Prof Nemur said I dont have to for a while but I shoud come in any way. He brout me a presint only it wasnt a presint but just for lend. He said its a teeching mashine that werks like TV. It talks and makes picturs and I got to tern it on just before I go to sleep. I said your kidding. Why shoud I tern on a TV before I go to sleep. But Prof Nemur said if I want to get smart I got to do what he says. So I told him I dint think I was goin to get smart anyway.

Then Dr. Strauss came over and put his hand on my sholder and said Charlie you dont know it yet but your getting smarter all the time. You wont notise it for a while like you dont notise how the hour hand on a clock moves. Thats the way it is with the changes in you. They are happining so slow you cant tell. But we can follow it from the tests and the way you act and talk and your progress reports. He said Charlie youve got to have fayth in us and in yourself. We cant be sure it will be permanint but we are confidant that soon your going to be a very intellijent young man.

I said okay and Prof Nemur showed me how to werk the TV that reely wasnt a TV. I askd him what did it do. First he lookd sore again because I asked him to explane me and he said I shoud just do what he told me. But Dr Strauss said he shoud explane it to me because I was beginning to questien authorety. I dont no what that meens but Prof Nemur looked like he was going to bite his lip off. Then he explaned me very slow that the mashine did lots of things to my mind. Somethings it did just before I fall asleep like teach me things when Im very sleepy and a little while after I start to fall asleep I still hear the talk even if I dont see the picturs anymore. Other things is at nite its suppose to make me have dreams and remembir things that happened a long time ago when I was a very littel kid.

Its scary.

Oh yes I forgot. I asked Prof Nemur when I can go back to Miss Kinnians class at the adult center and he said soon Miss Kinnian will come to the collidge testing center to teach me speshul. I am glad about that. I dint see her so much since the operashun but she is nice.

March 25—That crazy TV kept me up all nite. How can I sleep with something yelling crazy things all night in my ears. And the nutty picturs. Wow. I dont know what it says when Im up so how am I going to know when Im sleeping. I asked Burt about it and he says its ok. He says my branes are lerning just before I got to sleep and that will help me when Miss Kinnian starts my lessons at the testing center. The testing center isnt a hospitil for animils like I thougt before. Its a labortory for sience. I dont know what sience is exept Im helping it with this experimint.

Anyway I dont know about that TV. I think its crazy. If you can get smart when your going to sleep why do pepul go to school. I dont think that thing will werk. I use to watch the late show and the late late show on TV all the time before I went to sleep and it never made me smart. Maybe only certin movies make you smart. Maybe like quizz shows.

March 26—How am I gonna work in the daytime if that thing keeps waking me up at nite. In the middel of the nite I woke up and I coudnt go back to sleep because it kept saying *remembir . . . remembir . . . remembir.* . . . So I think I remembird something. I dont remembir exackly but it was about Miss Kinnian and the school where I lerned about reading. And how I went their.

A long time ago once I asked Joe Carp how he lerned to read and if I coud lern to read to. He laffed like he always done when I say something funny and he says to me Charlie why waste your time they cant put any branes in where there aint none. But Fanny Birden herd me and she askd her cusin who is a collidge studint at Beekman and she told me about the adult center for retarded pepul at the Beekman collidge.

She rote the name down on a paper and Frank laffed and said dont go getting so eddicated that you wont talk to your old frends. I said dont worry I will always keep my old frends even if I can read and rite. He was laffing and Joe Carp was laffing but Gimpy came in and told them to get back to making rolls. They are all good frends to me.

After werk I walked over six blocks to the school and I

was scared. I was so happy I was going to lern to read that I bougt a newspaper to take home with me and read after I lerned.

When I got their it was a big long hall with lots of pepul. I got scared of saying somthing wrong to sombody so I startid to go home. But I dont know why I terned around and went inside agen.

I wated until most everbody went away exept some pepul going over by a big timeclock like the one we have at the bakery and I asked the lady if I coud lern to read and rite because I wanted to read all the things in the newspaper and I showed it to her. She was Miss Kinnian but I dint know it then. She said if you come back tomorow and rejister I will start to teach you how to read. But you got to understand it will take a long time maybe years to lern to read. I told her I dint know it took so long but I wantid to lern anyway because I made believe a lot of times. I meen I pretend to pepul I know how to read but it aint true and I wantid to lern.

She shaked my hand and said glad to meet you Mistre Gordon. I will be your teacher. My name is Miss Kinnian. So thats wear I went to lern and thats how I met Miss Kinnian.

Thinking and remembiring is hard and now I dont sleep so good any more. That TV is too loud.

March 27—Now that Im starting to have those dreams and remembiring Prof Nemur says I got to go to theripy sesions with Dr Strauss. He says theripy sesions is like when you feel bad you talk to make it better. I tolld him I dont feel bad and I do plenty of talking all day so why do I have to go to theripy but he got sore and says I got to go anyway.

What theripy is is that I got to lay down on a couch and Dr. Strauss sits in a chair near me and I talk about anything that comes into my head. For a long time I dint say nothing because I coudnt think of nothing to say. Then I told him about the bakery and the things they do there. But its silly for me to go to his office and lay down on the couch to talk because I rite it down in the progress reports anyway and he could read it. So today I brout the progress report with me and I told him maybe he could just read it and I could take a nap on the couch. I was very tired because that TV kept me up all nite but he said no it dont work that way. I got to talk. So I talked but then I fell asleep on the couch anyway—rite in the middle.

March 28—I got a headake. Its not from that TV this time. Dr Strauss showed me how to keep the TV turned low so now I can sleep. I dont hear a thing. And I still dont understand what it says. A few times I play it over in the morning to find out what I lerned before I fell asleep and while I was sleeping and I dont even know the words. Maybe its another langwidge or something. But most times it sounds american. But it talks too fast.

I askd Dr Strauss what good is it to get smart in my sleep if I want to be smart when Im awake. He says its the same thing and I have two minds. Theres the SUB-CONSCIOUS *and the* CONSCIOUS (thats how you spell it) and one dont tell the other what its doing. They dont even talk to each other. Thats why I dream. And boy have I been having crazy dreams. Wow. Ever since that night TV. The late late late late late movie show.

I forgot to ask Dr Strauss if it was only me or if everybody has two minds like that.

(I just looked up the word in the dicshunery Dr Strauss gave me. SUBCONSCIOUS. *adj. Of the nature of mental operations yet not present in consciousness; as, subconscious conflict of desires.*) Theres more but I still dont know what it meens. This isnt a very good dicshunery for dumb people like me.

Anyway the headake is from the party. Joe Carp and Frank Reilly invited me to go with them after work to Hallorans Bar for some drinks. I dont like to drink wiskey but they said we will have lots of fun. I had a good time. We played games with me doing a dance on the top of the bar with a lampshade on my head and everyone laffing.

Then Joe Carp said I shoud show the girls how I mop out the toilet in the bakery and he got me a mop. I showed them and everyone laffed when I told them that Mr Donner said I was the best janiter and errand boy he ever had because I like my job and do it good and never come late or miss a day exept for my operashun.

I said Miss Kinnian always told me Charlie be proud of the work you do because you do your job good.

Everybody laffed and Frank said that Miss Kinnian must be some cracked up piece if she goes for Charlie and Joe said hey Charlie are you making out with her. I said I dint know what that meens. They gave me lots of drinks and Joe said Charlie is a card when hes potted. I think that means they like me. We have some good times but I cant wait to be smart like my best frends Joe Carp and Frank Reilly.

I dont remember how the party was over but they asked me to go around the corner to see if it was raining and when I came back there was no one their. Maybe they went to find me. I looked for them all over till it was late. But I got lost and I felt bad at myself for getting lost because I bet Algernon coud go up and down those streets a hundrid times and not get lost like I did.

Then I dont remember so good but Mrs Flynn says a nice poleecman brought me back home.

That same nite I dreamed about my mother and father only I coudnt see her face it was all wite and she was blurry. I was crying because we were in a big departmint store and I was losst and I coudnt find them and I ran up and down the rows around all the big cownters in the store. Then a man came and took me in a big room with benches and gave me a lolypop and tolld me a big boy like me shoudnt cry because my mother and father woud come to find me.

Anyway thats the dream and I got a headake and a big lump on my head and black and blue marks all over. Joe Carp says mabye I got rolled or the cop let me have it. I dont think poleecmen do things like that. But anyway I dont think Ill drink wiskey anymore.

March 29—I beet Algernon. I dint even know I beet him until Burt Selden told me. Then the second time I lost because I got so exited. But after that I beet him 8 more times. I must be getting smart to beat a smart mouse like Algernon. But I dont feel smarter.

I wanted to race some more but Burt said thats enough for one day. He let me hold Algernon for a minit. Algernon is a nice mouse. Soft like cotton. He blinks and when he opens his eyes their black and pink on the eges.

I asked can I feed him because I felt bad to beat him and I wanted to be nice and make frends. Burt said no Algernon is a very speshul mouse with an operashun like mine. He was the first of all the animals to stay smart so long and he said that Algernon is so smart he has to solve a problem with a lock that changes every time he goes in to eat so he has to lern something new to get his food. That made me sad because if he coudnt lern he woudnt be able to eat and he would be hungry.

I dont think its right to make you pass a test to eat. How woud Burt like to have to pass a test every time he wants to eat. I think Ill be frends with Algernon.

That reminds me. Dr Strauss says I shoud write down all my dreams and the things I think so when I come to his office I can tell them. I tolld him I dont know how to think yet but he says he means more things like what I wrote about my mom and dad and about when I started school at Miss Kinnians or anything that happened before the operation is thinking and I wrote them in my progress report.

I didnt know I was thinking and remembering. Maybe that means something is happining to me. I dont feel different but Im so exited I cant sleep.

Dr Strauss gave me some pink pills to make me sleep good. He says I got to get lots of sleep because thats when most of the changes happin in my brane. It must be true because Uncle Herman use to sleep in our house all the time when he was out of werk on the old sofa in the parler. He was fat and it was hard for him to get a job because he use to paint pepuls houses and he got very slow going up and down the ladder.

When I once tolld my mom I wantid to be a painter like Uncle Herman my sister Norma said yeah Charlies going to be the artist of the family. And dad slappd her face and tolld her not to be so goddam nasty to her brother. I dont no what a artist is but if Norma got slappd for saying it I gess its not a nice thing. I always feeled bad when Norma got slappd for being meen to me. When I get smart Ill go visit her.

March 30—Tonite after werk Miss Kinnian came to the teeching room near the labatory. She looked glad to see me but nervus. She looks yunger then I remembired her.

I tolld her I was trying very hard to be smart. She said I have confidense in you Charlie the way you strugled so much to reed and rite better then all the others. I know you can do it. At werst you will have it all for a little wile and your doing somthing for other retarded pepul.

We startid to reed a very hard book. I never red such a hard book before. Its called Robinson Crusoe about a man who gets merooned on a dessert iland. Hes smart and figgers out all kinds of things so he can have a house and food and hes a good swimmer. Only I feel sorry for him because hes all alone and he has no frends. But I think their must be somebody else on the iland because theres a picture of him with his funny umbrela looking at feet-prints. I hope he gets a frend and not be so lonely.

March 31—Miss Kinnian teeches me how to spel better. She says look at a werd and close your eyes and say it over and over again until you remember. I have lots of truble with *through* that you say THREW and *enough* and *tough* that you dont say ENEW and TEW. You got to say ENUFF and TUFF. Thats how I use to rite it before I started to get smart. Im mixd up but Miss Kinnian says dont worry spelling is not suppose to make sence.

PROGRESS REPORT 9

April 1—Everbody in the bakery came to see me today where I started my new job working by the dough-mixer. It happined like this. Oliver who works on the mixer quit yesterday. I used to help him out before bringing the bags of flour over for him to put in the mixer. Anyway I dint know that I knew how to work the mixer. Its very hard and Oliver went to bakers school for one year before he could learn how to be an assistint baker.

But Joe Carp hes my friend he said Charlie why dont you take over Olivers job. Everybody on the floor came around and they were ~~laff~~ *laughing* and Frank Reilly said yes Charlie you been here long ~~enuff~~ *enough*. Go ahead. Gimpy aint around and he wont know you tryed it. I was scared because Gimpy is the head baker and he told me never to go near the mixer because I would get hurt. Everyone said do it exept Fannie Birden who said stop it why dont you leave the poor man alone.

Frank Reilly said shut up Fanny its April fools day and if Charlie works on the mixer he might fix it good so we will all have the day off. I said I coudnt fix the mashine but I could work it because I been watching Oliver ever since I got back.

I worked the dough-mixer and everybody was surprised espeshully Frank Reilly. Fanny Birden got exited because she said it took Oliver 2 years to learn how to mix the dough right and he went to bakers school. Bernie Bate who helps on the mashine said I did it faster then Oliver did and better. Nobody laffed. When Gimpy came back and Fanny told him he got sore at me for working on the mixer.

But she said watch him and see how he does it. They were playing him for an April Fool joke and he foold them instead. Gimpy watched and I knew he was sore at me because he dont like when people dont do what he tells them just like Prof Nemur. But he saw how I worked the mixer and he skratched his head and said I see it but I dont believe it. Then he called Mr Donner and told me to work it again so Mr Donner could see it.

I was scared he was going to be angry and holler at me so after I was finished I said can I go back to my own job now. I got to sweep out the front of the bakery behind the counter. Mr Donner looked at me funny for a long time. Then he said this must be some kind of April fools joke you guys are playing on me. Whats the catch.

Gimpy said thats what I thought it was some kind of a gag. He limped all around the mashine and he said to Mr Donner I dont understand it either but Charlie knows how to handle it and I got to admit it he does a better job then Oliver.

Everybody was crowded around and talking about it and I got scared because they all looked at me funny and they were exited. Frank said I told you there is something peculier lately about Charlie. And Joe Carp says yeah I know what you mean. Mr Donner sent everybody back to work and he took me out to the front of the store with him.

He said Charlie I dont know how you done it but it

looks like you finally learned something. I want you to be carefull and do the best you can do. You got yourself a new job with a 5 doller raise.

I said I dont want a new job because I like to clean up and sweep and deliver and do things for my friends but Mr Donner said never mind your friends I need you for this job. I dont think much of a man who dont want to advance.

I said whats advance mean. He scratched his head and looked at me over his glasses. Never mind that Charlie. From now on you work that mixer. Thats advance.

So now instead of delivering packiges and washing out the toilets and dumping the garbage. Im the new mixer. Thats advance. Tomorrow I will tell Miss Kinnian. I think she will be happy but I dont know why Frank and Joe are mad at me. I asked Fanny and she said never mind those fools. This is April Fools day and the joke backfired and made them the fools instead of you.

I asked Joe to tell me what was the joke that backfired and he said go jump in the lake. I guess their mad at me because I worked the mashine but they didnt get the day off like they thought. Does that mean Im getting smarter.

April 3—Finished Robinson Crusoe. I want to find out more about what happens to him but Miss Kinnian says thats all there is. WHY.

April 4—Miss Kinnian says Im learning fast. She read some of my progress reports and she looked at me kind of funny. She says Im a fine person and Ill show them all. I asked her why. She said never mind but I shouldnt feel bad if I find out that everybody isnt nice like I think. She said for a person who God gave so little to you did more than a lot of people with brains they never even used. I said that all my friends are smart people and their good. They like me and they never did anything that wasnt nice. Then she got something in her eye and she had to run out to the ladys room.

While I was sitting in the teaching room waiting for her I was wondering about how Miss Kinnian was a nice lady like my mother use to be. I think I remember my mother told me to be good and always be friendly to people. She said but always be careful because some people dont understand and they might think you are trying to make trouble.

That makes me remember when mom had to go away and they put me to stay in Mrs Leroys house who lived next door. Mom went to the hospital. Dad said she wasnt sick or nothing but she went to the hospital to bring me back a baby sister or a brother. (I still dont know how they do that) I told them I want a baby brother to play with and I dont know why they got me a sister instead but she was nice like a doll. Only she cryd all the time.

I never hurt her or nothing.

They put her in a crib in their room and once I heard Dad say dont worry Charlie wouldnt harm her.

She was like a bundle all pink and screaming sometimes that I couldnt sleep. And when I went to sleep she woke me up in the nighttime. One time when they were in the kitchen and I was in my bed she was crying. I got up to pick her up and hold her to get quiet the way mom does. But then Mom came in yelling and took her away. And she slapped me so hard I fell on the bed.

Then she startid screaming. Dont you ever touch her again. Youll hurt her. Shes a baby. You got no business touching her. I dint know it then but I guess I know it now that she thought I was going to hurt the baby because I was too dumb to know what I was doing. Now that makes me feel bad because I would never of hurt the baby.

When I go to Dr Straus office I got to tell him about that.

April 6—Today, I learned, the *comma,* this is, a, comma (,) a period, with, a tail, Miss Kinnian, says its, importent, because, it makes writing, better, she said, somebody, could lose, a lot, of money, if a comma, isnt in, the right, place, I got, some money, that I, saved from, my job, and what, the foundation, pays me, but not, much and, I dont, see how, a comma, keeps, you from, losing it,

But, she says, everybody, uses commas, so Ill, use them, too,,,,,

April 7—I used the comma wrong. Its *punctuation*. Miss Kinnian told me to look up long words in the dictionary to learn to spell them. I said whats the difference if you can read it anyway. She said its part of your education so from now on Ill look up all the words Im not sure how to spell. It takes a long time to write that way but I think Im remembering more and more.

Anyway thats how come I got the word *punctuation* right. Its that way in the dictionary. Miss Kinnian says a period is punctuation too, and there are lots of other marks to learn. I told her I thought she meant all the periods had to have tails and be called commas. But she said no.

She said; You, got. to-mix?them!up: She showd? me" how, to mix! them; up, and now! I can. mix (up all? kinds of punctuation— in, my. writing! There" are lots, of rules; to learn? but. Im' get'ting them in my head:

One thing? I, like: about, Dear Miss Kinnian: (thats, the way? it goes; in a business, letter (if I ever go! into business?) is that, she: always; gives me' a reason" when—I ask. She"s a gen'ius! I wish? I cou'd be smart-like-her;

Punctuation, is? fun!

April 8—What a dope I am! I didn't even understand what she was talking about. I read the grammar book last night and it explains the whole thing. Then I saw it was the same way as Miss Kinnian was trying to tell me, but I didn't get it. I got up in the middle of the night and the whole thing straightened out in my mind.

Miss Kinnian said that the TV working, just before I fell asleep and during the night, helped out. She said I reached a *plateau*. That's like the flat top of a hill.

After I figured out how punctuation worked, I read over all my old progress reports from the beginning. Boy, did I have crazy spelling and punctuation! I told Miss Kinnian I ought to go over the pages and fix all the mistakes, but she said, "No, Charlie, Professor Nemur wants them just as they are. That's why he lets you keep them after they're photostated—to see your own progress. You're coming along fast, Charlie."

That made me feel good. After the lesson I went down and played with Algernon. We don't race any more.

April 10—I feel sick. Not like for a doctor, but inside my chest it feels empty, like getting punched and a heartburn at the same time.

I wasn't going to write about it, but I guess I got to, because it's important. Today was the first day I ever stayed home from work on purpose.

Last night Joe Carp and Frank Reilly invited me to a party. There were lots of girls and Gimpy was there and Ernie too. I remembered how sick I got last time I drank too much, so I told Joe I didn't want to drink anything. He gave me a plain coke instead. It tasted funny, but I thought it was just a bad taste in my mouth.

We had a lot of fun for a while.

"Dance with Ellen," Joe said. "She'll teach you the steps." Then he winked at her like he had something in his eye.

She said, "Why don't you leave him alone?"

He slapped me on the back. "This is Charlie Gordon, my buddy, my pal. He's no ordinary guy—he's been promoted to working on the dough-mixing machine. All I did was ask you to dance with him and give him a good time. What's wrong with that?"

He pushed me up close against her. So she danced with me. I fell three times and I couldn't understand why because no one else was dancing besides Ellen and me. And all the time I was tripping because somebody's foot was always sticking out.

They were all around in a circle watching and laughing at the way we were doing the steps. They laughed harder every time I fell, and I was laughing too because it was so funny. But the last time it happened I didn't laugh. I picked myself up and Joe pushed me down again.

Then I saw the look on Joe's face and it gave me a funny feeling in my stomach.

"He's a scream," one of the girls said. Everybody was laughing.

"Oh, you were right, Frank," choked Ellen. "He's a one man side show." Then she said, "Here, Charlie, have a fruit." She gave me an apple, but when I bit into it, it was fake.

Then Frank started laughing and he said, "I told ya he'd eat it. C'n you imagine anyone dumb enough to eat wax fruit?"

29

Joe said, "I ain't laughed so much since we sent him around the corner to see if it was raining that night we ditched him at Halloran's."

Then I saw a picture that I remembered in my mind when I was a kid and the children in the block let me play with them, hide-and-go-seek and I was IT. After I counted up to ten over and over on my fingers I went to look for the others. I kept looking until it got cold and dark and I had to go home.

But I never found them and I never knew why.

What Frank said reminded me. That was the same thing that happened at Halloran's. And that was what Joe and the rest of them were doing. Laughing at me. And the kids playing hide-and-go-seek were playing tricks on me and they were laughing at me too.

The people at the party were a bunch of blurred faces all looking down and laughing at me.

"Look at him. His face is red."

"He's blushing. Charlie's blushing."

"Hey, Ellen, what'd you do to Charlie? I never saw him act like this before."

"Boy, Ellen sure got him worked up."

I didn't know what to do or where to turn. Her rubbing up against me made me feel funny. Everyone was laughing at me and all of a sudden I felt naked. I wanted to hide myself so they wouldn't see. I ran out of the apartment. It was a large apartment house with lots of halls and I couldn't find my way to the staircase. I forgot all about the elevator. Then, after, I found the stairs and ran out into the street and walked for a long time before I went to my room. I never knew before that Joe and Frank and the others liked to have me around just to make fun of me.

Now I know what they mean when they say "to pull a Charlie Gordon."

I'm ashamed.

And another thing. I dreamed about that girl Ellen dancing and rubbing up against me and when I woke up the sheets were wet and messy.

April 13—Still didn't go back to work at the bakery. I told Mrs. Flynn, my landlady, to call and tell Mr. Donner I'm sick. Mrs. Flynn looks at me lately like she's scared of me.

I think it's a good thing about finding out how everybody laughs at me. I thought about it a lot. It's because I'm so dumb and I don't even know when I'm doing something dumb. People think it's funny when a dumb person can't do things the same way they can.

Anyway, now I know I'm getting a little smarter every day. I know punctuation, and I can spell good. I like to look up all the hard words in the dictionary and I remember them. And I try to write these progress reports very careful but that's hard to do. I am reading a lot now, and Miss Kinnian says I read very fast. And I even understand a lot of the things I'm reading about, and they stay in my mind. There are times when I can close my eyes and think of a page and it all comes back like a picture.

But other things come into my head too. Sometimes I close my eyes and I see a clear picture. Like this morning just after I woke up, I was laying in bed with my eyes open. It was like a big hole opened up in the walls of my mind and I can just walk through. I think its far back . . . a long time ago when I first started working at Donner's Bakery. I see the street where the bakery is. Fuzzy at first and then it gets patchy with some things so real they are right here now in front of me, and other things stay blurred, and I'm not sure. . . .

A little old man with a baby carriage made into a pushcart with a charcoal burner, and the smell of roasting chestnuts, and snow on the ground. A young fellow, skinny with wide eyes and a scared look on his face looking up at the store sign. What does it say? Blurred letters in a way that don't make sense. I know *now* that the sign says DONNER'S BAKERY, but looking back in my memory at the sign I can't read the words through his eyes. None of the signs make sense. I think that fellow with the scared look on his face is me.

Bright neon lights. Christmas trees and sidewalk peddlers. People bundled in coats with collars up and scarves around their necks. But he has no gloves. His hands are cold and he puts down a heavy bundle of brown paper bags. He's stopping to watch the little mechanical toys that the peddler winds up—the tumbling bear, the dog jumping, the seal spinning a ball on its nose. Tumbling, jumping, spinning. If he had all those toys for himself he would be the happiest person in the world.

He wants to ask the red-faced peddler, with his fingers sticking through the brown cotton gloves, if he can hold the tumbling bear for a minute, but he is afraid. He picks up the bundle of paper bags and puts it on his shoulder. He is skinny but he is strong from many years of hard work.

"Charlie! Charlie! . . . fat head barley!"

Children circle around him laughing and teasing him like little dogs snapping at his feet. Charlie smiles at them. He would like to put down his bundle and play games with them, but when he thinks about it the skin on his back twitches and he feels the way the older boys throw things at him.

Coming back to the bakery he sees some boys standing in the door of a dark hallway.

"Hey look, there's Charlie!"

"Hey, Charlie. What you got there? Want to shoot some craps?"

"C'mere. We won't hurtya."

But there is something about the doorway—the dark hall, the laughing, that makes his skin twitch again. He tries to know what it is but all he can remember is their dirt and piss all over his clothes, and Uncle Herman shouting when he came home all covered with filth, and how Uncle Herman ran out with a hammer in his hand to find the boys who did that to him. Charlie backs away from the boys laughing in the hallway, drops the bundle. Picks it up again and runs the rest of the way to the bakery.

"What took you so long, Charlie?" shouts Gimpy from the doorway to the back of the bakery.

Charlie pushes through the swinging doors to the back of the bakery and sets down the bundle on one of the skids. He leans against the wall shoving his hands into his pockets. He wishes he had his spinner.

He likes it back here in the bakery where the floors are white with flour—whiter than the sooty walls and ceiling. The thick soles of his own high shoes are crusted with white and there is white in the stitching and lace-eyes, and under his nails and in the cracked chapped skin of his hands.

He relaxes here—squatting against the wall—leaning back in a way that tilts his baseball cap with the *D* forward over his eyes. He likes the smell of flour, sweet dough, bread and cakes and rolls baking. The oven is crackling and makes him sleepy.

Sweet . . . warm . . . sleep . . .

Suddenly, falling, twisting, head hitting against the wall. Someone has kicked his legs out from under him.

That's all I can remember. I can see it all clearly, but I don't know why it happened. It's like when I used to go to the movies. The first time I never understood because they went too fast but after I saw the picture three or four times I used to understand what they were saying. I've got to ask Dr. Strauss about it.

April 14—Dr. Strauss says the important thing is to keep recalling memories like the one I had yesterday and to write them down. Then when I come into his office we can talk about them.

Dr. Strauss is a psychiatrist and a neurosurgeon. I didn't know that. I thought he was just a plain doctor. But when I went to his office this morning, he told me about how important it is for me to learn about myself so that I can understand my problems. I said I didn't have any problems.

He laughed and then he got up from his chair and went to the window. "The more intelligent you become the more problems you'll have, Charlie. Your intellectual growth is going to outstrip your emotional growth. And I think you'll find that as you progress, there will be many things you'll want to talk to me about. I just want you to remember that this is the place for you to come when you need help."

I still don't know what it's all about, but he said even if I don't understand my dreams or memories or why I have them, some time in the future they're all going to connect up, and I'll learn more about myself. He said the important thing is to find out what those people in my memories are saying. It's all about me when I was a boy and I've got to remember what happened.

I never knew about these things before. It's like if I get intelligent enough I'll understand all the words in my mind, and I'll know about those boys standing in the hallway, and about my Uncle Herman and my parents. But what he means is then I'm going to feel bad about it all and I might get sick in my mind.

So I've got to come into his office twice a week now to talk about the things that bother me. We just sit there, and I talk, and Dr. Strauss listens. It's called therapy, and that means talking about things will make me feel better. I told him one of the things that bothers me is about women. Like dancing with that girl Ellen got me all excited. So we talked about it and I got a funny feeling while I was talking, cold and sweaty, and a buzzing inside my head and I thought I was going to throw up. Maybe because I always thought it was dirty and bad to talk about that. But Dr. Strauss said what happened to me after the party was a wet dream, and it's a natural thing that happens to boys.

So even if I'm getting intelligent and learning a lot of new things, he thinks I'm still a boy about women. It's confusing, but I'm going to find out all about my life.

April 15—I'm reading a lot these days and almost everything is staying in my mind. Besides history and geography and arithmetic, Miss Kinnian says I should start learning foreign languages. Prof. Nemur gave me some more tapes to play while I sleep. I still don't know how the conscious and unconscious mind works, but Dr. Strauss says not to worry yet. He made me promise that when I start learning college subjects in a couple of weeks I won't read any books on psychology—that is, until he gives me permission. He says it will confuse me and make me think about psychological theories instead of about my own ideas and feelings. But it's okay to read novels. This week I read *The Great Gatsby, An American Tragedy,* and *Look Homeward, Angel.* I never knew about men and women doing things like that.

April 16—I feel a lot better today, but I'm still angry that all the time people were laughing and making fun of me. When I become intelligent the way Prof. Nemur says, with much more than twice my I.Q. of 70, then maybe people will like me and be my friends.

I'm not sure what I.Q. is anyway. Prof. Nemur said it was something that measured how intelligent you were—like a scale in the drugstore weighs pounds. But Dr. Strauss had a big argument with him and said an I.Q. didn't *weigh* intelligence at all. He said an I.Q. showed how much intelligence you could get, like the numbers on the outside of a measuring cup. You still had to fill the cup up with stuff.

When I asked Burt Seldon, who gives me my intelligence tests and works with Algernon, he said that some people would say both of them were wrong and according to the things he's been reading up on, the I.Q. measures a lot of different things including some of the things you learned already and it really isn't a good measure of intelligence at all.

So I still don't know what I.Q. is, and everybody says it's something different. Mine is about a hundred now, and it's going to be over a hundred and fifty soon, but they'll still have to fill me up with the stuff. I didn't want to say anything, but I don't see how if they don't know *what* it is, or *where* it is—how they know *how much* of it you've got.

Prof Nemur says I have to take a *Rorschach Test* the day after tomorrow. I wonder what that is.

April 17—I had a nightmare last night, and this morning, after I woke up, I free-associated the way Dr. Strauss told me to do when I remember my dreams. Think about the dream and just let my mind wander until other thoughts come up in my mind. I keep on doing that until my mind goes blank. Dr. Strauss says that it means I've reached a point where my subconscious is trying to block my conscious from remembering. It's a wall between the present and the past. Sometimes the wall stays up and sometimes it breaks down and I can remember what's behind it.

Like this morning.

The dream was about Miss Kinnian reading my progress reports. In the dream I sit down to write but I can't write or read any more. It's all gone. I get frightened so I ask Gimpy at the bakery to write for me. But when Miss

Kinnian reads the report she gets angry and tears the pages up because they've got dirty words in them.

When I get home Prof. Nemur and Dr. Strauss are waiting for me and they give me a beating for writing dirty things in the progress report. When they leave me I pick up the torn pages but they turn into lace valentines with blood all over them.

It was a horrible dream but I got out of bed and wrote it all down and then I started to free associate.

Bakery . . . baking . . . the urn . . . someone kicking me . . . fall down . . . bloody all over . . . writing . . . big pencil on a red valentine . . . a little gold heart . . . a locket . . . a chain . . . all covered with blood . . . and he's laughing at me . . .

The chain is from a locket . . . spinning around . . . flashing the sunlight into my eyes. And I like to watch it spin . . . watch the chain . . . all bunched up and twisting and spinning . . . and a little girl is watching me.

Her name is Miss Kin—I mean Harriet.

"Harriet . . . Harriet . . . we all love Harriet."

And then there's nothing. It's blank again.

Miss Kinnian reading my progress reports over my shoulder.

Then we're at the Adult Center for the Retarded, and she's reading over my shoulder as I write my ~~composishuns~~ compositions.

School changes into P.S. 13 and I'm eleven years old and Miss Kinnian is eleven years old too, but now she's not Miss Kinnian. She's a little girl with dimples and long curls and her name is Harriet. We all love Harriet. It's Valentines Day.

I remember . . .

I remember what happened at P.S. 13 and why they had to change my school and send me to P.S. 222. It was because of Harriet.

I see Charlie—eleven years old. He has a little gold-color locket he once found in the street. There's no chain, but he has it on a string, and he likes to twirl the locket so that it bunches up the string, and then watch it unwind, spinning around with the sun flicking into his eyes.

Sometimes when the kids play catch they let him play in the middle and he tries to get the ball before one of them catches it. He likes to be in the middle—even if he never catches the ball—and once when Hymie Roth dropped the ball by mistake and he picked it up they wouldn't let him throw it but he had to go in the middle again.

When Harriet passes by, the boys stop playing and look at her. All the boys love Harriet. When she shakes her head her curls bounce up and down, and she has dimples. Charlie doesn't know why they make such a fuss about a girl and why they always want to talk to her (he'd rather play ball or kick-the-can, or ringo-levio than talk to a girl) but all the boys are in love with Harriet so he is in love with her too.

She never teases him like the other kids, and he does tricks for her. He walks on the desks when the teacher isn't there. He throws erasers out the window, scribbles all over the blackboard and walls. And Harriet always screeches and giggles, "Oh, lookit Charlie. Ain't he funny? Oh, ain't he silly?"

It's Valentine's Day, and the boys are talking about valentines they're going to give Harriet, so Charlie says, "I'm gonna give Harriet a valentime too."

They laugh and Barry says, "Where you gonna get a valentime?"

"I'm gonna get her a pretty one. You'll see."

But he doesn't have any money for a valentine, so he decides to give Harriet his locket that is heart-shaped like the valentines in the store windows. That night he takes tissue paper from his mother's drawer, and it takes a long time to wrap and tie it with a piece of red ribbon. Then he takes it to Hymie Roth the next day during lunch period in school and asks Hymie to write on the paper for him.

He tells Hymie to write: *Dear Harriet, I think you are the most prettiest girl in the whole world. I like you very much and I love you. I want you to be my valentime. Your friend, Charlie Gordon.*

Hymie prints very carefully in large letters on the paper, laughing all the time, and he tells Charlie, "Boy, this will knock her eyes out. Wait'll she sees this."

Charlie is scared, but he wants to give Harriet that locket, so he follows her home from school and waits until she goes into her house. Then he sneaks into the hall and hangs the package on the inside of the doorknob. He rings the bell twice and runs across the street to hide behind the tree.

When Harriet comes down she looks around to see who rang the bell. Then she sees the package. She takes it and goes upstairs. Charlie goes home from school and he gets a spanking because he took the tissue paper and ribbon out of his mother's drawer without telling her. But he doesn't care. Tomorrow Harriet will wear the locket and tell all the boys he gave it to her. Then they'll see.

The next day he runs all the way to school, but it's too early. Harriet isn't there yet, and he's excited.

But when Harriet comes in she doesn't even look at him. She isn't wearing the locket. And she looks sore.

He does all kinds of things when Mrs. Janson isn't watching: He makes funny faces. He laughs out loud. He stands up on his seat and wiggles his fanny. He even throws a piece of chalk at Harold. But Harriet doesn't look at him even once. Maybe she forgot. Maybe she'll wear it tomorrow. She passes by in the hallway, but when he comes over to ask her she pushes past him without saying a word.

Down in the schoolyard her two big brothers are waiting for him.

Gus pushes him. "You little bastard, did you write this dirty note to my sister?"

Charlie says he didn't write any dirty notes. "I just gave her a valentine."

Oscar who was on the football team before he graduated from high school grabs Charlie's shirt and tears off two buttons. "You keep away from my kid sister, you degenerate. You don't belong in this school anyway."

He pushes Charlie over to Gus who catches him by the throat. Charlie is scared and starts to cry.

Then they start to hurt him. Oscar punches him in the nose, and Gus knocks him on the ground and kicks him in the side and then both of them kick him, one and then the other, and some of the other kids in the yard—Charlie's friends—come running screaming and clapping hands: "Fight! Fight! They're beating up Charlie!"

His clothes are torn and his nose is bleeding and one of his teeth is broken, and after Gus and Oscar go away he sits on the sidewalk and cries. The blood tastes sour. The other kids just laugh and shout: "Charlie got a licking! Charlie got a licking!" And then Mr. Wagner, one of the caretakers from the school, comes and chases them away. He takes Charlie into the boys' room and tells him to wash off the blood and dirt from his face and hands before he goes back home. . . .

I guess I was pretty dumb because I believed what people told me. I shouldn't have trusted Hymie or anyone.

I never remembered any of this before today, but it came back to me after I thought about the dream. It has something to do with the feeling about Miss Kinnian reading my progress reports. Anyway, I'm glad now I don't have to ask anyone to write things for me. Now I can do it for myself.

But I just realized something. Harriet never gave me back my locket.

April 18—I found out what a Rorschach is. It's the test with the inkblots, the one I took before the operation. As soon as I saw what it was, I got frightened. I knew Burt was going to ask me to find the pictures, and I knew I wouldn't be able to. I was thinking, if only there was some way of knowing what kind of pictures were hidden there. Maybe there weren't any pictures at all. Maybe it was just a trick to see if I was dumb enough to look for something that wasn't there. Just thinking about it made me sore at him.

"All right, Charlie," he said, "you've seen these cards before, remember?"

"Of course, I remember."

The way I said it, he knew I was angry, and he looked up at me surprised.

"Anything wrong, Charlie?"

"No, nothing's wrong. Those inkblots upset me."

He smiled and shook his head. "Nothing to be upset about. This is just one of the standard personality tests. Now I want you to look at this card. What might this be? What do you see on this card? People see all sorts of things in these inkblots. Tell me what it might be for you—what it makes you think of."

I was shocked. I stared at the card and then at him.

That wasn't what I had expected him to say at all. "You mean there are no pictures hidden in those inkblots?"

Burt frowned and took off his glasses. "What?"

"Pictures! Hidden in the inkblots! Last time you told me that everyone could see them and you wanted me to find them too."

"No, Charlie. I couldn't have said that."

"What do you mean?" I shouted at him. Being so afraid of the inkblots had made me angry at myself and at Burt too. "That's what you said to me. Just because you're smart enough to go to college doesn't mean you have to make fun of me. I'm sick and tired of everybody laughing at me."

I don't recall ever being so angry before. I don't think it was at Burt himself, but suddenly everything exploded. I tossed the Rorschach cards on the table and walked out. Professor Nemur was passing by in the hall, and when I rushed past him without saying hello he knew something was wrong. He and Burt caught up with me as I was about to go down in the elevator.

"Charlie," said Nemur, grabbing my arm. "Wait a minute. What is this all about?"

I shook free and nodded at Burt. "I'm sick and tired of people making fun of me. That's all. Maybe before I didn't know any better, but now I do, and I don't like it."

"Nobody's making fun of you here, Charlie," said Nemur.

"What about the inkblots? Last time Burt told me there were pictures in the ink—that everyone could see, and I—"

"Look, Charlie, would you like to hear the exact words Burt said to you, and your answers as well? We have a tape-recording of that testing session. We can replay it and let you hear exactly what was said."

I went back with them to the psych office with mixed feelings. I was sure they had made fun of me and tricked me when I was too ignorant to know better. My anger was an exciting feeling, and I didn't give it up easily. I was ready to fight.

As Nemur went to the files to get the tape, Burt explained: "Last time, I used almost the exact words I used today. It's a requirement of these tests that the procedure be the same each time it's administered."

"I'll believe that when I hear it."

A look passed between them. I felt the blood rush to my face again. They were laughing at me. But then I realized what I had just said, and hearing myself I understood the reason for the look. They weren't laughing. They knew what was happening to me. I had reached a new level, and anger and suspicion were my first reactions to the world around me.

Burt's voice boomed over the tape recorder:

"Now I want you to look at this card, Charlie. What might this be? What do you see on this card? People see all kinds of things in these inkblots. Tell me what it makes you think of . . ."

The same words, almost the same tone of voice he had used minutes ago in the lab. And then I heard my answers—childish, impossible things. And I dropped limply into the chair beside Professor Nemur's desk. "Was that really me?"

I went back to the lab with Burt, and we went on with the Rorschach. We went through the cards slowly. This time my responses were different. I "saw" things in the inkblots. A pair of bats tugging at each other. Two men fencing with swords. I imagined all sorts of things. But even so, I found myself not trusting Burt completely any more. I kept turning the cards around, checking the backs to see if there was anything there I was supposed to catch.

I peeked, while he was making his notes. But it was all in code that looked like this:

WF + A DdF-Ad orig. WF — A SF + obj

The test still doesn't make sense. It seems to me that anyone could make up lies about things he didn't really see. How could they know I wasn't making fools of them by saying things I didn't really imagine?

Maybe I'll understand it when Dr. Strauss lets me read up on psychology. It's getting harder for me to write down all my thoughts and feelings because I know that people are reading them. Maybe it would be better if I

41

could keep some of these reports private for a while. I'm going to ask Dr. Strauss. Why should it suddenly start to bother me?

PROGRESS REPORT 10

April 21—I figured out a new way to set up the mixing machines in the bakery to speed up production. Mr. Donner says he will save labor costs and increase profits. He gave me a fifty-dollar bonus and a ten-dollar-a-week raise.

I wanted to take Joe Carp and Frank Reilly out to lunch to celebrate, but Joe had to buy some things for his wife, and Frank was meeting his cousin for lunch. I guess it will take time for them to get used to the changes in me.

Everyone seems frightened of me. When I went over to Gimpy and tapped him on the shoulder to ask him something, he jumped up and dropped his cup of coffee all over himself. He stares at me when he thinks I'm not looking. Nobody at the place talks to me any more, or kids around the way they used to. It makes the job kind of lonely.

Thinking about it makes me remember the time I fell asleep standing up and Frank kicked my legs out from under me. The warm sweet smell, the white walls, the roar of the oven when Frank opens the door to shift the loaves.

Suddenly falling . . . twisting . . . everything out from under me and my head cracking against the wall.

It's me, and yet it's like someone else lying there—another Charlie. He's confused . . . rubbing his head . . . staring up at Frank, tall and thin, and then at Gimpy nearby, massive, hairy, gray-faced Gimpy with bushy eye-brows that almost hide his blue eyes.

"Leave the kid alone," says Gimp. "Jesus, Frank, why do you always gotta pick on him?"

"It don't mean nothing," laughs Frank. "It don't hurt him. He don't know any better. Do you, Charlie?"

Charlie rubs his head and cringes. He doesn't know what he's done to deserve this punishment, but there is always the chance that there will be more.

"But you know better," says Gimpy, clumping over on his orthopedic boot, "so what the hell you always picking on him for?" The two men sit down at the long table, the tall Frank and the heavy Gimp shaping the dough for the rolls that have to be baked for the evening orders.

They work in silence for a while, and then Frank stops and tips his white cap back. "Hey, Gimp, think Charlie could learn to bake rolls?"

Gimp leans an elbow on the worktable. "Why don't we just leave him alone?"

"No, I mean it, Gimp—seriously. I bet he could learn something simple like making rolls."

The idea seems to appeal to Gimpy who turns to stare at Charlie. "Maybe you got something there. Hey, Charlie, come here a minute."

As he usually does when people are talking about him, Charlie has been keeping his head down, staring at his shoelaces. He knows how to lace and tie them. He could make rolls. He could learn to pound, roll, twist and shape the dough into the small round forms.

Frank looks at him uncertainly. "Maybe we shouldn't, Gimp. Maybe it's wrong. If a moron can't learn maybe we shouldn't start anything with him."

"You leave this to me," says Gimpy who has now taken over Frank's idea. "I think maybe he can learn. Now listen, Charlie. You want to learn something? You want me to teach you how to make rolls like me and Frank are doing?

Charlie stares at him, the smile melting from his face. He understands what Gimpy wants, and he feels cornered. He wants to please Gimpy, but there is something about the words *learn* and *teach*, something to remember about being punished severely, but he doesn't recall what it is—only a thin white hand upraised, hitting him to make him learn something he couldn't understand.

Charlie backs away but Gimpy grabs his arm. "Hey, kid, take it easy. We ain't gonna hurt you. Look at him shaking like he's gonna fall apart. Look, Charlie. I got a nice new shiny good-luck piece for you to play with." He holds out his hand and reveals a brass chain with a shiny

43

brass disc that says STA-BRITE METAL POLISH. He holds the chain by one end and the gleaming gold disc rotates slowly, catching the light of the fluorescent bulbs. The pendant is a brightness that Charlie remembers but he doesn't know why or what.

He doesn't reach for it. He knows you get punished if you reach out for other people's things. If someone puts it into your hand that is all right. But otherwise it's wrong. When he sees that Gimpy is offering it to him, he nods and smiles again.

"That he knows," laughs Frank. "Give him something bright and shiny." Frank, who has let Gimpy take over the experiment, leans forward excitedly. "Maybe if he wants that piece of junk bad enough and you tell him he'll get it if he learns to shape the dough into rolls—maybe it'll work."

As the bakers set to the task of teaching Charlie, others from the shop gather around. Frank clears an area between them on the table, and Gimpy pulls off a medium sized piece of dough for Charlie to work with. There is talk of betting on whether or not Charlie can learn to make rolls.

"Watch us carefully," says Gimpy, putting the pendant beside him on the table where Charlie can see it. "Watch and do everything we do. If you learn how to make rolls, you'll get this shiny good-luck piece."

Charlie hunches over on his stool, intently watching Gimpy pick up the knife and cut off a slab of dough. He studies each movement as Gimpy rolls out the dough into a long roll, breaks it off and twists it into a circle, pausing now and then to sprinkle it with flour.

"Now watch me," says Frank, and he repeats Gimpy's performance. Charlie is confused. There are differences. Gimpy holds his elbows out as he rolls the dough, like a bird's wings, but Frank keeps his arms close to his sides. Gimpy keeps his thumbs together with the rest of his fingers as he kneads the dough, but Frank works with the flat of his palms, keeping thumbs apart from his other fingers and up in the air.

Worrying about these things makes it impossible for Charlie to move when Gimpy says, "Go ahead, try it."

Charlie shakes his head.

"Look, Charlie, I'm gonna do it again slow. Now you

44

watch everything I do, and do each part along with me. Okay? But try to remember everything so then you'll be able to do the whole thing alone. Now come on—like this."

Charlie frowns as he watches Gimpy pull off a section of dough and roll it into a ball. He hesitates, but then he picks up the knife and slices off a piece of dough and sets it down in the center of the table. Slowly, keeping his elbows out exactly as Gimpy does, he rolls it into a ball.

He looks from his own hands to Gimpy's, and he is careful to keep his fingers exactly the same way, thumbs together with the rest of his fingers—slightly cupped. He has to do it right, the way Gimpy wants him to do it. There are echoes inside him that say, do it right and they will like you. And he wants Gimpy and Frank to like him.

When Gimpy has finished working his dough into a ball, he stands back, and so does Charlie. "Hey, that's great. Look, Frank, he made it into a ball."

Frank nods and smiles. Charlie sighs and his whole frame trembles as the tension builds. He is unaccustomed to this rare moment of success.

"All right now," says Gimpy. "Now we make a roll." Awkwardly, but carefully, Charlie follows Gimpy's every move. Occasionally, a twitch of his hand or arm mars what he is doing, but in a little while he is able to twist off a section of the dough and fashion it into a roll. Working beside Gimpy he makes six rolls, and sprinkling them with flour he sets them carefully alongside Gimpy's in the large flour-covered tray.

"All right, Charlie." Gimpy's face is serious. "Now, let's see you do it by yourself. Remember all the things you did from the beginning. Now, go ahead."

Charlie stares at the huge slab of dough and at the knife that Gimpy has pushed into his hand. And once again panic comes over him. What did he do first? How did he hold his hand? His fingers? Which way did he roll the ball? . . . A thousand confusing ideas burst into his mind at the same time and he stands there smiling. He wants to do it, to make Frank and Gimpy happy and have them like him, and to get the bright good-luck piece that Gimpy has promised him. He turns the smooth, heavy piece of dough around and around on the table, but he cannot bring himself to start. He cannot cut into it because he knows he will fail and he is afraid.

"He forgot already," said Frank. "It don't stick."

He wants it to stick. He frowns and tries to remember: first you start to cut off a piece. Then you roll it out into a ball. But how does it get to be a roll like the ones in the tray? That's something else. Give him time and he'll remember. As soon as the fuzziness passes away he'll remember. Just another few seconds and he'll have it. He wants to hold on to what he's learned—for a little while. He wants it so much.

"Okay, Charlie," sighs Gimpy, taking the cutter out of his hand. "That's all right. Don't worry about it. It's not your work anyway."

Another minute and he'll remember. If only they wouldn't rush him. Why does everything have to be in such a hurry?

"Go ahead, Charlie. Go sit down and look at your comic book. We got to get back to work."

Charlie nods and smiles, and pulls the comic book out of his back pocket. He smooths it out, and puts it on his head as a make-believe hat. Frank laughs and Gimpy finally smiles.

"Go on, you big baby," snorts Gimpy. "Go sit down there until Mr. Donner wants you."

Charlie smiles at him and goes back to the flour sacks in the corner near the mixing machines. He likes to lean back against them while he sits on the floor cross-legged and looks at the pictures in his comic book. As he starts to turn the pages, he feels like crying, but he doesn't know why. What is there to feel sad about? The fuzzy cloud comes and goes, and now he looks forward to the pleasure of the brightly colored pictures in the comic book that he has gone through thirty, forty times. He knows all of the figures in the comic—he has asked their names over and over again (of almost everyone he meets)—and he understands that the strange forms of letters and words in the white balloons above the figures means that they are saying something. Would he ever learn to read what was in the balloons? If they gave him enough time—if they didn't rush him or push him too fast—he would get it. But nobody has time.

Charlie pulls his legs up and opens the comic book to

the first page where the Batman and Robin are swinging up a long rope to the side of a building. Someday, he decides, he is going to read. And then he will be able to read the story. He feels a hand on his shoulder and he looks up. It is Gimpy holding out the brass disc and chain, letting it swing and twirl around so that it catches the light.

"Here," he says gruffly, tossing it into Charlie's lap, and then he limps away. . . .

I never thought about it before, but that was a nice thing for him to do. Why did he? Anyway, that is my memory of the time, clearer and more complete than anything I have ever experienced before. Like looking out of the kitchen window early when the morning light is still gray. I've come a long way since then, and I owe it all to Dr. Strauss and Professor Nemur, and the other people here at Beekman. But what must Frank and Gimpy think and feel now, seeing how I've changed?

April 22—People at the bakery are changing. Not only ignoring me. I can feel the hostility. Donner is arranging for me to join the baker's union, and I've gotten another raise. The rotten thing is that all of the pleasure is gone because the others resent me. In a way, I can't blame them. They don't understand what has happened to me, and I can't tell them. People are not proud of me the way I expected—not at all.

Still, I've got to have someone to talk to. I'm going to ask Miss Kinnian to go to a movie tomorrow night to celebrate my raise. If I can get up the nerve.

April 24—Professor Nemur finally agreed with Dr. Strauss and me that it will be impossible for me to write down everything if I know it's immediately read by people at the lab. I've tried to be completely honest about everything, no matter who I was talking about, but there are things I can't put down unless I can keep them private—at least for a while.

Now, I'm allowed to keep back some of these more personal reports, but before the final report to the Welberg Foundation, Professor Nemur will read through everything to decide what part of it should be published.

What happened today at the lab was very upsetting.

I dropped by the office earlier this evening to ask Dr. Strauss or Professor Nemur if they thought it would be all right for me to ask Alice Kinnian out to a movie, but before I could knock I heard them arguing with each other. I shouldn't have stayed, but it's hard to break the habit of listening because people have always spoken and acted as if I weren't there, as if they never cared what I overheard.

I heard someone bang on the desk, and then Professor Nemur shouted: "I've already informed the convention committee that we will present the paper at Chicago."

Then I heard Dr. Strauss' voice: "But you're wrong, Harold. Six weeks from now is still too soon. He's still changing."

And then Nemur: "We've predicted the pattern correctly so far. We're justified in making an interim report. I tell you, Jay, there's nothing to be afraid of. We've succeeded. It's all positive. Nothing can go wrong now."

Strauss: "This is too important to all of us to bring it out into the open prematurely. You're taking the authority on yourself—"

Nemur: "You forget that I'm the senior member of this project."

Strauss: "And you forget that you're not the only one with a reputation to consider. If we claim too much now, our whole hypothesis will come under fire."

Nemur: "I'm not afraid of regression any more. I've checked and rechecked everything. An interim report will do no harm. I feel sure nothing can go wrong now."

The argument went on that way with Strauss saying that Nemur had his eye on the Chair of Psychology at Hallston, and Nemur saying that Strauss was riding on the coattails of his psychological research. Then Strauss said that the project had as much to do with his techniques in psychosurgery and enzyme-injection patterns, as with Nemur's theories, and that someday thousands of neurosurgeons all over the world would be using *his* methods, but at this point Nemur reminded him that those new techniques would never have come about if not for *his* original theory.

They called each other names—*opportunist, cynic, pessimist*—and I found myself frightened. Suddenly, I realized I no longer had the right to stand there outside the office and listen to them without their knowing it. They might not have cared when I was too feeble-minded to know what was going on, but now that I could understand they wouldn't want me to hear it. I left without waiting for the outcome.

It was dark, and I walked for a long time trying to figure out why I was so frightened. I was seeing them clearly for the first time—not gods or even heroes, but just two men worried about getting something out of their work. Yet, if Nemur is right and the experiment is a success, what does it matter? There's so much to do, so many plans to make.

I'll wait until tomorrow to ask them about taking Miss Kinnian to a movie to celebrate my raise.

April 26—I know I shouldn't hang around the college when I'm through at the lab, but seeing the young men and women going back and forth carrying books and hearing them talk about all the things they're learning in their classes excites me. I wish I could sit and talk with them over coffee in the Campus Bowl Luncheonette when they get together to argue about books and politics and ideas. It's exciting to hear them talking about poetry and science and philosophy—about Shakespeare and Milton; Newton and Einstein and Freud; about Plato and Hegel and Kant, and all the other names that echo like great church bells in my mind.

Sometimes I listen in on the conversations at the tables around me, and pretend I'm a college student, even though I'm a lot older than they are. I carry books around, and I've started to smoke a pipe. It's silly, but since I belong at the lab I feel as if I'm a part of the university. I hate to go home to that lonely room.

April 27—I've made friends with some of the boys at the Campus Bowl. They were arguing about whether or not Shakespeare really wrote Shakespeare's plays. One of the boys—the fat one with the sweaty face—said that Marlowe wrote all of Shakespeare's plays. But Lenny, the short kid with the dark glasses, didn't believe that business about Marlowe, and he said that everyone knew that Sir Francis Bacon wrote the plays because Shakespeare had never been to college and never had the education that shows up in those plays. That's when the one with the freshman beanie said he had heard a couple of guys in the men's room talking about how Shakespeare's plays were really written by a lady.

And they talked about politics and art and God. I never before heard anyone say that there might not be a God. That frightened me, because for the first time I began to think about what God means.

Now I understand one of the important reasons for going to college and getting an education is to learn that the things you've believed in all your life aren't true, and that nothing is what it appears to be.

All the time they talked and argued, I felt the excitement bubble up inside me. This was what I wanted to do—go to college and hear people talk about important things.

I spend most of my free time at the library now, reading and soaking up what I can from books. I'm not concentrating on anything in particular, just reading a lot of fiction now—Dostoevski, Flaubert, Dickens, Hemingway, Faulkner—everything I can get my hands on—feeding a hunger that can't be satisfied.

April 28—In a dream last night I heard Mom screaming at Dad and the teacher at the elementary school P.S. 13 (my first school before they transferred me to P.S. 222). . . .

"He's normal! He's normal! He'll grow up like other people. Better than others." She was trying to scratch the teacher, but Dad was holding her back. "He'll go to college someday. He'll be *somebody*." She kept screaming it, clawing at Dad so he'd let go of her. "He'll go to college someday and he'll be somebody."

We were in the principal's office and there were a lot of people looking embarrassed, but the assistant principal was smiling and turning his head so no one would see it.

The principal in my dream had a long beard, and was floating around the room and pointing at me. "He'll have to go to a special school. Put him into the Warren State Home and Training School. We can't have him here."

Dad was pulling Mom out of the principal's office, and

she was shouting and crying too. I didn't see her face, but her big red teardrops kept splashing down on me. . . .

This morning I could recall the dream, but now there's more than that—I can remember through the blur, back to when I was six years old and it all happened. Just before Norma was born. I see Mom, a thin, dark-haired woman who talks too fast and uses her hands too much. As always her face is blurred. Her hair is up in a bun, and her hand goes to touch it, pat it smooth, as if she has to make sure it's still there. I remember that she was always fluttering like a big, white bird—around my father, and he too heavy and tired to escape her pecking.

I see Charlie, standing in the center of the kitchen, playing with his spinner, bright colored beads and rings threaded on a string. He holds the string up in one hand turns the rings so they wind and unwind in bright spinning flashes. He spends long hours watching his spinner. I don't know who made it for him, or what became of it, but I see him standing there fascinated as the string untwists and sets the rings spinning. . . .

She is screaming at him—no, she's screaming at his father. "I'm not going to take him. There's nothing wrong with him!"

"Rose, it won't do any good pretending any longer that nothing is wrong. Just look at him, Rose. Six years old, and—"

"He's not a dummy. He's normal. He'll be just like everyone else."

He looks sadly at his son with the spinner and Charlie smiles and holds it up to show him how pretty it is when it goes around and around.

"Put that thing away!" Mom shrieks and suddenly she knocks the spinner from Charlie's hand, and it crashes across the kitchen floor. "Go play with your alphabet blocks."

He stands there, frightened by the sudden outburst. He cowers, not knowing what she will do. His body begins to shake. They're arguing, and the voices back and forth make a squeezing pressure inside him and a sense of panic.

"Charlie, go to the bathroom. Don't you dare do it in your pants."

He wants to obey her, but his legs are too soft to move. His arms go up automatically to ward off blows.

"For God's sake, Rose. Leave him alone. You've got him terrified. You always do this, and the poor kid—"

"Then why don't you help me? I have to do it all by myself. Every day I try to teach him—to help him catch up to the others. He's just slow, that's all. But he can learn like everyone else."

"You're fooling yourself, Rose. It's not fair to us or to him. Pretending he's normal. Driving him as if he were an animal that could learn to do tricks. Why don't you leave him alone?"

"Because I want him to be like everyone else."

As they argue, the feeling that grips Charlie's insides becomes greater. His bowels feel as if they will burst and he knows he should go to the bathroom as she has told him so often. But he can't walk. He feels like sitting down right there in the kitchen, but it is wrong and she will slap him.

He wants his spinner. If he has his spinner and he watches it going round and round, he will be able to control himself and not make in his pants. But the spinner is all apart with some of the rings under the table and some under the sink, and the cord is near the stove.

It is very strange that although I can recall the voices clearly their faces are still blurred, and I can see only general outlines. Dad massive and slumped. Mom thin and quick. Hearing them now, arguing with each other across the years, I have the impulse to shout at them: "Look at him. There, down there! Look at Charlie. He has to go to the toilet!"

Charlie stands clutching and pulling at his red checkered shirt as they argue over him. The words are angry sparks between them—an anger and a guilt he can't identify.

"Next September he's going to go back to P.S. 13 and do the term's work over again."

"Why can't you let yourself see the truth? The teacher says he's not capable of doing the work in a regular class."

"That bitch a teacher? Oh, I've got better names for her. Let her start with me again and I'll do more than just write to the board of education. I'll scratch that dirty slut's eyes out. Charlie, why are you twisting like that? Go to the bathroom. Go by yourself. You know how to go."

"Can't you see he wants you to take him? He's frightened."

"Keep out of this. He's perfectly capable of going to the bathroom himself. The book says it gives him confidence and a feeling of achievement."

The terror that waits in that cold tile room overwhelms him. He is afraid to go there alone. He reaches up for her hand and sobs out: "Toi— toi . . ." and she slaps his hand away.

"No more," she says sternly. "You're a big boy now. You can go by yourself. Now march right into that bathroom and pull your pants down the way I taught you. I warn you if you make in your pants you'll get spanked."

I can almost feel it now, the stretching and knotting in his intestines as the two of them stand over him waiting to see what he will do. His whimper becomes a soft crying as suddenly he can control no longer, and he sobs and covers his face with his hands as he dirties himself.

It is soft and warm and he feels the confusion of relief and fear. It is his, but she will take it away from him as she always does. She will take it away and keep it for herself. And she will spank him. She comes toward him, screaming that he is a bad boy, and Charlie runs to his father for help.

Suddenly, I remember that her name is Rose and his name is Matt. It's odd to have forgotten your parents' names. And what about Norma? Strange I haven't thought about them all for a long time. I wish I could see Matt's face now, to know what he was thinking at that moment. All I remember is that as she began to spank me, Matt Gordon turned and walked out of the apartment.

I wish I could see their faces more clearly.

PROGRESS REPORT 11

May 1—Why haven't I ever noticed how beautiful Alice Kinnian is? She has pigeon-soft brown eyes and feathery brown hair down to the hollow of her neck. When she smiles, her full lips look as if she's pouting.

We went to a movie and then to dinner. I didn't see much of the first picture because I was too conscious of her sitting next to me. Twice her bare arm touched mine on the armrest, and both times the fear that she would become annoyed made me pull back. All I could think about was her soft skin just inches away. Then I saw, two rows ahead of us, a young man with his arm around his girl, and I wanted to put my arm around Miss Kinnian. Terrifying. But if I did it slowly . . . first resting my arm on the back of her seat . . . moving up . . . inch by inch . . . to rest near her shoulders and the back of her neck . . . casually . . .

I didn't dare.

The best I could do was rest my elbow on the back of her seat, but by the time I got there I had to shift position to wipe the perspiration off my face and neck.

Once, her leg accidentally brushed against mine.

It became such an ordeal—so painful—that I forced myself to take my mind off her. The first picture had been a war film, and all I caught was the ending where the G.I. goes back to Europe to marry the woman who saved his life. The second picture interested me. A psychological film about a man and woman apparently in love but actually destroying each other. Everything suggests that the man is going to kill his wife but at the last moment, something she screams out in a nightmare makes him recall something that happened to him during his childhood. The sudden memory shows him that his hatred is really directed at a depraved governess who had terrified him with frightening stories and left a flaw in his personality. Excited at discovering this, he cries out with joy so that his wife awakens. He takes her in his arms and the implication is that all his problems have been solved. It was pat and cheap, and I must have shown my anger because Alice wanted to know what was wrong. "It's a lie," I explained, as we walked out into the lobby. "Things just don't happen that way."

"Of course not." She laughed. "It's a world of make-believe."

"Oh, no! That's no answer." I insisted. "Even in the world of make-believe there have to be rules. The parts have to be consistent and belong together. This kind of picture is a lie. Things are forced to fit because the writer or the director or somebody wanted something in that didn't belong. And it doesn't feel right."

She looked at me thoughtfully as we walked out into the bright dazzling night-lights of Times Square. "You're coming along fast."

"I'm confused. I don't know what I know any more."

"Never mind that," she insisted. "You're beginning to see and understand things." She waved her hand to take in all of the neon and glitter around us as we crossed over to Seventh Avenue. "You're beginning to see what's behind the surface of things. What you say about the parts having to belong together—that was a pretty good insight."

"Oh, come on now. I don't feel as if I'm accomplishing anything. I don't understand about myself or my past. I don't even know where my parents are, or what they look like. Do you know that when I see them in a flash of memory or in a dream the faces are a blur? I want to see their expressions. I can't understand what's going on unless I can see their faces—"

"Charlie, calm down." People were turning to stare. She slipped her arm through mine and pulled me close to restrain me. "Be patient. Don't forget you're accomplishing in weeks what takes others a lifetime. You're a giant sponge soaking in knowledge. Soon you'll begin to connect things up, and you'll see how all the different worlds of learning are related. All the levels, Charlie, like steps on a giant ladder. And you'll climb higher and higher to see more and more of the world around you."

As we entered the cafeteria on Forty-fifth Street and picked up our trays, she spoke animatedly. "Ordinary people," she said, "can see only a little bit. They can't change much or go any higher than they are, but you're a genius. You'll keep going up and up, and see more and more. And each step will reveal worlds you never even knew existed."

People on the line who heard her turned to stare at me, and only when I nudged her to stop did she lower her voice. "I just hope to God," she whispered, "that you don't get hurt."

For a little while after that I didn't know what to say. We ordered our food at the counter and carried it to our table and ate without talking. The silence made me nervous. I knew what she meant about her fear, so I joked about it.

"Why should I get hurt? I couldn't be any worse off than I was before. Even Algernon is still smart, isn't he? As long as he's up there I'm in good shape." She toyed with her knife making circular depressions in a pat of butter and the movement hypnotized me. "And besides," I told her, "I overheard something—Professor Nemur and Dr. Strauss were arguing, and Nemur said he's positive that nothing can go wrong."

"I hope so," she said. "You have no idea how afraid I've been that something might go wrong. I feel partly responsible." She saw me staring at the knife and she put it down carefully beside her plate.

"I never would have done it but for you," I said.

She laughed and it made me tremble. That's when I saw that her eyes were soft brown. She looked down at the tablecloth quickly and blushed.

"Thank you, Charlie," she said, and took my hand.

It was the first time anyone had ever done that, and it made me bolder. I leaned forward, holding on to her hand, and the words came out. "I like you very much." After I said it, I was afraid she'd laugh, but she nodded and smiled.

"I like you too, Charlie."

"But it's more than liking. What I mean is . . . oh, hell! I don't know what I mean." I knew I was blushing, and I didn't know where to look or what to do with my hands. I dropped a fork, and when I tried to retrieve it, I knocked over a glass of water and it spilled on her dress. Suddenly, I had become clumsy and awkward again, and when I tried to apologize I found my tongue had become too large for my mouth.

"That's all right, Charlie," she tried to reassure me. "It's only water. Don't let it upset you this way."

In the taxi on the way home, we were silent for a long time, and then she put down her purse and straightened my tie and puffed up my breast pocket handkerchief. "You were very upset tonight, Charlie."

"I feel ridiculous."

"I upset you by talking about it. I made you self-conscious."

"It's not that. What bothers me is that I can't put into words the way I feel."

"These feelings are new to you. Not everything has to . . . be put into words."

I moved closer to her and tried to take her hand again, but she pulled away. "No, Charlie. I don't think this is good for you. I've upset you, and it might have a negative effect."

When she put me off, I felt awkward and ridiculous at the same time. It made me angry with myself and I pulled back to my side of the seat and stared out the window. I hated her as I had never hated anyone before—with her easy answers and maternal fussing. I wanted to slap her face, to make her crawl, and then to hold her in my arms and kiss her.

"Charlie, I'm sorry if I've upset you."

"Forget it."

"But you've got to understand what's happening."

"I understand," I said, "and I'd rather not talk about it."

By the time the cab reached her apartment on Seventy-seventh Street, I was thoroughly miserable.

"Look," she said, "this is my fault. I shouldn't have gone out with you tonight."

"Yes, I see that now."

"What I mean is, we have no right to put this on a personal . . . emotional level. You have so much to do. I have no right to come into your life at this time."

"That's my worry, isn't it?"

"Is it? This isn't your private affair any more, Charlie. You've got obligations now—not only to Professor Nemur and Dr. Strauss, but to the millions who may follow in your footsteps."

The more she talked that way, the worse I felt. She

highlighted my awkwardness, my lack of knowledge about the right things to say and do. I was a blundering adolescent in her eyes, and she was trying to let me down easy.

As we stood at the door to her apartment, she turned and smiled at me and for a moment I thought she was going to invite me in, but she just whispered: "Good night, Charlie. Thank you for a wonderful evening."

I wanted to kiss her good night. I had worried about it earlier. Didn't a woman expect you to kiss her? In the novels I'd read and the movies I'd seen, the man makes the advances. I had decided last night that I would kiss her. But I kept thinking: what if she turns me down?

I moved closer and reached for her shoulders, but she was too quick for me. She stopped me and took my hand in hers. "We'd better just say good night this way, Charlie. We can't let this get personal. Not yet."

And before I could protest, or ask what she meant by *not yet,* she started inside. "Good night, Charlie, and thank you again for a lovely . . . lovely time." And closed the door.

I was furious at her, myself, and the world, but by the time I got home, I realized she was right. Now, I don't know whether she cares for me or if she was just being kind. What could she possibly see in me? What makes it so awkward is that I've never experienced anything like this before. How does a person go about learning how to act toward another person? How does a man learn how to behave toward a woman?

The books don't help much.

But next time, I'm going to kiss her good night.

May 3—One of the things that confuses me is never really knowing when something comes up from my past, whether it really happened that way, or if that was the way it seemed to be at the time, or if I'm inventing it. I'm like a man who's been half-asleep all his life, trying to find out what he was like before he woke up. Everything is strangely slow-motion and blurred.

I had a nightmare last night, and when I woke up I remembered something.

First the nightmare: I'm running down a long corridor, half blinded by the swirls of dust. At times I run forward and then I float around and run backwards, but I'm afraid because I'm hiding something in my pocket. I don't know what it is or where I got it, but I know they want to take it away from me and that frightens me.

The wall breaks down and suddenly there is a red-haired girl with her arms outstretched to me—her face is a blank mask. She takes me into her arms, kisses and caresses me, and I want to hold her tightly but I'm afraid. The more she touches me, the more frightened I become because I know I must never touch a girl. Then, as her body rubs up against mine, I feel a strange bubbling and throbbing inside me that makes me warm. But when I look up I see a bloody knife in her hands.

I try to scream as I run, but no sound comes out of my throat, and my pockets are empty. I search in my pockets but I don't know what it is I've lost or why I was hiding it. I know only that it's gone, and there is blood on my hands too.

When I woke up, I thought of Alice, and I had the same feeling of panic as in the dream. What am I afraid of? Something about the knife.

I made myself a cup of coffee and smoked a cigarette. I'd never had a dream like it before, and I knew it was connected with my evening with Alice. I have begun to think of her in a different way.

Free association is still difficult, because it's hard not to control the direction of your thoughts . . . just to leave your mind open and let anything flow into it . . . ideas bubbling to the surface like a bubble bath . . . a woman bathing . . . a girl . . . Norma taking a bath . . . I am watching through the keyhole . . . and when she gets out of the tub to dry herself I see that her body is different from mine. Something is missing.

Running down the hallway . . . somebody chasing me . . . not a person . . . just a big flashing kitchen knife . . . and I'm scared and crying but no voice comes out because my neck is cut and I'm bleeding . . .

"Mama, Charlie is peeking at me through the keyhole . . ."

Why is she different? What happened to her? . . . blood . . . bleeding . . . a dark cubbyhole . . .

Three blind mice . . . three blind mice,
See how they run! See how they run!
They all run after the farmer's wife,
She cut off their tails with a carving knife,
Did you ever see such a sight in your life,
As three . . . blind . . . mice?

Charlie, alone in the kitchen early in the morning. Everyone else asleep, and he amuses himself playing with his spinner. One of the buttons pops off his shirt as he bends over, and it rolls across the intricate line-pattern of the kitchen linoleum. It rolls towards the bathroom and he follows, but then he loses it. Where is the button? He goes into the bathroom to find it. There is a closet in the bathroom where the clothes hamper is, and he likes to take out all the clothes and look at them. His father's things and his mother's . . . and Norma's dresses. He would like to try them on and make believe he is Norma, but once when he did that his mother spanked him for it. There in the clothes hamper he finds Norma's underwear with dried blood. What had she done wrong? He was terrified. Whoever had done it might come looking for him. . . .

Why does a memory like that from childhood remain with me so strongly, and why does it frighten me now? Is it because of my feelings for Alice?

Thinking about it now, I can understand why I was taught to keep away from women. It was wrong for me to express my feelings to Alice. I have no right to think of a woman that way—not yet.

But even as I write these words, something inside shouts that there is more. I'm a person. I was somebody before I went under the surgeon's knife. And I have to love someone.

May 8—Even now that I have learned what has been going on behind Mr. Donner's back, I find it hard to believe. I first noticed something was wrong during the rush hour two days ago. Gimpy was behind the counter wrapping a birthday cake for one of our regular customers—a cake that sells for $3.95. But when Gimpy rang up the sale the register showed only $2.95. I started to tell him he had made a mistake, but in the mirror behind the counter I saw a wink and smile that passed from the customer to Gimpy and the answering smile on Gimpy's face. And when the man took his change, I saw the flash of a large silver coin left behind in Gimpy's hand, before his fingers closed on it, and the quick movement with which he slipped the half-dollar into his pocket.

"Charlie," said a woman behind me, "are there any more of those cream-filled éclairs?"

"I'll go back and find out."

I was glad of the interruption because it gave me time to think about what I had seen. Certainly, Gimpy had not made a mistake. He had deliberately undercharged the customer, and there had been an understanding between them.

I leaned limply against the wall not knowing what to do. Gimpy had worked for Mr. Donner for over fifteen years. Donner—who always treated his workers like close friends, like relatives—had invited Gimpy's family to his house for dinner more than once. He often put Gimpy in charge of the shop when he had to go out, and I had heard stories of the times Donner gave Gimpy money to pay his wife's hospital bills.

It was incredible that anyone would steal from such a man. There had to be some other explanation. Gimpy had really made a mistake in ringing up the sale, and the half-dollar was a tip. Or perhaps Mr. Donner had made some special arrangement for this one customer who regularly bought cream cakes. Anything rather than believe that Gimpy was stealing. Gimpy had always been so nice to me.

I no longer wanted to know. I kept my eyes averted from the register as I brought out the tray of éclairs and sorted out the cookies, buns, and cakes.

But when the little red-haired woman came in—the one who always pinched my cheek and joked about finding a girl friend for me—I recalled that she came in most often when Donner was out to lunch and Gimpy was behind the counter. Gimpy had often sent me out to deliver orders to her house.

Involuntarily, my mind totaled her purchases to $4.53. But I turned away so that I would not see what Gimpy rang up on the cash register. I wanted to know the truth, and yet I was afraid of what I might learn.

"Two forty-five, Mrs. Wheeler," he said.

The ring of the sale. The counting of change. The slam of the drawer. "Thank you, Mrs. Wheeler." I turned just in time to see him putting his hand into his pocket, and I heard the faint clink of coins.

How many times had he *used me* as a go-between to deliver packages to her, undercharging her so that later they could split the difference? Had he used me all these years to help him steal?

I couldn't take my eyes off Gimpy as he clomped around behind the counter, perspiration streaming down from under his paper cap. He seemed animated and good-natured, but looking up he caught my eye, frowned and turned away.

I wanted to hit him. I wanted to go behind the counter and smash his face in. I don't remember ever hating anyone before—but this morning I hated Gimpy with all my heart.

Pouring this all out on paper in the quiet of my room has not helped. Every time I think of Gimpy stealing from Mr. Donner I want to smash something. Fortunately, I don't think I'm capable of violence. I don't think I ever hit anyone in my life.

But I still have to decide what to do. Tell Donner that his trusted employee has been stealing from him all these years? Gimpy would deny it, and I could never prove it was true. And what would it do to Mr. Donner? I don't know what to do.

May 9—I can't sleep. This has gotten to me. I owe Mr. Donner too much to stand by and see him robbed this way. I'd be as guilty as Gimpy by my silence. And yet, is it my place to inform on him? The thing that bothers me most is that when he sent me on deliveries he used *me* to help him steal from Donner. Not knowing about it, I was outside it—not to blame. But now that I know, by my silence I am as guilty as he is.

Yet, Gimpy is a co-worker. Three children. What will he do if Donner fires him? He might not be able to get another job—especially with his club foot.

Is that my worry?

What's right? Ironic that all my intelligence doesn't help me solve a problem like this.

May 10—I asked Professor Nemur about it, and he insists that I'm an innocent bystander and there's no reason for me to become involved in what would be an unpleasant situation. The fact that I've been used as a go-between doesn't seem to bother him at all. If I didn't understand what was happening at the time, he says, then it doesn't matter. I'm no more to blame than the knife is to blame in a stabbing, or the car in a collision.

"But I'm not an inanimate object," I argued. "I'm a *person*."

He looked confused for a moment and then laughed. "Of course, Charlie. But I wasn't referring to now. I meant before the operation."

Smug, pompous—I felt like hitting him too. "I was a person before the operation. In case you forgot—"

"Yes, of course, Charlie. Don't misunderstand. But it was different . . ." And then he remembered that he had to check some charts in the lab.

Dr. Strauss doesn't talk much during our psychotherapy sessions, but today when I brought it up, he said that I was morally obligated to tell Mr. Donner. But the more I thought about it the less simple it became. I had to have someone else to break the tie, and the only one I could think of was Alice. Finally, at ten thirty I couldn't hold out any longer. I dialed three times, broke off in the middle each time, but on the fourth try, I managed to hold on until her voice.

At first she didn't think she should see me, but I begged her to meet me at the cafeteria where we had dinner together. "I respect you—you've always given me good advice." And when she still wavered, I insisted. "You *have* to help me. You're partly responsible. You said so yourself. If not for you I would never have gone into this in the first place. You just can't shrug me off now."

She must have sensed the urgency because she agreed to meet me. I hung up and stared at the phone. Why was it so important for me to know what *she* thought, how *she* felt? For more than a year at the Adult Center the only thing that mattered was pleasing her. Was that why I had agreed to the operation in the first place?

I paced up and back in front of the cafeteria until the policeman began to eye me suspiciously. Then I went in and bought coffee. Fortunately, the table we had used last time was empty. She would think of looking for me back there.

She saw me and waved to me, but stopped at the counter for coffee before she came over to the table. She smiled and I knew it was because I had chosen the same table. A foolish, romantic gesture.

"I know it's late," I apologized, "but I swear I was going out of my mind. I had to talk to you."

She sipped her coffee and listened quietly as I explained how I had found out about Gimpy's cheating, my own reaction, and the conflicting advice I'd gotten at the lab. When I finished, she sat back and shook her head.

"Charlie, you amaze me. In some ways you're so advanced, and yet when it comes to making a decision, you're still a child. I can't decide for you, Charlie. The answer can't be found in books—or be solved by bringing it to other people. Not unless you want to remain a child all your life. You've got to find the answer inside you— *feel* the right thing to do. Charlie, you've got to learn to trust yourself."

At first, I was annoyed at her lecture, but then suddenly —it began to make sense. "You mean, *I've* got to decide?" She nodded.

"In fact," I said, "now that I think of it, I believe I've already decided some of it! I think Nemur and Strauss are both wrong!"

She was watching me closely, excitedly. "Something is happening to you, Charlie. If you could only see your face."

"You're damned right, something is happening! A cloud of smoke was hanging in front of my eyes, and with one breath you blew it away. A simple idea. Trust *myself*. And it never occurred to me before."

"Charlie, you're wonderful."

I caught her hand and held it. "No, it's you. You touch my eyes and make me see."

She blushed and pulled her hand back.

"The last time we were here," I said, "I told you I liked you. I should have trusted myself to say I love you."

"Don't, Charlie. Not yet."

"Not yet?" I shouted. "That's what you said last time. Why not yet?"

"Shhhh . . . Wait a while, Charlie. Finish your studies. See where they lead you. You're changing too fast."

"What does that have to do with it? My feeling for you won't change because I'm becoming intelligent. I'll only love you more."

"But you're changing emotionally too. In a peculiar sense I'm the first woman you've ever been really aware of—in this way. Up to now I've been your teacher—someone you turn to for help and advice. You're bound to think you're in love with me. See other women. Give yourself more time."

"What you're saying is that young boys are always falling in love with their teachers, and that emotionally I'm still just a boy."

"You're twisting my words around. No, I don't think of you as a boy."

"Emotionally retarded then."

"No."

"Then, why?"

"Charlie, don't push me. I don't know. Already, you've gone beyond my intellectual reach. In a few months or even weeks, you'll be a different person. When you mature intellectually, we may not be able to communicate. When you mature emotionally, you may not even want me. I've got to think of myself too, Charlie. Let's wait and see. Be patient."

She was making sense, but I wasn't letting myself listen. "The other night—" I choked out, "You don't know how much I looked forward to that date. I was out of my mind wondering how to behave, what to say, wanting to make the best impression, and terrified I might say something to make you angry."

"You didn't make me angry. I was flattered."

"Then, when can I see you again?"

"I have no right to let you get involved."

"But I *am* involved!" I shouted, and then seeing people turn to look, I lowered my voice until it trembled with anger. "I'm a person—a man—and I can't live with just books and tapes and electronic mazes. You say, 'see other women.' How can I when I don't know any other women? Something inside is burning me up, and all I know is it makes me think of you. I'm in the middle of a page and I see your face on it—not blurred like those in my past, but clear and alive. I touch the page and your face is gone and I want to tear the book apart and throw it away."

"Please, Charlie . . ."

"Let me see you again."

"Tomorrow at the lab."

"You know that's not what I mean. Away from the lab. Away from the university. Alone."

I could tell she wanted to say yes. She was surprised by my insistence. I was surprised at myself. I only knew that I couldn't stop pressing her. And yet there was a terror in my throat as I begged her. My palms were damp. Was I afraid she'd say *no*, or afraid she'd say *yes?* If she hadn't broken the tension by answering me, I think I would have fainted.

"All right, Charlie. Away from the lab and the university, but not alone. I don't think we should be alone together."

"Anywhere you say," I gasped. "Just so I can be with you and not think of tests . . . statistics . . . questions . . . answers . . ."

She frowned for a moment. "All right. They have free spring concerts in Central Park. Next week you can take me to one of the concerts."

When we got to her doorway, she turned quickly and kissed my cheek. "Good night, Charlie. I'm glad you called me. I'll see you at the lab." She closed the door and I stood outside the building and looked at the light in her apartment window until it went out.

There is no question about it now. I'm in love.

May 11—After all this thinking and worrying, I realized Alice was right. I had to trust my intuition. At the bakery, I watched Gimpy more closely. Three times today, I saw him undercharging customers and pocketing his portion of the difference as the customers passed money back to him. It was only with certain regular customers that he did it, and it occurred to me that these people were as guilty as he. Without their agreement this could never take place. Why should Gimpy be the scapegoat?

That's when I decided on the compromise. It might not

be the perfect decision, but it was my decision, and it seemed to be the best answer under the circumstances. I would tell Gimpy what I knew and warn him to stop.

I got him alone back by the washroom, and when I came up to him he started away. "I've got something important to talk to you about," I said. "I want your advice for a friend who has a problem. He's discovered that one of his fellow employees is cheating his boss, and he doesn't know what to do about it. He doesn't like the idea of informing and getting the guy into trouble, but he won't stand by and let his boss—who has been good to both of them—be cheated."

Gimpy looked at me hard. "What does this friend of yours plan to do about it?"

"That's the trouble. He doesn't want to do anything. He feels if the stealing stops there would be nothing gained by doing anything at all. He would forget about it."

"Your friend ought to keep his nose in his own business," said Gimpy, shifting off his club foot. "He ought to keep his eyes closed to things like that and know who *his* friends are. A boss is a boss, and working people got to stick together."

"My friend doesn't feel that way."

"It's none of his business."

"He feels that if he knows about it he's partly responsible. So he's decided that if the thing stops, he's got nothing more to say. Otherwise, he'll tell the whole story. I wanted to ask your opinion. Do you think that under the circumstances the stealing will stop?"

It was a strain for him to conceal his anger. I could see that he wanted to hit me, but he just kept squeezing his fist.

"Tell your friend the guy doesn't seem to have any choice."

"That's fine," I said. "That will make my friend very happy."

Gimpy started away, and then he paused and looked back. "Your friend—could it be maybe he's interested in a cut? Is that his reason?"

"No, he just wants the whole thing to stop."

He glared at me. "I can tell you, you'll be sorry you stuck your nose in. I always stood up for you. I should of had my head examined." And then he limped off.

Perhaps I ought to have told Donner the whole story and had Gimpy fired—I don't know. Doing it this way has something to be said for it. It's over and done with. But how many people are there like Gimpy who use other people that way?

May 15—My studies are going well. The university library is my second home now. They've had to get me a private room because it takes me only a second to absorb the printed page, and curious students invariably gather around me as I flip through my books.

My most absorbing interests at the present time are etymologies of ancient languages, the newer works on the calculus of variations, and Hindu history. It's amazing the way things, apparently disconnected, hang together. I've moved up to another plateau, and now the streams of the various disciplines seem to be closer to each other as if they flow from a single source.

Strange how when I'm in the college cafeteria and hear the students arguing about history or politics or religion, it all seems so childish.

I find no pleasure in discussing ideas any more on such an elementary level. People resent being shown that they don't approach the complexities of the problem—they don't know what exists beyond the surface ripples. It's just as bad on a higher level, and I've given up any attempt to discuss these things with the professors at Beekman.

Burt introduced me to an economics professor at the faculty cafeteria, one well known for his work on the economic factors affecting interest rates. I had long wanted to talk to an economist about some of the ideas I had come across in my reading. The moral aspects of the military blockade as a weapon in times of peace had been bothering me. I asked him what he thought of the suggestion by some senators that we begin using such tactics as "blacklisting" and reinforcement of the navicert controls that had been used in World Wars I and II, against some of the smaller nations which now oppose us.

He listened quietly, staring off into space, and I assumed he was collecting his thoughts for an answer, but a few minutes later he cleared his throat and shook his head. That, he explained apologetically, was outside his area of specialization. His interest was in interest rates, and he hadn't given military economics much thought. He suggested I see Dr. Wessey, who once did a paper on War Trade Agreements during World War II. He might be able to help me.

Before I could say anything else, he grabbed my hand and shook it. He had been glad to meet me, but there were some notes he had to assemble for a lecture. And then he was gone.

The same thing happened when I tried to discuss Chaucer with an American literature specialist, questioned an Orientalist about the Trobriand Islanders, and tried to focus on the problems of automation-caused unemployment with a social psychologist who specialized in public opinion polls on adolescent behavior. They would always find excuses to slip away, afraid to reveal the narrowness of their knowledge.

How different they seem to be now. And how foolish I was ever to have thought that professors were intellectual giants. They're people—and afraid the rest of the world will find out. And Alice is a person too—a woman, not a goddess—and I'm taking her to the concert tomorrow night.

May 17—Almost morning and I can't fall asleep. I've got to understand what happened to me last night at the concert.

The evening started out well enough. The Mall at Central Park had filled up early, and Alice and I had to pick our way among the couples stretched out on the grass. Finally, far back from the path, we found an unused tree where—out of the range of lamplight—the only evidence of other couples was the protesting female laughter and the glow of lit cigarettes.

"This will be fine," she said. "No reason to be right on top of the orchestra."

"What's that they're playing now?" I asked.

"Debussy's *La Mer*. Do you like it?"

I settled down beside her. "I don't know much about this kind of music. I have to think about it."

"Don't think about it," she whispered. "Feel it. Let it sweep over you like the sea without trying to understand." She lay back on the grass and turned her face in the direction of the music.

I had no way of knowing what she expected of me. This was far from the clear lines of problem-solving and the systematic acquisition of knowledge. I kept telling myself that the sweating palms, the tightness in my chest, the desire to put my arms around her were merely biochemical reactions. I even traced the pattern of stimulus-and-reaction that caused my nervousness and excitement. Yet everything was fuzzy and uncertain. Should I put my arm around her or not? Was she waiting for me to do it? Would she get angry? I could tell I was still behaving like an adolescent and it angered me.

"Here," I choked, "why don't you make yourself more comfortable? Rest on my shoulder." She let me put my arm around her, but she didn't look at me. She seemed to be too absorbed in the music to realize what I was doing. Did she want me to hold her that way, or was she merely tolerating it? As I slipped my arm down to her waist, I felt her tremble, but still she kept staring in the direction of the orchestra. She was pretending to be concentrating on the music so that she wouldn't have to respond to me. She didn't want to know what was happening. As long as she looked away, and listened, she could pretend that my closeness, my arms around her, were without her knowledge or consent. She wanted me to make love to her body while she kept her mind on higher things. I reached over roughly and turned her chin. "Why don't you look at me? Are you pretending I don't exist?"

"No, Charlie," she whispered. "I'm pretending I don't exist."

When I touched her shoulder she stiffened and trembled, but I pulled her toward me. Then it happened. It started as a hollow buzzing in my ears . . . an electric saw . . . far away. Then the cold: arms and legs prickly, and finger numbing. Suddenly, I had the feeling I was being watched.

A sharp switch in perception. I saw, from some point in the darkness behind a tree, the two of us lying in each other's arms.

I looked up to see a boy of fifteen or sixteen, crouching nearby. "Hey!" I shouted. As he stood up, I saw his trousers were open and he was exposed.

"What's the matter?" she gasped.

I jumped up, and he vanished into the darkness. "Did you see him?"

"No," she said, smoothing her skirt nervously. "I didn't see anyone."

"Standing right here. Watching us. Close enough to touch you."

"Charlie, where are you going?"

"He couldn't have gotten very far."

"Leave him alone, Charlie. It doesn't matter."

But it mattered to me. I ran into the darkness, stumbling over startled couples, but there was no way to tell where he had gone.

The more I thought about him, the worse became the queasy feeling that comes before fainting. Lost and alone in a great wilderness. And then I caught hold of myself and found my way back to where Alice was sitting.

"Did you find him?"

"No, but he was there. I saw him."

She looked at me strangely. "Are you all right?"

"I will be . . . in a minute . . . Just that damned buzzing in my ears."

"Maybe we'd better go."

All the way back to her apartment, it was on my mind that the boy had been crouching there in the darkness, and for one second I had caught a glimpse of what he was seeing—the two of us lying in each other's arms.

"Would you like to come in? I could make some coffee."

I wanted to, but something warned me against it. "Better not. I've got a lot of work to do tonight."

"Charlie, is it anything I said or did?"

"Of course not. Just that kid watching us upset me."

She was standing close to me, waiting for me to kiss her. I put my arm around her, but it happened again. If I didn't get away quickly, I would pass out.

"Charlie, you look sick."

"Did you see him, Alice? The truth . . ."

She shook her head. "No. It was too dark. But I'm sure—"

"I've got to go. I'll call you." And before she could stop me, I pulled away. I had to get out of that building before everything caved in.

Thinking about it now, I'm certain it was a hallucination. Dr. Strauss feels that emotionally I'm still in that adolescent state where being close to a woman, or thinking of sex, sets off anxiety, panic, even hallucinations. He feels that my rapid intellectual development has deceived me into thinking I could live a normal emotional life. But

I've got to accept the fact that the fears and blocks triggered in these sexual situations reveal that emotionally I'm still an adolescent—sexually retarded. I guess he means I'm not ready for a relationship with a woman like Alice Kinnian. Not yet.

May 20—I've been fired from my job at the bakery. I know it was foolish of me to hang on to the past, but there was something about the place with its white brick walls browned by oven heat . . . It was home to me.

What did I do to make them hate me so?

I can't blame Donner. He's got to think of his business, and the other employees. And yet, he's been closer to me than a father.

He called me into his office, cleared the statements and bills off the solitary chair beside his roll-top desk, and without looking up at me, he said, "I've been meaning to talk to you. Now is as good a time as any."

It seems foolish now, but as I sat there staring at him—short, chubby, with the ragged light-brown moustache comically drooping over his upper lip—it was as if both of me, the old Charlie and the new, were sitting on that chair, frightened at what Old Mr. Donner was going to say.

"Charlie, your Uncle Herman was a good friend of mine. I kept my promise to him to keep you on the job, good times and bad, so that you didn't ever want for a dollar in your pocket and a place to lay your head without being put away in that home."

"The bakery is my home—"

"And I treated you like my own son who gave up his life for his country. And when Herman died—how old were you? seventeen? more like a six-year-old boy—I swore to myself . . . I said, Arthur Donner, as long as you got a bakery and a business over your head, you're going to look after Charlie. He is going to have a place to work, a bed to sleep in, and bread in his mouth. When they committed you to that Warren place, I told them how you would work for me, and I would take care of you. You didn't spend even one night in that place. I got you a room and I looked after you. Now, have I kept that solemn promise?"

I nodded, but I could see by the way he was folding and unfolding his bills that he was having trouble. And as much as I didn't want to know—I knew. "I've tried my best to do a good job. I've worked hard. . . ."

"I know, Charlie. Nothing's wrong with your work. But something happened to you, and I don't understand what it means. Not only me. Everyone has been talking about it. I've had them in here a dozen times in the last few weeks. They're all upset. Charlie, I got to let you go."

I tried to stop him but he shook his head.

"There was a delegation in to see me last night. Charlie, I got my business to hold together."

He was staring at his hands, turning the paper over and over as if he hoped to find something on it that was not there before. "I'm sorry, Charlie."

"But where will I go?"

He peered up at me for the first time since we'd walked into his cubbyhole office. "You know as well as I do that you don't *need* to work here any more."

"Mr. Donner, I've never worked anywhere else."

"Let's face it. You're not the Charlie who came in here seventeen years ago—not even the same Charlie of four months ago. You haven't talked about it. It's your own affair. Maybe a miracle of some kind—who knows? But you've changed into a very smart young man. And operating the dough mixer and delivering packages is no work for a smart young man."

He was right, of course, but something inside me wanted to make him change his mind.

"You've got to let me stay, Mr. Donner. Give me another chance. You said yourself that you promised Uncle Herman I would have a job here for as long as I needed it. Well, I still need it, Mr. Donner."

"You don't, Charlie. If you did then I'd tell them I don't care about their delegations and their petitions, and I'd stick up for you against all of them. But as it is now, they're all scared to death of you. I got to think of my own family too."

"What if they change their minds? Let me try to convince them." I was making it harder for him than he expected. I knew I should stop, but I couldn't control myself. "I'll make them understand," I pleaded.

"All right," he sighed finally. "Go ahead, try. But you're only going to hurt yourself."

As I came out of his office, Frank Reilly and Joe Carp

walked by me, and I knew what he had said was true. Having me around to look at was too much for them. I made them all uncomfortable.

Frank had just picked up a tray of rolls and both he and Joe turned when I called. "Look, Charlie, I'm busy. Maybe later—"

"No," I insisted. "Now—right now. Both of you have been avoiding me. Why?"

Frank, the fast talker, the ladies' man, the arranger, studied me for a moment and then set the tray down on the table. "Why? I'll tell you why. Because all of a sudden you're a big shot, a know-it-all, a brain! Now you're a regular whiz kid, an egghead. Always with a book—always with all the answers. Well, I'll tell you something. You think you're better than the rest of us here? Okay, go someplace else."

"But what did I do to you?"

"What did he do? Hear that, Joe? I'll tell you what you did, *Mister* Gordon. You come pushing in here with your ideas and suggestions and make the rest of us all look like a bunch of dopes. But I'll tell you something. To me you're still a moron. Maybe I don't understand some of them big words or the names of the books, but I'm as good as you are—better even."

"Yeah." Joe nodded, turning to emphasize the point to Gimpy who had just come up behind him.

"I'm not asking you to be my friends," I said, "or have anything to do with me. Just let me keep my job. Mr. Donner says it's up to you."

Gimpy glared at me and then shook his head in disgust. "You got a nerve," he shouted. "You can go to hell!" Then he turned and limped off heavily.

And so it went. Most of them felt the way Joe and Frank and Gimpy did. It had been all right as long as they could laugh at me and appear clever at my expense, but now they were feeling inferior to the moron. I began to see that by my astonishing growth I had made them shrink and emphasized their inadequacies. I had betrayed them, and they hated me for it.

Fanny Birden was the only one who didn't think I should be forced to leave, and despite their pressure and threats, she had been the only one not to sign the petition.

"Which don't mean to say," she remarked, "that I don't think there's something mighty strange about you,

74

Charlie. The way you've changed! I don't know. You used to be a good, dependable man—ordinary, not too bright maybe, but honest—and who knows what you done to yourself to get so smart all of a sudden. Like everybody's been saying—it ain't right."

"But what's wrong with a person wanting to be more intelligent, to acquire knowledge, and understand himself and the world?"

"If you'd read your Bible, Charlie, you'd know that it's not meant for man to know more than was given to him to know by the Lord in the first place. The fruit of that tree was forbidden to man. Charlie, if you done anything you wasn't supposed to—you know, like with the devil or something—maybe it ain't too late to get out of it. Maybe you could go back to being the good simple man you was before."

"There's no going back, Fanny. I haven't done anything wrong. I'm like a man born blind who has been given a chance to see light. That can't be sinful. Soon there'll be millions like me all over the world. Science can do it, Fanny."

She stared down at the bride and groom on the wedding cake she was decorating and I could see her lips barely move as she whispered: "It was evil when Adam and Eve ate from the *tree of knowledge*. It was evil when they saw they was naked, and learned about lust and shame. And they was driven out of Paradise and the gates was closed to them. If not for that none of us would have to grow old and be sick and die."

There was nothing more to say, to her or to the rest of them. None of them would look into my eyes. I can still feel the hostility. Before, they had laughed at me, despising me for my ignorance and dullness; now, they hated me for my knowledge and understanding. Why? What in God's name did they want of me?

This intelligence has driven a wedge between me and all the people I knew and loved, driven me out of the bakery. Now, I'm more alone than ever before. I wonder what would happen if they put Algernon back in the big cage with some of the other mice. Would *they* turn against him?

May 25—So this is how a person can come to despise himself—knowing he's doing the wrong thing and not being able to stop. Against my will I found myself drawn to Alice's apartment. She was surprised but she let me in.

"You're soaked. The water is streaming down your face."

"It's raining. Good for the flowers."

"Come on in. Let me get you a towel. You'll catch pneumonia."

"You're the only one I can talk to," I said. "Let me stay."

"I've got a pot of fresh coffee on the stove. Go ahead and dry yourself and then we can talk."

I looked around while she went to get the coffee. It was the first time I had ever been inside her apartment. I felt a sense of pleasure, but there was something disturbing about the room.

Everything was neat. The porcelain figurines were in a straight line on the window-ledge, all facing the same way. And the throw-pillows on the sofa hadn't been thrown at all, but were regularly spaced on the clear plastic covers that protected the upholstery. Two of the end tables had magazines, neatly stacked so that the titles were clearly visible. On one table: *The Reporter, The Saturday Review, The New Yorker;* on the other: *Mademoiselle, House Beautiful,* and *Reader's Digest.*

On the far wall, across from the sofa, hung an ornately framed reproduction of Picasso's "Mother and Child," and directly opposite, above the sofa, was a painting of a dashing Renaissance courtier, masked, sword in hand, protecting a frightened, pink-cheeked maiden. Taken all together, it was wrong. As if Alice couldn't make up her mind who she was and which world she wanted to live in.

"You haven't been to the lab for a few days," she called from the kitchen. "Professor Nemur is worried about you."

"I couldn't face them," I said. "I know there's no reason for me to be ashamed, but it's an empty feeling not going in to work every day—not seeing the shop, the ovens, the people. It's too much. Last night and the night before, I had nightmares of drowning."

She set the tray in the center of the coffee table—the napkins folded into triangles, and the cookies laid out in a circular display pattern. "You mustn't take it so hard, Charlie. It has nothing to do with you."

"It doesn't help to tell myself that. Those people—for

all these years—were my family. It was like being thrown out of my own home."

"That's just it," she said. "This has become a symbolic repetition of experiences you had as a child. Being rejected by your parents . . . being sent away . . ."

"Oh, Christ! Never mind giving it a nice neat label. What matters is that before I got involved in this experiment I had friends, people who cared for me. Now I'm afraid—"

"You've still got friends."

"It's not the same."

"Fear is a normal reaction."

"It's more than that. I've been afraid before. Afraid of being strapped for not giving in to Norma, afraid of passing Howells Street where the gang used to tease me and push me around. And I was afraid of the schoolteacher, Mrs. Libby, who tied my hands so I wouldn't fidget with things on my desk. But those things were real— something I was justified in being afraid of. This terror at being kicked out of the bakery is vague, a fear I don't understand."

"Get hold of yourself."

"*You* don't feel the panic."

"But, Charlie, it's to be expected. You're a new swimmer forced off a diving raft and terrified of losing the solid wood under your feet. Mr. Donner *was* good to you, and you *were* sheltered all these years. Being driven out of the bakery this way is an even greater shock than you expected."

"Knowing it intellectually doesn't help. I can't sit alone in my room any more. I wander into the streets at all hours of the day or night, not knowing what I'm looking for . . . walking until I'm lost . . . finding myself outside the bakery. Last night I walked all the way from Washington Square to Central Park, and I slept in the park. What the hell am I searching for?"

The more I talked, the more upset she became. "What can I do to help you, Charlie?"

"I don't know. I'm like an animal who's been locked out of his nice, safe cage."

She sat beside me on the couch. "They're pushing you too fast. You're confused. You want to be an adult, but there's still a little boy inside you. Alone and frightened." She put my head on her shoulder, trying to comfort me, and as she stroked my hair I knew that she needed me the way I needed her.

"Charlie," she whispered after a while, "whatever you want . . . don't be afraid of me. . . ."

I wanted to tell her I was waiting for the panic.

Once—during a bakery delivery—Charlie had nearly fainted when a middle-aged woman, just out of the bath, amused herself by opening her bathrobe and exposing herself. Had he ever seen a woman without clothes on? Did he know how to make love? His terror—his whining—must have frightened her because she clutched her robe together and gave him a quarter to forget what had happened. She was only testing him, she warned, to see if he was a good boy.

He tried to be good, he told her, and not look at women, because his mother used to beat him whenever that happened in his pants. . . .

Now he had the clear picture of Charlie's mother, screaming at him, holding a leather belt in her hand, and his father trying to hold her back. "Enough, Rose! You'll kill him! Leave him alone!" His mother straining forward to lash at him, just out of reach now so that the belt swishes past his shoulder as he writhes and twists away from it on the floor.

"Look at him!" Rose screams. "He can't learn to read and write, but he knows enough to look at a girl that way. I'll beat that filth out of his mind."

"He can't help it if he gets an erection. It's normal. He didn't do anything."

"He's got no business to think that way about girls. A friend of his sister's comes to the house and he starts thinking like that! I'll teach him so he never forgets. Do you hear? If you ever touch a girl, I'll put you away in a cage, like an animal, for the rest of your life. Do you hear me? . . ."

I still hear her. But perhaps I had been released. Maybe the fear and nausea was no longer a sea to drown in. but only a pool of water reflecting the past alongside the now. Was I free?

If I could reach Alice in time—without thinking about it, before it overwhelmed me—maybe the panic wouldn't happen. If only I could make my mind a blank. I managed to choke out: "You . . . you do it! Hold me!" And before I knew what she was doing, she was kissing me, holding me closer than anyone had ever held me before. But at the moment I should have come closest of all, it started: the buzzing, the chill, and the nausea. I turned away from her.

She tried to soothe me, to tell me it didn't matter, that there was no reason to blame myself. But ashamed, and no longer able to control my anguish, I began to sob. There in her arms I cried myself to sleep, and I dreamed of the courtier and the pink-cheeked maiden. But in my dream it was the maiden who held the sword.

PROGRESS REPORT 12

June 5—Nemur is upset because I haven't turned in any progress reports in almost two weeks (and he's justified because the Welberg Foundation has begun paying me a salary out of the grant so that I won't have to look for a job). The International Psychological Convention at Chicago is only a week away. He wants his preliminary report to be as full as possible, since Algernon and I are the prime exhibits for his presentation.

Our relationship is becoming increasingly strained. I resent Nemur's constant references to me as a laboratory specimen. He makes me feel that before the experiment I was not really a human being.

I told Strauss that I was too involved in thinking, reading, and digging into myself, trying to understand who and what I am, and that writing was such a slow process it made me impatient to get my ideas down. I followed his suggestion that I learn to type, and now that I can type nearly seventy-five words a minute, it's easier to get it all down on paper.

Strauss again brought up my need to speak and write simply and directly so that people will understand me. He reminds me that language is sometimes a barrier instead of a pathway. Ironic to find myself on the other side of the intellectual fence.

I see Alice occasionally, but we don't discuss what happened. Our relationship remains platonic. But for three nights after I left the bakery there were the nightmares. Hard to believe it was two weeks ago.

I am pursued down the empty streets at night by ghostly figures. Though I always run to the bakery, the door is locked, and the people inside never turn to look at me. Through the window, the bride and groom on the wedding cake point at me and laugh—the air becomes charged with laughter until I can't stand it—and the two cupids wave their flaming arrows. I scream. I pound on the door, but there is no sound. I see Charlie staring back at me from inside. Is it only a reflection? Things clutch at my legs and drag me away from the bakery down into the shadows of the alleyway, and just as they begin to ooze all over me I wake up.

Other times the window of the bakery opens into the past and looking through it I see other things and other people.

It's astonishing how my power of recall is developing. I cannot control it completely yet, but sometimes when I'm busy reading or working on a problem, I get a feeling of intense clarity.

I know it's some kind of subconscious warning signal, and now instead of waiting for the memory to come to me, I close my eyes and reach out for it. Eventually, I'll be able to bring this recall completely under control, to explore not only the sum of my past experiences, but also all of the untapped faculties of the mind.

Even now, as I think about it, I feel the sharp stillness. I see the bakery window . . . reach out and touch it . . . cold and vibrating, and then the glass becomes warm . . . hotter . . . fingers burning. The window reflecting my image becomes bright, and as the glass turns into a mirror, I see little Charlie Gordon—fourteen or fifteen— looking out at me through the window of his house, and it's doubly strange to realize how different he was. . . .

He has been waiting for his sister to come from school, and when he sees her turn the corner onto Marks Street, he waves and calls her name and runs out onto the porch to meet her.

Norma waves a paper. "I got an *A* in my history test. I knew all the answers. Mrs. Baffin said it was the best paper in the whole class."

She is a pretty girl with light brown hair carefully

braided and coiled about her head in a crown, and as she looks up at her big brother the smile turns to a frown and she skips away, leaving him behind as she darts up the steps into the house.

Smiling, he follows her.

His mother and father are in the kitchen, and Charlie, bursting with the excitement of Norma's good news, blurts it out before she has a chance.

"She got an *A!* She got an *A!*"

"No!" shrieks Norma. "Not you. You don't tell. It's my mark, and I'm going to tell."

"Now wait a minute, young lady." Matt puts his newspaper down and addresses her sternly. "That's no way to talk to your brother."

"He had no right to tell!"

"Never mind." Matt glares at her over his warning finger. "He meant no harm by it, and you musn't shout at him that way."

She turns to her mother for support. "I got an *A*—the best mark in class. Now I can have a dog? You promised. You said if I got a good mark in my test. And I got an *A*. A brown dog with white spots. And I'm going to call him Napoleon because that was the question I answered best on the test. Napoleon lost the battle of Waterloo."

Rose nods. "Go out on the porch and play with Charlie. He's been waiting over an hour for you to come home from school."

"I don't want to play with him."

"Go out on the porch," says Matt.

Norma looks at her father and then at Charlie. "I don't have to. Mother said I don't have to play with him if I don't want to."

"Now, young lady"—Matt rises out of his chair and comes toward her—"you just apologize to your brother."

"I don't have to," she screeches, rushing behind her mother's chair. "He's like a baby. He can't play Monopoly or checkers or anything . . . he gets everything all mixed up. I won't play with him any more."

"Then go to your room!"

"Can I have a dog now, Mama?"

Matt hits the table with his fist. "There'll be no dog in this house as long as you take this attitude, young lady."

"I promised her a dog if she did well in school—"

"A brown one with white spots!" adds Norma.

Matt points to Charlie standing near the wall. "Did you forget you told your son he couldn't have one because we didn't have the room, and no one to take care of it. Remember? When he asked for a dog? Are you going back on what you said to him?"

"But I can take care of my own dog," insists Norma. "I'll feed him, and wash him, and take him out . . ."

Charlie, who has been standing near the table, playing with his large red button at the end of a string, suddenly speaks out.

"I'll help her take care of the dog! I'll help her feed it and brush it and I won't let the other dogs bite it!"

But before either Matt or Rose can answer, Norma shrieks: "No! It's going to be my dog. Only my dog!"

Matt nods. "You see?"

Rose sits beside her and strokes her braids to calm her. "But we have to share things, dear. Charlie can help you take care of it."

"No! Only mine! . . . I'm the one who got the *A* in history—not him! He never gets good marks like me. Why should he help with the dog? And then the dog will like him more than me, and it'll be his dog instead of mine. No! If I can't have it for myself I don't want it."

"That settles it," says Matt picking up his newspaper and settling down in his chair again. "No dog."

Suddenly, Norma jumps off the couch and grabs the history test she had brought home so eagerly just a few minutes earlier. She tears it and throws the pieces into Charlie's startled face. "I hate you! I hate you!"

"Norma, stop that at once!" Rose grabs her but she twists away.

"And I hate school! I hate it! I'll stop studying, and I'll be a dummy like him. I'll forget everything I learned and then I'll be just like him." She runs out of the room, shrieking: "It's happening to me already. I'm forgetting everything . . . I'm forgetting . . . I don't remember anything I learned any more!"

Rose, terrified, runs after her. Matt sits there staring at the newspaper in his lap. Charlie, frightened by the hysteria and the screaming, shrinks into a chair whimpering softly. What has he done wrong? And feeling the wetness in his trousers and the trickling down his leg, he sits there

82

waiting for the slap he knows will come when his mother returns.

The scene fades, but from that time Norma spent all her free moments with her friends, or playing alone in her room. She kept the door to her room closed, and I was forbidden to enter without her permission.

I recall once overhearing Norma and one of her girl friends playing in her room, and Norma shouting: "He is not my real brother! He's just a boy we took in because we felt sorry for him. My mamma told me, and she said I can tell everyone now that he's not really my brother at all."

I wish this memory were a photograph so that I could tear it up and throw it back into her face. I want to call back across the years and tell her I never meant to stop her from getting her dog. She could have had it all to herself, and I wouldn't have fed it, or brushed it, or played with it—and I would never have made it like me more than it liked her. I only wanted her to play games with me the way we used to. I never meant to do anything that would hurt her at all.

June 6—My first real quarrel with Alice today. My fault. I wanted to see her. Often, after a disturbing memory or dream, talking to her—just being with her—makes me feel better. But it was a mistake to go down to the Center to pick her up.

I had not been back to the Center for Retarded Adults since the operation, and the thought of seeing the place was exciting. It's on Twenty-third Street, east of Fifth Avenue, in an old schoolhouse that has been used by the Beekman University Clinic for the last five years as a center for experimental education—special classes for the handicapped. The sign outside on the doorway, framed by the old spiked gateway, is just a gleaming brass plate that says *C. R. A. Beekman Extension.*

Her class ended at eight, but I wanted to see the room where—not so long ago—I had struggled over simple reading and writing and learned to count change of a dollar.

I went inside, slipped up to the door, and, keeping out

of sight, I looked through the window. Alice was at her desk, and in a chair beside her was a thin-faced woman I didn't recognize. She was frowning that open frown of unconcealed puzzlement, and I wondered what Alice was trying to explain.

Near the blackboard was Mike Dorni in his wheelchair, and there in his usual first-row first-seat was Lester Braun, who, Alice said, was the smartest in the group. Lester had learned easily what I had struggled over, but he came when he felt like it, or he stayed away to earn money waxing floors. I guess if he had cared at all—if it had been important to him as it was to me—they would have used him for this experiment. There were new faces, too, people I didn't know.

Finally, I got up the nerve to go in.

"It's Charlie!" said Mike, whirling his wheelchair around.

I waved to him.

Bernice, the pretty blonde with empty eyes, looked up and smiled dully. "Where ya been, Charlie? That's a nice suit."

The others who remembered me waved to me and I waved back. Suddenly, I could see by Alice's expression that she was annoyed.

"It's almost eight o'clock," she announced. "Time to put things away."

Each person had an assigned task, the putting away of chalk, erasers, papers, books, pencils, note paper, paints, and demonstration material. Each one knew his job and took pride in doing it well. They all started on their tasks except Bernice. She was staring at me.

"Why ain't Charlie been coming to school?" asked Bernice. "What's the matter, Charlie? Are you coming back?"

The others looked up at me. I looked to Alice, waiting for her to answer for me, and there was a long silence. What could I tell them that would not hurt them?

"This is just a visit," I said.

One of the girls started to giggle—Francine, whom Alice was always worried about. She had given birth to three children by the time she was eighteen, before her parents arranged for a hysterectomy. She wasn't pretty—not nearly as attractive as Bernice—but she had been an easy mark for dozens of men who bought her something pretty, or paid her way to the movies. She lived at a boarding house approved for outside work trainees by the Warren State Home, and was permitted out in the evenings to come to the Center. Twice she hadn't shown up—picked up by men on the way to school—and now she was allowed out only with an escort.

"He talks like a big shot now," she giggled.

"All right," said Alice, breaking in sharply. "Class dismissed. I'll see you all tomorrow night at six."

When they were gone, I could see by the way she was slamming her own things into her closet, that she was angry.

"I'm sorry," I said. "I was going to wait for you downstairs, and then I got curious about the old classroom. My *alma mater*. I just wanted to look through the window. And before I knew what I was doing I came in. What's bothering you?"

"Nothing—nothing's bothering me."

"Come on. Your anger is all out of proportion to what's happened. Something's on your mind."

She slammed down a book she was holding. "All right. You want to know? You're different. You've changed. And I'm not talking about your I.Q. It's your attitude toward people—you're not the same kind of human being—"

"Oh, come on now! Don't—"

"Don't interrupt me!" The real anger in her voice pushed me back. "I mean it. There was something in you before. I don't know . . . a warmth, an openness, a kindness that made everyone like you and like to have you around. Now, with all your intelligence and knowledge, there are differences that—"

I couldn't let myself listen. "What did you expect? Did you think I'd remain a docile pup, wagging my tail and licking the foot that kicks me? Sure, all this has changed me and the way I think about myself. I no longer have to take the kind of crap that people have been handing me all my life."

"People have not been bad to you."

"What do you know about it? Listen, the best of them

85

have been smug and patronizing—using me to make themselves superior and secure in their own limitations. Anyone can feel intelligent beside a moron."

After I said it, I knew she was going to take it the wrong way.

"You put me in that category too, I suppose."

"Don't be absurd. You know damned well I—"

"Of course, in a sense, I guess you're right. Next to you I am rather dull-witted. Nowadays every time we see each other, after I leave you I go home with the miserable feeling that I'm slow and dense about everything. I review things I've said, and come up with all the bright and witty things I should have said, and I feel like kicking myself because I didn't mention them when we were together."

"That's a common experience."

"I find myself wanting to impress you in a way I never thought about doing before, but being with you has undermined my self-confidence. I question my motives now, about everything I do."

I tried to get her off the subject, but she kept coming back to it. "Look, I didn't come here to argue with you," I finally said. "Will you let me take you home? I need someone to talk to."

"So do I. But these days I can't talk to you. All I can do is listen and nod my head and pretend I understand all about cultural variants, and neo-Boulean mathematics, and post-symbolic logic, and I feel more and more stupid, and when you leave the apartment, I have to stare in the mirror and scream at myself: 'No, you're not growing duller every day! You're not losing your intelligence! You're not getting senile and dull-witted. It's Charlie exploding forward so quickly that it makes it appear as if you're slipping backwards.' I say that to myself, Charlie, but whenever we meet and you tell me something and look at me in that impatient way, I know you're laughing.

"And when you explain things to me, and I can't remember them, you think it's because I'm not interested and don't want to take the trouble. But you don't know how I torture myself when you're gone. You don't know the books I've struggled over, the lectures I've sat in on at Beekman, and yet whenever I talk about something, I see how impatient you are, as if it were all childish. I wanted you to be intelligent. I wanted to help you and share with you—and now you've shut me out of your life."

As I listened to what she was saying, the enormity of it dawned on me. I had been so absorbed in myself and what was happening to me that I never thought about what was happening to her.

She was crying silently as we left the school, and I found myself without words. All during the ride on the bus I thought to myself how upside-down the situation had become. She was terrified of me. The ice had broken between us and the gap was widening as the current of my mind carried me swiftly into the open sea.

She was right in refusing to torture herself by being with me. We no longer had anything in common. Simple conversation had become strained. And all there was between us now was the embarrassed silence and unsatisfied longing in a darkened room.

"You're very serious," she said, breaking out of her own mood and looking up at me.

"About us."

"It shouldn't make you so serious. I don't want to upset you. You're going through a great trial." She was trying to smile.

"But you did. Only I don't know what to do about it."

On the way from the bus stop to her apartment, she said, "I'm not going to the convention with you. I called Professor Nemur this morning and told him. There will be a lot for you to do there. Interesting people—the excitement of the spotlight for a while. I don't want to be in the way—"

"Alice—"

"—and no matter what you say about it now, I know that's how I'm going to *feel,* so if you don't mind, I'll hang on to my splintering ego—thank you."

"But you're making more of this than it is. I'm sure if you'll just—"

"You *know?* You're *sure?*" She turned and glared at me on the front steps of her apartment building. "Oh, how insufferable you've become. How do *you* know what I feel? You take liberties with other people's minds. You can't tell *how* I feel or *what* I feel or *why* I feel."

She started inside and then she looked back at me, her voice shaky: "I'll be here when you get back. I'm just upset, that's all, and I want both of us to have a chance to think this out while we're a good distance apart."

For the first time in many weeks she didn't ask me inside. I stared at the closed door with the anger mounting inside me. I wanted to create a scene, to bang on the door, to break it down. I wanted my anger to consume the building.

But as I walked away I felt a kind of simmering, then cooling, and finally a relief. I walked so fast I was drifting along the streets, and the feeling that hit my cheek was a cool breeze out of the summer night. Suddenly free.

I realize now that my feeling for Alice had been moving backward against the current of my learning, from worship. to love, to fondness, to a feeling of gratitude and responsibility. My confused feeling for her had been holding me back, and I had clung to her out of my fear of being forced out on my own, and cut adrift.

But with the freedom came a sadness. I wanted to be in love with her. I wanted to overcome my emotional and sexual fears, to marry, have children, settle down.

Now it's impossible. I am just as far away from Alice with an I.Q. of 185 as I was when I had an I.Q. of 70. And this time we both know it.

June 8—What drives me out of the apartment to prowl through the city? I wander through the streets alone—not the relaxing stroll of a summer night, but the tense hurry to get—where? Down alleyways, looking into doorways, peering into half-shuttered windows, wanting someone to talk to and yet afraid to meet anyone. Up one street, and down another, through the endless labyrinth, hurling myself against the neon cage of the city. Searching . . . for what?

I met a woman in Central Park. She was sitting on a bench near the lake, with a coat clutched around her despite the heat. She smiled and motioned for me to sit beside her. We looked at the bright skyline on Central Park South, the honeycomb of lighted cells against the blackness, and I wished I could absorb them all.

Yes, I told her, I was from New York. No, I had never been to Newport News, Virginia. That's where she was from, and where she had married this sailor who was at sea now, and she hadn't seen him in two and a half years.

She twisted and knotted a handkerchief, using it from time to time to wipe the beaded sweat from her forehead. Even in the dim light reflected from the lake, I could see that she wore a great deal of make-up, but she looked attractive with her straight dark hair loose to her shoulders—except that her face was puffy and swollen as if she had just gotten up from sleep. She wanted to talk about herself, and I wanted to listen.

Her father had given her a good home, an education, everything a wealthy shipbuilder could give his only daughter—but not forgiveness. He would never forgive her elopement with the sailor.

She took my hand as she spoke, and rested her head on my shoulder. "The night Gary and I were married," she whispered, "I was a terrified virgin. And he just went crazy. First, he had to slap me and beat me. And then he took me with no love-making. That was the last time we were ever together. I never let him touch me again."

She could probably tell by the trembling of my hand that I was startled. It was too violent and intimate for me. Feeling my hand stir, she gripped it tighter as if she had to finish her story before she could let me go. It was important to her, and I sat quietly as one sits before a bird that feeds from your palm.

"Not that I don't like men," she assured me with wide-eyed openness. "I've been with other men. Not him, but lots of others. Most men are gentle and tender with a woman. They make love slowly, with caresses and kisses first." She looked at me meaningfully, and let her open palm brush back and forth against mine.

It was what I had heard about, read about, dreamed about. I didn't know her name, and she didn't ask mine. She just wanted me to take her someplace where we could be alone. I wondered what Alice would think.

I caressed her awkwardly and kissed her still more hesitantly so that she looked up at me. "What's the matter?" she whispered. "What are you thinking?"

"About you."

"Do you have a place we can go?"

Each step forward was caution. At what point would the ground give way and plunge me into anxiety? Something kept me moving ahead to test my footing.

"If you don't have a place, the Mansion Hotel on

Fifty-third doesn't cost too much. And they don't bother you about luggage if you pay in advance."

"I have a room—"

She looked at me with new respect. "Well, that's fine."

Still nothing. And that in itself was curious. How far could I go without being overwhelmed by symptoms of panic? When we were alone in the room? When she undressed? When I saw her body? When we were lying together?

Suddenly, it was important to know if I could be like other men, if I could ever ask a woman to share a life with me. Having intelligence and knowledge wasn't enough. I wanted this, too. The sense of release and looseness was strong now with the feeling that it *was* possible. The excitement that came over me when I kissed her again communicated itself, and I was sure I could be normal with her. She was different from Alice. She was the kind of woman who had been around.

Then her voice changed, uncertain. "Before we go . . . Just one thing . . ." She stood up and took a step toward me in the spray of lamplight, opening her coat, and I could see the shape of her body as I had not imagined it all the time we were sitting next to each other in the shadows. "Only the fifth month," she said. "It doesn't make any difference. You don't mind, do you?"

Standing there with her coat open, she was superimposed as a double exposure on the picture of the middle-aged woman just out of the bathtub, holding open her bathrobe for Charlie to see. And I waited, as a blasphemer waits for lightning. I looked away. It was the last thing I had expected, but the coat wrapped tightly around her on such a hot night should have warned me that something was wrong.

"It's not my husband's," she assured me. "I wasn't lying to you about what I said before. I haven't seen him for years. It was a salesman I met about eight months ago. I was living with him. I'm not going to see him any more, but I'm going to keep the baby. We've just got to be careful—not rough or anything like that. But otherwise you don't have to worry."

Her voice ran down when she saw my anger. "That's filthy!" I shouted. "You ought to be ashamed of yourself."

She drew away, wrapping her coat quickly around her to protect what lay within.

As she made that protective gesture, I saw the second double image: my mother, heavy with my sister, in the days when she was holding me less, warming me less with her voice and touch, protecting me less against anyone who dared to say I was subnormal.

I think I grabbed her shoulder—I'm not sure, but then she was screaming, and I was sharply back to reality with the sense of danger. I wanted to tell her I had meant no harm—I would never hurt her or anyone. "Please, don't scream!"

But she was screaming, and I heard the running footsteps on the darkened path. This was something no one would understand. I ran into the darkness, to find an exit from the park, zig-zagging across one path and down another. I didn't know the park, and suddenly I crashed into something that threw me backwards. A wire-mesh fence—a dead end. Then I saw the swings and slides and realized it was a children's playground locked up for the night. I followed the fence, and kept going, half-running, stumbling over twisted roots. At the lake that curved around near the playground, I doubled back, found another path, went over the small footbridge and then around and under it. No exit.

"What is it? What happened, lady?"

"A maniac?"

"You all right?"

"Which way did he go?"

I had circled back to where I had started from. I slipped behind the huge outcropping of a rock and a screen of bramble and dropped flat on my stomach.

"Get a cop. There's never a cop when you need one."

"What happened?"

"A degenerate tried to rape her."

"Hey, some guy down there is chasing him. There he goes!"

"Come on! Get the bastard before he gets outta the park!"

"Careful. He's got a knife and a gun. . . ."

It was obvious that the shouting had flushed out the night crawlers because the cry of "there he goes!" was echoed from behind me, and looking out from behind the rock I could see a lone runner being chased down the lamplit path into the darkness. Seconds later, another one passed in front of the rock and disappeared into the shadows. I pictured myself being caught by this eager mob and beaten and torn by them. I deserved it. I almost wanted it.

I stood up, brushed the leaves and dirt from my clothing and walked slowly down the path in the direction from which I had come. I expected every second to be grabbed from behind and pulled down into the dirt and darkness, but soon I saw the bright lights of Fifty-ninth Street and Fifth Avenue, and I came out of the park.

Thinking about it now, in the security of my room, I am shaken with the rawness that touched me. Remembering how my mother looked before she gave birth to my sister is frightening. But even more frightening is the feeling that I wanted them to catch me and beat me. Why did I want to be punished? Shadows out of the past clutch at my legs and drag me down. I open my mouth to scream, but I am voiceless. My hands are trembling, I feel cold, and there is a distant humming in my ears.

PROGRESS REPORT 13

June 10—We're on a Strato-jet about to take off for Chicago. I owe this progress report to Burt who had the bright idea that I could dictate this on a transistor tape recorder and have a public stenographer in Chicago type it up. Nemur likes the idea. In fact, he wants me to use the recorder up to the last minute. He feels it will add to the report if they play the most recent tape at the end of the session.

So here I am, sitting off by myself in our private section of a jet on the way to Chicago, trying to get used to thinking aloud, and to the sound of my own voice. I suppose the typist can get rid of all the *uhm's, er's* and *ah's,* and make it all seem natural on paper (I can't help the paralysis that comes over me when I think hundreds of people are going to listen to the words I'm saying now).

My mind is a blank. At this point my feelings are more important than anything else.

The idea of going up in the air terrifies me.

As far as I can tell, in the days before the operation, I never really understood what planes were. I never connected the movies and TV close-ups of planes with the things that I saw zooming overhead. Now that we're about to take off I can think only of what might happen if we crash. A cold feeling, and the thought that I don't want to die. Brings to mind those discussions about God.

I've thought about death often in recent weeks, but not really about God. My mother took me to church occasionally—but I don't recall ever connecting that up with the thought of God. She mentioned Him quite often, and I had to pray to Him at night, but I never thought much about it. I remember Him as a distant uncle with a long beard on a throne (like Santa Claus in the department store on his big chair, who picks you up on his knee and asks you if you've been good, and what would you like him to give you?). She was afraid of Him, but asked favors anyway. My father never mentioned Him—it was as if God was one of Rose's relatives he'd rather not get involved with.

* * *

"We're ready to take off, sir. May I help you fasten your seat belt?"

"Do I have to? I don't like to be strapped down."

"Until we're airborne."

"I'd rather not, unless it's necessary. I've got this fear of being strapped in. It'll probably make me sick."

"It's regulations, sir. Here, let me help you."

"No! I'll do it myself."

"No . . . that one goes through here."

"Wait, uh. . . . Okay."

* * *

Ridiculous. There's nothing to be afraid of. Seat belt isn't too tight—doesn't hurt. Why should putting on the damned seat belt be so terrifying? That, and the vibrations of the plane taking off. Anxiety all out of proportion to the situation . . . so it must be something . . . what? . . . flying up into and through dark clouds . . . fasten your seat belts . . . strapped down . . . straining forward . . . odor of sweaty leather . . . vibrations and a roaring sound in my ears.

Through the window—in the clouds—I see Charlie. Age is difficult to tell, about five years old. Before Norma . . .

"Are you two ready yet?" His father comes to the doorway, heavy, especially in the sagging fleshiness of his face and neck. He has a tired look. "I said, are you ready?"

"Just a minute," answers Rose. "I'm getting my hat on. See if his shirt is buttoned, and tie his shoelaces."

"Come on, let's get this thing over with."

"Where?" asks Charlie. "Where . . . Charlie . . . go?"

His father looks at him and frowns. Matt Gordon never knows how to react to his son's questions.

Rose appears in the doorway of her bedroom, adjusting the half-veil of her hat. She is a birdlike woman, and her arms—up to her head, elbows out—look like wings. "We're going to the doctor who is going to help you get smart."

The veil makes it look as if she were peering down at him through a wire screen. He is always frightened when they dress up to go out this way, because he knows he will have to meet other people and his mother will become upset and angry.

He wants to run, but there is no place for him to go.

"Why do you have to tell him that?" said Matt.

"Because it's the truth. Dr. Guarino can help him."

Matt paces the floor like a man who has given up hope but will make one last attempt to reason. "How do you know? What do you know about this man? If there was anything that could be done, the doctors would have told us long ago."

"Don't say that," she screeches. "Don't tell me there's nothing they can do." She grabs Charlie and presses his head against her bosom. "He's going to be normal, whatever we have to do, whatever it costs."

"It's not something money can buy."

"It's Charlie I'm talking about. Your son . . . your only child." She rocks him from side to side, near hysteria now. "I won't listen to that talk. They don't know, so they say nothing can be done. Dr. Guarino explained it all to me. They won't sponsor his invention, he says, because it will prove they're wrong. Like it was with those other scientists, Pasteur and Jennings, and the rest of them. He told me all about your fine medical doctors afraid of progress."

Talking back to Matt this way, she becomes relaxed and sure of herself again. When she lets go of Charlie, he goes to the corner and stands against the wall frightened and shivering.

"Look," she says, "you got him upset again."

"Me?"

"You always start these things in front of him."

"Oh, Christ! Come on, let's get this damned thing over with."

All the way to Dr. Guarino's office they avoid speaking to each other. Silence on the bus, and silence walking three blocks from the bus to the downtown office building. After about fifteen minutes, Dr. Guarino comes out to the waiting room to greet them. He is fat and balding, and he looks as if would pop through his white lab jacket. Charlie is fascinated by the thick white eyebrows and white moustache that twitch from time to time. Sometimes the moustache twitches first, followed by the raising of both eyebrows, but sometimes the brows go up first and the moustache twitch follows.

The large white room into which Guarino ushers them smells recently painted, and it is almost bare—two desks on one side of the room, and on the other, a huge machine with rows of dials and four long arms like dentist's drills. Nearby is a black leather examination table with thick, webbed, restraining straps.

"Well, well, well," says Guarino, raising his eyebrows, "so this is Charlie." He grips the boy's shoulders firmly. "We're going to be friends."

"Can you really do anything for him, Dr. Guarino?" says Matt. "Have you ever treated this kind of thing before? We don't have much money."

The eyebrows come down like shutters as Guarino frowns. "Mr. Gordon, have I said anything yet about what I could do? Don't I have to examine him first? Maybe something can be done, maybe not. First there will have to be physical and mental tests to determine the causes of the pathology. There will be enough time later to talk of prognosis. Actually, I'm very busy these days. I only agreed to look into this case because I'm doing a special study of this type of neural retardation. Of course, if you have qualms, then perhaps . . ."

His voice trails off sadly, and he turns away, but Rose Gordon jabs at Matt with her elbow. "My husband doesn't mean that at all, Dr. Guarino. He talks too much." She glares at Matt again to warn him to apologize.

Matt sighs. "If there is any way you can help Charlie, we'll do anything you ask. Things are slow these days. I sell barbershop supplies, but whatever I have I'll be glad to—"

"Just one thing I must insist on," says Guarino, pursing his lips as if making a decision. "Once we start, the treatment must continue all the way. In cases of this type, the results often come suddenly after long months without any sign of improvement. Not that I am promising you success, mind you. Nothing is guaranteed. But you must give the treatment a chance, otherwise you're better off not starting at all."

He frowns at them to let his warning sink in, and his brows are white shades from under which his bright blue eyes stare. "Now, if you'll just step outside and let me examine the boy."

Matt hesitates to leave Charlie alone with him, but Guarino nods. "This is the best way," he says, ushering them both outside to the waiting room. "The results are always more significant if the patient and I are alone when the psychosubstantiation tests are performed. External distractions have a deleterious effect on the ramified scores."

Rose smiles at her husband triumphantly, and Matt follows her meekly outside.

Alone with Charlie, Dr. Guarino pats him on the head. He has a kindly smile.

"Okay, kid. On the table."

When Charlie doesn't respond, he lifts him gently onto the leather-padded table and straps him down securely with heavy webbed straps. The table smells of deeply in-grained sweat, and leather.

"Maaaa!"

"She's outside. Don't worry, Charlie. This won't hurt a bit."

"Want Ma!" Charlie is confused at being restrained this way. He has no sense of what is being done to him, but there have been other doctors who were not so gentle after his parents left the room.

Guarino tries to calm him. "Take it easy, kid. Nothing to be scared of. You see this big machine here? Know what I'm going to do with it?"

Charlie cringes, and then he recalls his mother's words. "Make me smart."

"That's right. At least you know what you're here for. Now, just close your eyes and relax while I turn on these switches. It'll make a loud noise, like an airplane, but it won't hurt you. And we'll see if we can make you a little bit smarter than you are now."

Guarino snaps on the switch that sets the huge machine humming, red and blue lights blinking on and off. Charlie is terrified. He cringes and shivers, straining against the straps that hold him fast to the table.

He starts to scream, but Guarino quickly pushes a wad of cloth into his mouth. "Now, now, Charlie. None of that. You be a good little boy. I told you it won't hurt."

He tries to scream again, but all that comes out is a muffled choking that makes him want to throw up. He feels the wetness and the stickiness around his legs, and the odor tells him that his mother will punish him with the spanking and the corner for making in his pants. He could not control it. Whenever he feels trapped and panic sets in, he loses control and dirties himself. Choking . . . sick . . . nausea . . . and everything goes black . . .

There is no way of knowing how much time passes, but when Charlie opens his eyes, the cloth is out of his mouth, and the straps have been removed. Dr. Guarino pretends he does not smell the odor. "Now that didn't hurt you a bit, did it?"

"N-no . . ."

"Well, then what are you trembling like that for? All I did was use that machine to make you smarter. How does it feel to be smarter now than you were before?"

Forgetting his terror, Charlie stares wide-eyed at the machine. "Did I get smart?"

"Of course you did. Uh, stand back over there. How does it feel?"

"Feels wet. I made."

"Yes, well—uh—you won't do that next time, will you? You won't be scared any more, now that you know it doesn't hurt. Now I want you to tell your mom how smart you feel, and she'll bring you here twice a week for short-wave encephalo-reconditioning, and you'll get smarter, and smarter, and smarter."

Charlie smiles. "I can walk backwards."

"You can? Let's see," says Guarino closing his folder in mock excitement. "Let me see."

Slowly, and with great effort, Charlie takes several steps backward, stumbling against the examination table as he goes. Guarino smiles and nods. "Now that's what I call something. Oh, you wait. You're going to be the smartest boy on your block before we're through with you."

Charlie flushes with pleasure at this praise and attention. It is not often that people smile at him and tell him he has done something well. Even the terror of the machine, and of being strapped down to the table, begins to fade.

"On the whole block?" The thought fills him as if he cannot take enough air into his lungs no matter how he tries. "Even smarter than Hymie?"

Guarino smiles again and nods. "Smarter than Hymie."

Charlie looks at the machine with new wonder and respect. The machine will make him smarter than Hymie who lives two doors away and knows how to read and write and is in the Boy Scouts. "Is that your machine?"

"Not yet. It belongs to the bank. But soon it'll be mine, and then I'll be able to make lots of boys like you smart." He pats Charlie's head and says, "You're a lot nicer than some of the normal kids whose mothers bring them here hoping I can make geniuses out of them by raising their I.Q.'s."

"Do they be jean-asses if you raise their eyes?" He put his hands to his face to see if the machine had done anything to raise his eyes. "You gonna make me a jean-ass?"

Guarino's laugh is friendly as he squeezes Charlie's

shoulder. "No, Charlie. Nothing for you to worry about. Only nasty little donkeys become jean-asses. You'll stay just the way you are—a nice kid." And then, thinking better of it he adds: "Of course, a little smarter than you are now."

He unlocks the door and leads Charlie out to his parents. "Here he is, folks. None the worse for the experience. A good boy. I think we're going to be good friends, eh, Charlie?"

Charlie nods. He wants Dr. Guarino to like him, but he is terrified when he sees the expression on his mother's face. "Charlie! What did you do?"

"Just an accident, Mrs. Gordon. He was frightened the first time. But don't blame him or punish him. I wouldn't want him to connect punishment with coming here."

But Rose Gordon is sick with embarrassment. "It's disgusting. I don't know what to do, Dr. Guarino. Even at home he forgets—and sometimes when we have people in the house. I'm so ashamed when he does that."

The look of disgust on his mother's face sets him trembling. For a short while he had forgotten how bad he is, how he makes his parents suffer. He doesn't know how, but it frightens him when she says he makes her suffer, and when she cries and screams at him, he turns his face to the wall and moans softly to himself.

"Now don't upset him, Mrs. Gordon, and don't worry. Bring him to me on Tuesday and Thursday each week at the same time."

"But will this really do any good?" asks Matt. "Ten dollars is a lot of—"

"Matt!" she clutches at his sleeve. "Is that anything to talk about at a time like this? Your own flesh and blood, and maybe Dr. Guarino can make him like other children, with the Lord's help, and you talk about money!"

Matt Gordon starts to defend himself, but then, thinking better of it, he pulls out his wallet.

"Please . . ." sighs Guarino, as if embarrassed at the sight of money. "My assistant at the front desk will take care of all the financial arrangements. Thank you." He half bows to Rose, shakes Matt's hand and pats Charlie on the back. "Nice boy. Very nice." Then, smiling again, he disappears behind the door to the inner office.

They argue all the way home, Matt complaining that

barber supply sales have fallen off, and that their savings are dwindling, Rose screeching back that making Charlie normal is more important than anything else.

Frightened by their quarreling, Charlie whimpers. The sound of anger in their voices is painful to him. As soon as they enter the apartment, he pulls away and runs to the corner of the kitchen, behind the door and stands with his forehead pressed against the tile wall, trembling and moaning.

They pay no attention to him. They have forgotten that he has to be cleaned and changed.

"I'm not hysterical. I'm just sick of you complaining every time I try to do something for your son. You don't care. You just don't care."

"That's not true! But I realize there's nothing we can do. When you've got a child like him it's a cross, and you bear it, and love it. Well, I can bear him, but I can't stand your foolish ways. You've spent almost all our savings on quacks and phonies—money I could have used to set me up in a nice business of my own. Yes. Don't look at me that way. For all the money you've thrown down the sewer to do something that can't be done, I could have had a barbershop of my own instead of eating my heart out selling for ten hours a day. My own place with people working for *me!*"

"Stop shouting. Look at him, he's frightened."

"The hell with you. Now I know who's the dope around here. Me! For putting up with you." He storms out, slamming the door behind him.

*   *   *

"Sorry to interrupt you, sir, but we're going to be landing in a few minutes. You'll have to fasten your seat belt again . . . Oh, you have it on, sir. You've had it on all the way from New York. Close to two hours . . ."

"I forgot all about it. I'll just leave it on until we land. It doesn't seem to bother me any more."

*   *   *

Now I can see where I got the unusual motivation for becoming *smart* that so amazed everyone at first. It was something Rose Gordon lived with day and night. Her fear, her guilt, her shame that Charlie was a moron. Her dream that something could be done. The urgent question always: whose fault was it, hers or Matt's? Only after Norma proved to her that she was capable of having normal children, and that I was a freak, did she stop trying to make me over. But I guess I never stopped wanting to be the smart boy she wanted me to be, so that she would love me.

A funny thing about Guarino. I should resent him for what he did to me, and for taking advantage of Rose and Matt, but somehow I can't. After that first day, he was always pleasant to me. There was always the pat on the shoulder, the smile, the encouraging word that came my way so rarely.

He treated me—even then—as a human being.

It may sound like ingratitude, but that is one of the things that I resent here—the attitude that I am a guinea pig. Nemur's constant references to having *made me what I am,* or that someday there will be others like me who *will become real human beings.*

How can I make him understand that he did not create me?

He makes the same mistake as the others when they look at a feeble-minded person and laugh because they don't understand there are human feelings involved. He doesn't realize that I was a person before I came here.

I am learning to control my resentment, not to be so impatient, to wait for things. I guess I'm growing up. Each day I learn more and more about myself, and the memories that began as ripples now wash over me in high-breaking waves. . . .

June 11—The confusion began from the moment we arrived at the Chalmers Hotel in Chicago and discovered that by error our rooms would not be vacant until the next night and until then we would have to stay at the nearby Independence Hotel. Nemur was furious. He took it as a personal affront and quarrelled with everyone in the line of hotel command from the bellhop to the manager. We waited in the lobby as each hotel official went off in search of his superior to see what could be done.

In the midst of all the confusion—luggage drifting in

and piling up all around the lobby, bellboys hustling back and forth with their little baggage carts, members who hadn't seen each other in a year, recognizing and greeting each other—we stood there feeling increasingly embarrassed as Nemur tried to collar officials connected with the International Psychological Association.

Finally, when it became apparent that nothing could be done about it, he accepted the fact that we would have to spend our first night in Chicago at the Independence.

As it turned out, most of the younger psychologists were staying at the Independence, and that was where the big first-night parties were. Here, people had heard about the experiment, and most of them knew who I was. Wherever we went, someone came up and asked my opinions on everything from the effects of the new tax to the latest archaeological discoveries in Finland. It was challenging, and my storehouse of general knowledge made it easy for me to talk about almost anything. But after a while I could see that Nemur was annoyed at all the attention I was getting.

When an attractive young clinician from Falmouth College asked me if I could explain some of the causes of my own retardation, I told her that Professor Nemur was the man to answer that.

It was the chance he had been waiting for to show his authority, and for the first time since we'd known each other he put his hand on my shoulder. "We don't know exactly what causes the type of phenylketonuria that Charlie was suffering from as a child—some unusual biochemical or genetic situation, possibly ionizing radiation or natural radiation or even a virus attack on the fetus—whatever it was resulted in a defective gene which produces a, shall we say, 'maverick enzyme' that creates defective biochemical reactions. And, of course, newly produced amino acids compete with the normal enzymes causing brain damage."

The girl frowned. She had not expected a lecture, but Nemur had seized the floor and he went on in the same vein. "I call it *competitive inhibition of enzymes*. Let me give you an example of how it works. Think of the enzyme produced by the defective gene as *a wrong key which fits* into the chemical lock of the central nervous system—*but won't turn*. Because it's there, the true

102

key—the right enzyme—can't even enter the lock. It's blocked. Result? Irreversible destruction of proteins in the brain tissue."

"But if it is irreversible," intruded one of the other psychologists who had joined the little audience, "how is it possible that Mr. Gordon here is no longer retarded?"

"Ah!" crowed Nemur, "I said the destruction to the tissue was irreversible, not the process itself. Many researchers have been able to reverse the process through injections of chemicals which combine with the defective enzymes, changing the molecular shape of the interfering key, as it were. This is central to our own technique as well. But first, we remove the damaged portions of the brain and permit the implanted brain tissue which has been chemically revitalized to produce brain proteins at a supernormal rate—"

"Just a minute, Professor Nemur," I said, interrupting him at the height of his peroration. "What about Rahajamati's work in that field?"

He looked at me blankly. "Who?"

"Rahajamati. His article attacks Tanida's theory of enzyme fusion—the concept of changing the chemical structure of the enzyme blocking the step in the metabolic pathway."

He frowned. "Where was that article translated?"

"It hasn't been translated yet. I read it in the *Hindu Journal of Psychopathology* just a few days ago."

He looked at his audience and tried to shrug it off. "Well, I don't think we have anything to worry about. Our results speak for themselves."

"But Tanida himself first propounded the theory of blocking the maverick enzyme through combination, and now he points out that—"

"Oh, come now, Charlie. Just because a man is the first to come forth with a theory doesn't make him the final word on its experimental development. I think everyone here will agree that the research done in the United States and Britain far outshines the work done in India and Japan. We still have the best laboratories and the best equipment in the world."

"But that doesn't answer Rahajamati's point that—"

"This is not the time or place to go into that. I'm certain all of these points will be adequately dealt with in tomorrow's session." He turned to talk to someone about an old college friend, cutting me off completely, and I stood there dumbfounded.

I managed to get Strauss off to one side, and I started questioning him. "All right, now. You've been telling me I'm too sensitive to him. What did I say that upset him that way?"

"You're making him feel inferior and he can't take it."

"I'm serious, for God's sake. Tell me the truth."

"Charlie, you've got to stop thinking that everyone is laughing at you. Nemur couldn't discuss those articles because he hasn't read them. He can't read those languages."

"Not read Hindi and Japanese? Oh, come on now."

"Charlie, not everyone has your gift for languages."

"But then how can he refute Rahajamati's attack on this method, and Tanida's challenge to the validity of this kind of control? He must know about those—"

"No . . . ," said Strauss thoughtfully. "Those papers must be recent. There hasn't been time to get translations made."

"You mean you haven't read them either?"

He shrugged. "I'm an even worse linguist than he is. But I'm certain before the final reports are turned in, all the journals will be combed for additional data."

I didn't know what to say. To hear him admit that both of them were ignorant of whole areas in their own fields was terrifying. "What languages do you know?" I asked him.

"French, German, Spanish, Italian, and enough Swedish to get along."

"No Russian, Chinese, Portuguese?"

He reminded me that as a practicing psychiatrist and neurosurgeon he had very little time for languages. And the only ancient languages that he could read were Latin and Greek. Nothing of the ancient Oriental tongues.

I could see he wanted to end the discussion at that point, but somehow I couldn't let go. I had to find out just how much he knew.

I found out.

Physics: nothing beyond the quantum theory of fields. Geology: nothing about geomorphology or stratigraphy or even petrology. Nothing about the micro- or macro-economic theory. Little in mathematics beyond the elementary level of calculus of variations, and nothing at all about Banach algebra or Riemannian manifolds. It was the first inkling of the revelations that were in store for me this weekend.

I couldn't stay at the party. I slipped away to walk and think this out. Frauds—both of them. They had pretended to be geniuses. But they were just ordinary men working blindly, pretending to be able to bring light into the darkness. Why is it that everyone lies? No one I know is what he appears to be. As I turned the corner I caught a glimpse of Burt coming after me.

"What's the matter?" I said as he caught up to me. "Are you following me?"

He shrugged and laughed uncomfortably. "Exhibit *A*, star of the show. Can't have you run down by one of these motorized Chicago cowboys or mugged and rolled on State Street."

"I don't like being kept in custody."

He avoided my gaze as he walked beside me, his hands deep in his pockets. "Take it easy, Charlie. The old man is on edge. This convention means a lot to him. His reputation is at stake."

"I didn't know you were so close to him," I taunted, recalling all the times Burt had complained about the professor's narrowness and pushing.

"I'm not close to him." He looked at me defiantly. "But he's put his whole life into this. He's no Freud or Jung or Pavlov or Watson, but he's doing something important and I respect his dedication—maybe even more because he's just an ordinary man trying to do a great man's work, while the great men are all busy making bombs."

"I'd like to hear you call him ordinary to his face."

"It doesn't matter what he thinks of himself. Sure he's egotistic, so what? It takes that kind of ego to make a man attempt a thing like this. I've seen enough of men like him to know that mixed in with that pompousness and self-assertion is a goddamned good measure of uncertainty and fear."

"And phoniness and shallowness," I added. "I see

them now as they really are, phonies. I suspected it of Nemur. He always seemed frightened of something. But Strauss surprised me."

Burt paused and let out a long stream of breath. We turned into a luncheonette for coffee, and I didn't see his face, but the sound revealed his exasperation.

"You think I'm wrong?"

"Just that you've come a long way kind of fast," he said. "You've got a superb mind now, intelligence that can't really be calculated, more knowledge absorbed by now than most people pick up in a long lifetime. But you're lopsided. You know things. You see things. But you haven't developed understanding, or—I have to use the word—tolerance. You call them phonies, but when did either of them ever claim to be perfect, or superhuman? They're ordinary people. You're the genius."

He broke off awkwardly, suddenly aware that he was preaching at me.

"Go ahead."

"Ever meet Nemur's wife?"

"No."

"If you want to understand why he's under tension all the time, even when things are going well at the ab and in his lectures, you've got to know Bertha Nemur. Did you know she's got him his professorship? Did you know she used her father's influence to get him the Welberg Foundation grant? Well, now she's pushed him into this premature presentation at the convention. Until you've had a woman like her riding you, don't think you can understand the man who has."

I didn't say anything, and I could see he wanted to get back to the hotel. All the way back we were silent.

Am I a genius? I don't think so. Not yet anyway. As Burt would put it, mocking the euphemisms of educational jargon, I'm *exceptional*—a democratic term used to avoid the damning labels of *gifted* and *deprived* (which used to mean *bright* and *retarded*) and as soon as *exceptional* begins to mean anything to anyone they'll change it. The idea seems to be: use an expression only as long as it doesn't mean anything to anybody. *Exceptional* refers to both ends of the spectrum, so all my life I've been exceptional.

Strange about learning; the farther I go the more I see that I never knew even existed. A short while ago I foolishly thought I could learn everything—all the knowledge in the world. Now I hope only to be able to know of its existence, and to understand one grain of it.

Is there time?

Burt is annoyed with me. He finds me impatient and the others must feel the same. But they hold me back and try to keep me in my place. What is my place? Who and what am I now? Am I the sum of my life or only of the past months? Oh, how impatient they get when I try to discuss it with them. They don't like to admit that they don't know. It's paradoxical that an ordinary man like Nemur presumes to devote himself to making other people geniuses. He would like to be thought of as the discoverer of new laws of learning—the Einstein of psychology. And he has the teacher's fear of being surpassed by the student, the master's dread of having the disciple discredit his work. (Not that I am in any real sense Nemur's student or disciple as Burt is.)

I guess Nemur's fear of being revealed as a man walking on stilts among giants is understandable. Failure at this point would destroy him. He is too old to start all over again.

As shocking as it is to discover the truth about men I had respected and looked up to, I guess Burt is right. I must not be too impatient with them. Their ideas and brilliant work made the experiment possible. I've got to guard against the natural tendency to look down on them now that I have surpassed them.

I've got to realize that when they continually admonish me to speak and write simply so that people who read these reports will be able to understand me, they are talking about themselves as well. But still it's frightening to realize that my fate is in the hands of men who are not the giants I once thought them to be, men who don't know all the answers.

June 13—I'm dictating this under great emotional strain. I've walked out on the whole thing. I'm on a plane headed back to New York alone, and I have no idea what I'm going to do when I get there.

At first, I admit, I was in awe at the picture of an international convention of scientists and scholars, gathered for an exchange of ideas. Here, I thought, was where it all really happened. Here it would be different from the sterile college discussions, because these were the men on the highest levels of psychological research and education, the scientists who wrote the books and delivered the lectures, the authorities people quoted. If Nemur and Strauss were ordinary men working beyond their abilities, I felt sure it would be different with the others.

When it was time for the meeting, Nemur steered us through the gigantic lobby with its heavy baroque furnishings and huge curving marble staircases, and we moved through the thickening knots of handshakers, nodders, and smilers. Two other professors from Beekman who had arrived in Chicago just this morning joined us. Professors White and Clinger walked a little to the right and a step or two behind Nemur and Strauss, while Burt and I brought up the rear.

Standees parted to make a path for us into the Grand Ballroom, and Nemur waved to the reporters and photographers who had come to hear at first hand about the startling things that had been done with a retardate adult in just a little over three months.

Nemur had obviously sent out advance publicity releases.

Some of the psychological papers delivered at the meeting were impressive. A group from Alaska showed how stimulation of various portions of the brain caused a significant development in learning ability, and a group from New Zealand had mapped out those portions of the brain that controlled perception and retention of stimuli.

But there were other kinds of papers too—P. T. Zellerman's study on the difference in the length of time it took white rats to learn a maze when the corners were curved rather than angular, or Worfel's paper on the effect of intelligence level on the reaction-time of rhesus monkeys. Papers like these made me angry. Money, time, and energy squandered on the detailed analysis of the trivial. Burt was right when he praised Nemur and Strauss for devoting themselves to something important and uncertain rather than to something insignificant and safe.

If only Nemur would look at me as a human being.

After the chairman announced the presentation from

Beekman University, we took our seats on the platform behind the long table—Algernon in his cage between Burt and me. We were the main attraction of the evening, and when we were settled, the chairman began his introduction. I half expected to hear him boom out: *Laideezzz and gentulmennnnnn. Step right this way and see the side show! An act never before seen in the scientific world! A mouse and a moron turned into geniuses before your very eyes!*

I admit I had come here with a chip on my shoulder.

All he said was: "The next presentation really needs no introduction. We have all heard about the startling work being done at Beekman University, sponsored by the Welberg Foundation grants, under the direction of the chairman of the psychology department, Professor Nemur, in co-operation with Dr. Strauss of the Beekman Neuropsychiatric Center. Needless to say, this is a report we have all been looking forward to with great interest. I turn the meeting over to Professor Nemur and Dr. Strauss."

Nemur nodded graciously at the chairman's introductory praise and winked at Strauss in the triumph of the moment.

The first speaker from Beekman was Professor Clinger.

I was becoming irritated, and I could see that Algernon, upset by the smoke, the buzzing, the unaccustomed surroundings, was moving around in his cage nervously. I had the strangest compulsion to open his cage and let him out. It was an absurd thought—more of an itch than a thought—and I tried to ignore it. But as I listened to Professor Clinger's stereotyped paper on "The effects of left-handed goal boxes in a T-maze versus right-handed goal boxes in a T-maze," I found myself toying with the release-lock mechanism of Algernon's cage.

In a short while (before Strauss and Nemur would unveil their crowning achievement) Burt would read a paper describing the procedures and results of administering intelligence and learning tests he had devised for Algernon. This would be followed by a demonstration as Algernon was put through his paces of solving a problem in order to get his meal (something I have never stopped resenting!).

Not that I had anything against Burt. He had always

been straightforward with me—more so than most of the others—but when he described the white mouse who had been given intelligence, he was as pompous and artificial as the others. As if he were trying on the mantle of his teachers. I restrained myself at that point more out of friendship for Burt than anything else. Letting Algernon out of his cage would throw the meeting into chaos, and after all this was Burt's debut into the rat-race of academic preferment.

I had my finger on the cage door release, and as Algernon watched the movement of my hand with his pink-candy eyes, I'm certain he knew what I had in mind. At that moment Burt took the cage for his demonstration. He explained the complexity of the shifting lock, and the problem-solving required each time the lock was to be opened. (Thin plastic bolts fell into place in varying patterns and had to be controlled by the mouse, who depressed a series of levers in the same order.) As Algernon's intelligence increased, his problem-solving speed increased—that much was obvious. But then Burt revealed one thing I had *not* known.

At the peak of his intelligence, Algernon's performance had become variable. There were times, according to Burt's report, when Algernon refused to work at all—even when apparently hungry—and other times when he would solve the problem but, instead of taking his food reward, would hurl himself against the walls of his cage.

When someone from the audience asked Burt if he was suggesting that this erratic behavior was directly caused by increased intelligence, Burt ducked the question. "As far as I am concerned," he said, "there's not enough evidence to warrant that conclusion. There are other possibilities. It is possible that both the increased intelligence and the erratic behavior at this level were created by the original surgery, instead of one being a function of the other. It's also possible that this erratic behavior is unique to Algernon. We didn't find it in any of the other mice, but then none of the others achieved as high a level of intelligence nor maintained it for as long as Algernon has."

I realized immediately that this information had been withheld from me. I suspected the reason, and I was annoyed, but that was nothing to the anger I felt when they brought out the films.

I had never known that my early performances and tests in the laboratory were filmed. There I was, at the table beside Burt, confused and open-mouthed as I tried to run the maze with the electric stylus. Each time I received a shock, my expression changed to an absurd wide-eyed stare, and then that foolish smile again. Each time it happened the audience roared. Race after race, it was repeated, and each time they found it funnier than before.

I told myself they were not gawking curiosity seekers, but scientists here in search of knowledge. They couldn't help finding these pictures funny—but still, as Burt caught the spirit and made amusing comments on the films, I was overcome with a sense of mischief. It would be even funnier to see Algernon escape from his cage, and to see all these people scattering and crawling around on their hands and knees trying to retrieve a small, white, scurrying genius.

But I controlled myself, and by the time Strauss took the podium the impulse had passed.

Strauss dealt largely with the theory and techniques of neurosurgery, describing in detail how pioneer studies on the mapping of hormone control centers enabled him to isolate and stimulate these centers while at the same time removing the hormone-inhibitor producing portion of the cortex. He explained the enzyme-block theory and went on to describe my physical condition before and after surgery. Photographs (I didn't know they had been taken) were passed around and commented on, and I could see by the nods and smiles that most people there agreed with him that the "dull, vacuous facial expression" had been transformed into an "alert, intelligent appearance." He also discussed in detail the pertinent aspects of our therapy sessions—especially my changing attitudes toward free association on the couch.

I had come there as part of a scientific presentation, and I had expected to be put on exhibition, but everyone kept talking about me as if I were some kind of newly created thing they were presenting to the scientific world. No one in this room considered me an individual—a

111

human being. The constant juxtaposition of "Algernon and Charlie," and "Charlie and Algernon," made it clear that they thought of both of us as a couple of experimental animals who had no existence outside the laboratory. But, aside from my anger, I couldn't get it out of my mind that something was wrong.

Finally, it was Nemur's turn to speak—to sum it all up as the head of the project—to take the spotlight as the author of a brilliant experiment. This was the day he had been waiting for.

He was impressive as he stood up there on the platform, and, as he spoke, I found myself nodding with him, agreeing with things I knew to be true. The testing, the experiment, the surgery, and my subsequent mental development were described at length, and his talk was enlivened by quotations from my progress reports. More than once I found myself hearing something personal or foolish read to this audience. Thank God I had been careful to keep most of the details about Alice and myself in my private file.

Then, at one point in his summary, he said it: "We who have worked on this project at Beekman University have the satisfaction of knowing we have taken one of nature's mistakes and by our new techniques created a superior human being. When Charlie came to us he was outside of society, alone in a great city without friends or relatives to care about him, without the mental equipment to live a normal life. No past, no contact with the present, no hope for the future. It might be said that Charlie Gordon did not really exist before this experiment. . . ."

I don't know why I resented it so intensely to have them think of me as something newly minted in their private treasury, but it was—I am certain—echoes of that idea that had been sounding in the chambers of my mind from the time we had arrived in Chicago. I wanted to get up and show everyone what a fool he was, to shout at him: *I'm a human being, a person—with parents and memories and a history—and I was before you ever wheeled me into that operating room!*

At the same time deep in the heat of my anger there was forged an overwhelming insight into the thing that had disturbed me when Strauss spoke and again when Nemur amplified his data. They had made a mistake—of course! The statistical evaluation of the waiting period necessary to prove the permanence of the change had been based on earlier experiments in the field of mental development and learning, on waiting periods with normally dull or normally intelligent animals. But it was obvious that the waiting period would have to be extended in those cases where an animal's intelligence had been increased two or three times.

Nemur's conclusions had been premature. For both Algernon and myself, it would take more time to see if this change would stick. The professors had made a mistake, and no one else had caught it. I wanted to jump up and tell them, but I couldn't move. Like Algernon, I found myself behind the mesh of the cage they had built around me.

Now there would be a question period, and before I would be allowed to have my dinner, I would be required to perform before this distinguished gathering. No. I had to get out of there.

". . . In one sense, he was the result of modern psychological experimentation. In place of a feeble-minded shell, a burden on the society that must fear his irresponsible behavior, we have a man of dignity and sensitivity, ready to take his place as a contributing member of society. I should like you all to hear a few words from Charlie Gordon. . . ."

God damn him. He didn't know what he was talking about. At that point, the compulsion overwhelmed me. I watched in fascination as my hand moved, independent of my will, to pull down the latch of Algernon's cage. As I opened it he looked up at me and paused. Then he turned, darted out of his cage, and scampered across the long table.

At first, he was lost against the damask tablecloth, a blur of white on white, until a woman at the table screamed, knocking her chair backwards as she leaped to her feet. Beyond her, pitchers of water overturned, and then Burt shouted. "Algernon's loose!" Algernon jumped down from the table, onto the platform and then to the floor.

"Get him! Get him!" Nemur screeched as the audience, divided in its aims, became a tangle of arms and legs. Some of the women (non-experimentalists?) tried to stand on the unstable folding chairs while others, trying to help corner Algernon, knocked them over.

"Close those back doors!" shouted Burt, who realized Algernon was smart enough to head in that direction.

"Run," I heard myself shout. "The side door!"

"He's gone out the side door," someone echoed.

"Get him! Get him!" begged Nemur.

The crowd surged out of the Grand Ballroom into the corridor, as Algernon, scampering along the maroon carpeted hallway, led them a merry chase. Under Louis XIV tables, around potted palms, up stairways, around corners, down stairways, into the main lobby, picking up other people as we went. Seeing them all running back and forth in the lobby, chasing a white mouse smarter than many of them, was the funniest thing that had happened in a long time.

"Go ahead, laugh!" snorted Nemur, who nearly bumped into me, "but if we don't find him, the whole experiment is in danger."

I pretended to be looking for Algernon under a waste basket. "Do you know something?" I said. "You've made a mistake. And after today, maybe it just won't matter at all."

Seconds later, half a dozen women came screaming out of the powder room, skirts clutched frantically around their legs.

"He's in there," someone yelled. But for a moment, the searching crowd was stayed by the handwriting on the wall—*Ladies*. I was the first to cross the invisible barrier and enter the sacred gates.

Algernon was perched on top of one of the washbasins, glaring at his reflection in the mirror.

"Come on," I said. "We'll get out of here together."

He let me pick him up and put him into my jacket pocket. "Stay in there quietly until I tell you."

The others came bursting through the swinging doors—looking guiltily as if they expected to see screaming nude females. I walked out as they searched the washroom, and I heard Burt's voice. "There's a hole in that ventilator. Maybe he went up there."

"Find out where it leads to," said Strauss.

"You go up to the second floor," said Nemur, waving to Strauss. "I'll go down to the basement."

At this point they burst out of the ladies' room and the forces split. I followed behind the Strauss contingent up to the second floor as they tried to discover where the ventilator led to. When Strauss and White and their half-dozen followers turned right down Corridor B, I turned left up Corridor C and took the elevator to my room.

I closed the door behind me, and patted my pocket. A pink snout and white fuzz poked out and looked around. "I'll just get my things packed," I said, "and we'll take off—just you and me—a couple of man-made geniuses on the run."

I had the bellhop put the bags and the tape-recorder into a waiting taxi, paid my hotel bill, and walked out the revolving door with the object of the search nestling in my jacket pocket. I used my return-flight ticket to New York.

Instead of going back to my place, I plan to stay at a hotel here in the city for one or two nights. We'll use that as a base of operations while I look for a furnished apartment, somewhere midtown. I want to be near Times Square.

Talking all this out makes me feel a lot better—even a little silly. I don't really know why I got so upset, or what I'm doing on a jet heading back to New York with Algernon in a shoebox under the seat. I mustn't panic. The mistake doesn't necessarily mean anything serious. It's just that things are not as definite as Nemur believed. But where do I go from here?

First, I've got to see my parents. As soon as I can.

I may not have all the time I thought I had. . . .

PROGRESS REPORT 14

June 15—Our escape hit the papers yesterday, and the tabloids had a field day. On the second page of the *Daily Press* there was an old picture of me and a sketch of a white mouse. The headline read: *Moron-Genius and Mouse Go Berserk*. Nemur and Strauss are reported as saying I had been under tremendous strain and that I would undoubtedly return soon. They offered a five-hundred-dollar reward for Algernon, not realizing we were together.

When I turned to the later story on the fifth page, I was stunned to find a picture of my mother and sister. Some reporter had obviously done his legwork.

SISTER UNAWARE OF MORON-GENIUS' WHEREABOUTS

(Special to the Daily Press)

Brooklyn, N.Y., June 14—Miss Norma Gordon, who lives with her mother, Rose Gordon, at 4136 Marks Street, Brooklyn, N.Y., denied any knowledge of her brother's whereabouts. Miss Gordon said, "We haven't seen him or heard from him in more than seventeen years."

Miss Gordon says she believed her brother dead until last March, when the head of the psychology department at Beekman University approached her for permission to use Charlie in an experiment.

"My mother told me he had been sent to the Warren place," (Warren State Home and Training School, in Warren, Long Island) said Miss Gordon, "and that he died there a few years later. I had no idea then that he was still alive."

Miss Gordon requests that anyone who has any news about her brother's whereabouts communicate with the family at their home address.

The father, Matthew Gordon, who is not living with his wife and daughter, now operates a barber-shop in the Bronx.

I stared at the news story for a while, and then I turned back and looked at the picture again. How can I describe them?

I can't say I remember Rose's face. Although the recent photograph is a clear one, I still see it through the gauze of childhood. I knew her, and I didn't know her. Had we passed on the street, I would not have recognized her, but now, knowing she is my mother, I can make out the faint details—yes!

Thin, drawn into exaggerated lines. Sharp nose and chin. And I can almost hear her chatter and bird-screech. Hair done up in a bun, severely. Piercing me with her dark eyes. I want her to take me into her arms and tell me I am a good boy, and at the same time I want to turn away to avoid a slap. Her picture makes me tremble.

And Norma—thin-faced too. Features not so sharp,

pretty, but very much like my mother. Her hair worn down to her shoulders softens her. The two of them are sitting on the living room couch.

It was Rose's face that brought back the frightening memories. She was two people to me, and I never had any way of knowing which she would be. Perhaps she would reveal it to others by a gesture of hand, a raised eyebrow, a frown—my sister knew the storm warnings, and she would always be out of range whenever my mother's temper flared—but it always caught me unawares. I would come to her for comforting, and her anger would break over me.

And other times there would be tenderness and holding-close like a warm bath, and hands stroking my hair and brow, and the words carved above the cathedral of my childhood:

> *He's like all the other children.*
> *He's a good boy.*

I see back through the dissolving photograph, myself and father leaning over a bassinet. He's holding me by the hand and saying, "There she is. You mustn't touch her because she's very little, but when she gets bigger you'll have a sister to play with."

I see my mother in the huge bed nearby, bleached and pasty, arms limp on the orchid-figured comforter, raising her head anxiously. "Watch him, Matt—"

That was before she had changed towards me, and now I realize it was because she had no way of knowing yet if Norma would be like me or not. It was later on, when she was sure her prayers had been answered, and Norma showed all signs of normal intelligence, that my mother's voice began to sound different. Not only her voice, but her touch her look, her very presence—all changed. It was as if her magnetic poles had reversed and where they had once attracted now repelled. I see now that when Norma flowered in our garden I became a weed, allowed to exist only where I would not be seen, in corners and dark places.

Seeing her face in the newspaper, I suddenly hated her. It would have been better if she had ignored the doctors and teachers and others who were so in a hurry to convince her that I was a moron, turning her away from me so that she gave me less love when I needed more.

What good would it do to see her now? What could she tell me about myself? And yet, I'm curious. How would she react?

To see her and trace back to learn what I was? Or to forget her? Is the past worth knowing? Why is it so important for me to say to her: "Mom, look at me. I'm not retarded any more. I'm normal. Better than normal. I'm a genius?"

Even as I try to get her out of my mind, the memories seep back from the past to contaminate the here and now. Another memory—when I was much older.

A quarrel.

Charlie lying in bed, with the covers pulled up around him. The room dark, except for the thin line of yellow light from the door ajar that penetrates the darkness to join both worlds. And he hears things, not understanding but feeling, because the rasp of their voices is linked to their talk of him. More and more, each day, he comes to associate that tone with a frown when they speak of him.

He has been almost asleep when through the bar of light the soft voices were raised to the pitch of argument—his mother's voice sharp with the threat of one used to having her way through hysteria. "He's got to be sent away. I don't want him in the house any more with her. Call Dr. Portman and tell him we want to send Charlie to the Warren State Home."

My father's voice is firm, steadying. "But you know Charlie wouldn't harm her. It can't make any difference to her at this age."

"How do we know? Maybe it has a bad effect on a child to grow up with . . . someone like him in the house."

"Dr. Portman said—"

"Portman said! Portman said! I don't care what he said! Think of what it will be like for her to have a brother like that. I was wrong all these years, trying to believe he would grow up like other children. I admit it now. Better for him to be put away."

"Now that you've got her, you've decided you don't want him any more. . . ."

"Do you think this is easy? Why are you making it harder for me? All these years everyone telling me he should be put away. Well, they were right. Put him away. Maybe at the Home with his own kind he'll have something. I don't know what's right or wrong any more. All I know is I'm not going to sacrifice my daughter for him now."

And though Charlie has not understood what passed between them, he is afraid and sinks beneath the covers, eyes open, trying to pierce the darkness that surrounds him.

As I see him now, he is not really afraid, just withdrawing, as a bird or squirrel backs off from the brusque movements of the feeder—involuntary, instinctive. The light through that door ajar comes to me again in luminous vision. Seeing Charlie huddled beneath the covers I wish I could give him comfort, explain to him that he has done nothing wrong, that it is beyond him to change his mother's attitude back to what it was before his sister came. There on the bed, Charlie did not understand what they were saying, but now it hurts. If I could reach out into the past of my memories, I would make her see how much she was hurting me.

This is no time to go to her. Not until I've had time to work it out for myself.

Fortunately, as a precaution, I withdrew my savings from the bank as soon as I arrived in New York. Eight hundred and eighty-six dollars won't last long, but it will give me time to get my bearings.

I've checked into the Camden Hotel on 41st Street, a block from Times Square. New York! All the things I've read about it! Gotham . . . the melting pot . . . Baghdad-on-the-Hudson. City of light and color. Incredible that I've lived and worked all my life just a few stops away on the subway and been to Times Square only once—with Alice.

It's hard to keep from calling her. I've started and stopped myself several times. I've got to keep away from her.

So many confusing thoughts to get down. I tell myself that as long as I keep taping my progress reports, nothing will be lost; the record will be complete. Let them be in the dark for a while; I was in the dark for more than thirty years. But I'm tired now. Didn't get to sleep on the plane yesterday, and I can't keep my eyes open. I'll pick up at this point tomorrow.

June 16—Called Alice, but hung up before she answered. Today I found a furnished apartment. Ninety-five dollars a month is more than I planned to spend, but it's on Forty-third and Tenth Avenue and I can get to the library in ten minutes to keep up with my reading and study. The apartment is on the fourth floor, four rooms, and there's a rented piano in it. The landlady says that one of these days the rental service will pull it out, but maybe by that time I can learn to play it.

Algernon is a pleasant companion. At mealtimes he takes his place at the small gateleg table. He likes pretzels, and today he took a sip of beer while we watched the ball game on TV. I think he rooted for the Yankees.

I'm going to move most of the furniture out of the second bedroom and use the room for Algernon. I plan to build him a three-dimensional maze out of scrap plastic that I can pick up cheaply downtown. There are some complex maze variations I'd like him to learn to be sure he keeps in shape. But I'm going to see if I can find some motivation other than food. There must be other rewards that will induce him to solve problems.

Solitude gives me a chance to read and think, and now that the memories are coming through again—to rediscover my past, to find out who and what I really am. If anything should go wrong, I'll have at least that.

June 19—Met Fay Lillman, my neighbor across the hall. When I came back with an armful of groceries, I discovered I had locked myself out, and I remembered that the front fire escape connected my living room window and the apartment directly across the hall.

The radio was on loud and brassy, so I knocked—softly at first, and then louder.

"Come on in! Door's open!"

I pushed the door, and froze, because standing in front

of an easel, painting, was a slender blonde in pink bra and panties.

"Sorry!" I gasped, closing the door again. From outside, I shouted. "I'm your neighbor across the hall. I locked myself out, and I wanted to use the fire escape to get over to my window."

The door swung open and she faced me, still in her underwear, a brush in each hand and hands on her hips.

"Didn't you hear me say come in?" She waved me into the apartment, pushing away a carton full of trash. "Just step over that pile of junk there."

I thought she must have forgotten—or not realized—she was undressed, and I didn't know which way to look. I kept my eyes averted, looking at the walls, ceiling, everywhere but at her.

The place was a shambles. There were dozens of little folding snack-tables, all covered with twisted tubes of paint, most of them crusted dry like shriveled snakes, but some of them alive and oozing ribbons of color. Tubes, brushes, cans, rags, and parts of frames and canvas were strewn everywhere. The place was thick with the odor compounded of paint, linseed oil, and turpentine—and after a few moments the subtle aroma of stale beer. Three overstuffed chairs and a mangy green couch were piled high with discarded clothing, and on the floor lay shoes, stockings and underthings, as if she were in the habit of undressing as she walked and flinging her clothes as she went. A fine layer of dust covered everything.

"Well, you're Mr. Gordon," she said, looking me over. "I've been dying to get a peek at you ever since you moved in. Have a seat." She scooped up a pile of clothing from one of the chairs and dumped it onto the crowded sofa. "So you finally decided to visit your neighbors. Get you a drink?"

"You're a painter," I burbled, for want of something to say. I was unnerved by the thought that any moment she would realize she was undressed and would scream and dash for the bedroom. I tried to keep my eyes moving, looking everywhere but at her.

"Beer or ale? Nothing else in the place right now except cooking sherry. You don't want cooking sherry, do you?"

"I can't stay," I said, getting hold of myself and fixing

my gaze at the beauty mark on the left side of her chin. "I've locked myself out of my apartment. I wanted to go across the fire escape. It connects our windows."

"Any time," she assured me. "Those lousy patent locks are a pain in the ass. I locked myself out of this place three times the first week I lived here—and once I was out in the hall stark naked for half an hour. Stepped out to get the milk, and the goddamned door swung shut behind me. I ripped the goddamned lock off and I haven't had one on my door since."

I must have frowned, because she laughed. "Well, you see what the damned locks do. They lock you out, and they don't protect much, do they? Fifteen burglaries in this goddamned building in the past year and every one of them in apartments that were locked. No one ever broke in here, even though the door was always open. They'd have a rotten time finding anything valuable here anyway."

When she insisted again on my having a beer with her, I accepted. While she was getting it from the kitchen, I looked around the room again. What I hadn't noticed before was that the part of the wall behind me had been cleared away—all the furniture pushed to one side of the room or the center, so that the far wall (the plaster of which had been torn off to expose the brick) served as an art gallery. Paintings were crowded to the ceiling and others were stacked against each other on the floor. Several of them were self-portraits, including two nudes. The painting she had been working on when I came in, the one on the easel, was a half-length nude of herself, showing her hair long (not the way she wore it now, up in blonde braids coiled around her head like a crown) down to her shoulders with part of her long tresses twisted around the front and resting between her breasts. She had painted her breasts uptilted and firm with the nipples an unrealistic lollipop-red. When I heard her coming back with the beer, I spun away from the easel quickly, stumbled over some books, and pretended to be interested in a small autumn landscape on the wall.

I was relieved to see that she had slipped into a thin ragged housecoat—even though it had holes in all the wrong places—and I could look directly at her for the first time. Not exactly beautiful, but her blue eyes and pert snub nose gave her a catlike quality that contrasted with her robust, athletic movements. She was about thirty-five, slender and well proportioned. She set the beers on the hardwood floor, curled up beside them in front of the sofa, and motioned for me to do the same.

"I find the floor more comfortable than chairs," she said, sipping the beer from the can. "Don't you?"

I told her I hadn't thought about it, and she laughed and said I had an honest face. She was in the mood to talk about herself. She avoided Greenwich Village, she said, because there, instead of painting, she would be spending all her time in bars and coffee shops. "It's better up here. away from the phonies and the dilettantes. Here I can do what I want and no one comes to sneer. You're not a sneerer, are you?"

I shrugged, trying not to notice the gritty dust all over my trousers and my hands. "I guess we all sneer at something. You're sneering at the phonies and dilettantes, aren't you?"

After a while, I said I'd better be getting over to my own apartment. She pushed a pile of books away from the window—and I climbed over newspapers and paper bags filled with empty quart beer bottles. "One of these days," she sighed, "I've got to cash them in."

I climbed onto the window sill and out to the fire escape. When I got my window open, I came back for my groceries, but before I could say thanks and good-bye, she started out onto the fire escape after me. "Let's see your place. I've never been there. Before you moved in, the two little old Wagner sisters wouldn't even say good morning to me." She crawled through my window behind me and sat on the ledge.

"Come on in," I said, putting the groceries on the table.

"I don't have any beer, but I can make you a cup of coffee." But she was looking past me, her eyes wide in disbelief.

"My God! I've never seen a place as neat as this. Who would dream that a man living by himself could keep a place so orderly?"

"I wasn't always that way," I apologized. "It's just since I moved in here. It was neat when I moved in, and

123

I've had the compulsion to keep it that way. It upsets me now if anything is out of place."

She got down off the window sill to explore the apartment.

"Hey," she said, suddenly, "do you like to dance? You know—" She held out her arms and did a complicated step as she hummed a Latin beat. "Tell me you dance and I'll bust."

"Only the fox trot," I said, "and not very good at that."

She shrugged. "I'm nuts about dancing, but nobody I ever meet—that I like—is a good dancer. I've got to get myself all dolled up once in a while and go downtown to the Stardust Ballroom. Most of the guys hanging around there are kind of creepy, but they can dance."

She sighed as she looked around. "Tell you what I don't like about a place so goddamned orderly like this. As an artist . . . it's the lines that get me. All the straight lines in the walls, on the floors, in the corners that turn into boxes—like coffins. The only way I can get rid of the boxes is to take a few drinks. Then all the lines get wavy and wiggly, and I feel a lot better about the whole world. When things are all straight and lined up this way I get morbid. Ugh! If I lived here I would have to stay drunk all the time."

Suddenly, she swung around and faced me. "Say, could you let me have five until the twentieth? That's when my alimony check comes. I usually don't run short, but I had a problem last week."

Before I could answer, she screeched and started over to the piano in the corner. "I used to play the piano. I heard you fooling around with it a few times, and I said to myself that guy's goddamned good. That's how I know I wanted to meet you even before I saw you. I haven't played in such a goddamned long time." She was picking away at the piano as I went into the kitchen to make coffee.

"You're welcome to practice on it any time," I said. I don't know why I suddenly became so free with my place, but there was something about her that demanded complete unselfishness. "I don't leave the front door open yet, but the window isn't locked, and if I'm not here all you've got to do is climb in through the fire escape. Cream and sugar in your coffee?"

When she didn't answer, I looked back into the living room. She wasn't there, and as I started towards the window, I heard her voice from Algernon's room.

"Hey, what's this?" She was examining the three dimensional plastic maze I had built. She studied it and then let out another squeal. "Modern sculpture! All boxes and straight lines!"

"It's a special maze," I explained. "A complex learning device for Algernon."

But she was circling around it, excited. "They'll go mad for it at the Museum of Modern Art."

"It's not sculpture," I insisted. I opened the door to Algernon's living-cage attached to the maze, and let him into the maze opening.

"My God!" she whispered. "Sculpture with a *living element*. Charlie, it's the greatest thing since junkmobiles and tincannia."

I tried to explain, but she insisted that the living element would make sculpture history. Only when I saw the laughter in her wild eyes did I realize she was teasing me. "It could be self-perpetuating art," she went on, "a creative experience for the art lover. You get another mouse and when they have babies, you always keep one to reproduce the living element. Your work of art attains immortality, and all the fashionable people buy copies for conversation pieces. What are you going to call it?"

"All right," I sighed. "I surrender. . . ."

"No," she snorted, tapping the plastic dome where Algernon had found his way into the goal-box. "*I surrender* is too much of a cliché. How about: *Life is just a box of mazes?*"

"You're a nut!" I said.

"Naturally!" She spun around and curtsied. "I was wondering when you'd notice."

About then the coffee boiled over.

Halfway through the cup of coffee, she gasped and said she had to run because she had a date a half-hour earlier with someone she met at an art exhibit.

"You wanted some money," I said.

She reached into my half open wallet and pulled out a

125

five-dollar bill. "Till next week," she said, "when the check comes. Thanks a mill." She crumpled the money, blew Algernon a kiss, and before I could say anything she was out the window onto the fire escape, and out of sight. I stood there foolishly looking after her.

So damned attractive. So full of life and excitement. Her voice, her eyes—everything about her was an invitation. And she lived out the window and just a fire escape away.

June 20—Perhaps I should have waited before going to see Matt; or not gone to see him at all. I don't know. Nothing turns out the way I expect it to. With the clue that Matt had opened a barbershop somewhere in the Bronx, it was a simple matter to find him. I remembered he had sold for a barber supply company in New York. That led me to Metro Barber Shop Supplies who had a barbershop account under the name of *Gordons Barber Shop* on Wentworth Street in the Bronx.

Matt had often talked about a barbershop of his own. How he hated selling! What battles they had about it! Rose screaming that a salesman was at least a dignified occupation, but she would never have a barber for a husband. And oh, wouldn't Margaret Phinney snicker at the "barber's wife." And what about Lois Meiner whose husband was a claims examiner for the Alarm Casualty Company? Wouldn't she stick her nose up in the air!

During the years he worked as a salesman, hating every day of it (especially after he saw the movie version of *Death of a Salesman)* Matt dreamed that he would someday become his own boss. That must have been in his mind in those days when he talked about saving money and gave me my haircuts down in the basement. They were good haircuts too, he boasted, a lot better than I'd get in that cheap barbershop on Scales Avenue. When he walked out on Rose, he walked out on selling too, and I admired him for that.

I was excited at the thought of seeing him. Memories were warm ones. Matt had been willing to take me as I was. Before Norma: the arguments that weren't about money or impressing the neighbors were about me—that I should be let alone instead of being pushed to do what other kids did. And after Norma: that I had a right to a life of my own even though I wasn't like other children. Always defending me. I couldn't wait to see the expression on his face. He was someone I'd be able to share this with.

Wentworth Street was a rundown section of the Bronx. Most of the stores on the street had "For Rent" signs in the windows, and others were closed for the day. But halfway down the block from the bus stop there was a barber pole reflecting a candy cane of light from the window.

The shop was empty except for the barber reading a magazine in the chair nearest the window. When he looked up at me, I recognized Matt—stocky, red-cheeked, a lot older and nearly bald with a fringe of gray hair bordering the sides of his head—but still Matt. Seeing me at the door, he tossed the magazine aside.

"No waiting. You're next."

I hesitated, and he misunderstood. "Usually not open at this hour, mister. Had an appointment with one of my regulars, but he didn't show. Just about to close. Lucky for you I sat down to rest my feet. Best haircut and shave in the Bronx."

As I let myself be drawn into the shop, he bustled around, pulling out scissors and combs and a fresh neckcloth.

"Everything sanitary, as you can see, which is more than I can say for most barbershops in this neighborhood. Haircut and shave?"

I eased myself into the chair. Incredible that he didn't recognize me when I knew him so plainly. I had to remind myself that he had not seen me in more than fifteen years, and that my appearance had changed even more in the past months. He studied me in the mirror now that he had me covered with the striped neckcloth, and I saw a frown of faint recognition.

"The works," I said, nodding at the union-shop price list, "haircut, shave, shampoo, sun-tan . . ."

His eyebrows went up.

"I've got to meet someone I haven't seen in a long time," I assured him, "and I want to look my best."

It was a frightening sensation, having him cut my hair again. Later, as he stropped the razor against leather the harsh whisper made me cringe. I bent my head under the gentle press of his hand and felt the blade scrape carefully across my neck. I closed my eyes and waited. It was as if I were on the operating table again.

My neck muscle knotted, and without warning it twitched. The blade nicked me just above the Adam's apple.

"Hey!" he shouted. "Jesus . . . take it easy. You moved. Hey, I'm awful sorry."

He dashed to wet a towel at the sink.

In the mirror I watched the bright red bubble and the thin line dripping down my throat. Excited and apologizing, he got to it before it reached the neckcloth.

Watching him move, adroit for such a short, heavy man, I felt guilty at the deception. I wanted to tell him who I was and have him put his arm around my shoulder, so we could talk about the old days. But I waited while he dabbed at the cut with styptic powder.

He finished shaving me silently, and then brought the sun-tan lamp over to the chair and put cool white pads of cotton soaked in witch hazel over my eyes. There, in the bright red inner darkness I saw what happened the night he took me away from the house for the last time. . . .

Charlie is asleep in the other room, but he wakens to the sound of his mother shrieking. He has learned to sleep through quarrels—they are an everyday occurrence in his house. But tonight there is something terribly wrong in that hysteria. He shrinks back into the pillow and listens.

"I can't help it! He's got to go! We've got her to think about. I won't have her come home from school crying every day like this because the children tease her. We can't destroy her chance for a normal life because of him."

"What do you want to do? Turn him out into the street?"

"Put him away. Send him to the Warren State Home."

"Let's talk it over in the morning."

"No. All you do is talk, talk, and you don't do anything. I don't want him here another day. Now—tonight."

"Don't be foolish, Rose. It's too late to do anything . . . tonight. You're shouting so loud everyone will hear you."

"I don't care. He goes out tonight. I can't stand looking at him any more."

"You're being impossible, Rose. What are you doing?"

"I warn you. Get him out of here."

"Put that knife down."

"I'm not going to have her life destroyed."

"You're crazy. Put that knife away."

"He's better off dead. He'll never be able to live a normal life. He'll be better off—"

"You're out of your mind. For God's sake, control yourself!"

"Then take him away from here. Now—tonight."

"All right. I'll take him over to Herman tonight and maybe tomorrow we'll find out about getting him into the Warren State Home."

There is silence. From the darkness I feel the shudder pass over the house, and then Matt's voice, less panicky than hers. "I know what you've gone through with him, and I can't blame you for being afraid. But you've got to control yourself. I'll take him over to Herman. Will that satisfy you?"

"That's all I ask. Your daughter is entitled to a life, too."

Matt comes into Charlie's room and dresses his son, and though the boy doesn't understand what is happening, he is afraid. As they go out the door, she looks away. Perhaps she is trying to convince herself that he has already gone out of her life—that he no longer exists. On the way out, Charlie sees on the kitchen table the long carving knife she cuts roasts with, and he senses vaguely that she wanted to hurt him. She wanted to take something away from him, and give it to Norma.

When he looks back at her, she has picked up a rag to wash the kitchen sink. . . .

When the haircut, shave, sun treatment, and the rest were over, I sat in the chair limply, feeling light, and slick, and clean, and Matt whisked the neckcloth off and offered me a second mirror to see the reflection of the back of my head. Seeing myself in the front mirror looking into the back mirror, as he held it for me, it tilted for an instant into the one angle that produced the illusion of depth; endless corridors of myself . . . looking at myself

. . . looking at myself . . . looking at myself . . . looking . . .

Which one? Who was I?

I thought of not telling him. What good was it for him to know? Just go away and not reveal who I was. Then I remembered that I wanted him to know. He had to admit that I was alive, that I was someone. I wanted him to boast about me to the customers tomorrow as he gave haircuts and shaves. That would make it all real. If he knew I was his son, then I would be a person.

"Now that you've got the hair off my face, maybe you'll know me," I said as I stood up, waiting for a sign of recognition.

He frowned. "What is this? A gag?"

I assured him it was not a gag, and if he looked and thought hard enough he would know me. He shrugged and turned to put his combs and scissors away. "I got no time for guessing games. Got to close up. That'll be three-fifty."

What if he didn't remember me? What if this was only an absurd fantasy? His hand was out for the money, but I made no move toward my wallet. He had to remember me. He had to know me.

But no—of course not—and as I felt the sour taste in my mouth and the sweat in my palms, I knew that in a minute I would be sick. But I didn't want that in front of him.

"Hey, you all right?"

"Yes . . . just . . . wait . . ." I stumbled into one of the chrome chairs and bent forward gasping for breath, waiting for the blood to come back to my head. My stomach was churning. Oh, God, don't let me faint now. Don't let me look ridiculous in front of him.

"Water . . . some water, please . . ." Not so much for the drink as to make him turn away. I didn't want him to see me like this after all these years. By the time he returned with a glass, I felt a little better.

"Here, drink this. Rest a minute. You'll be okay." He stared at me as I sipped the cool water, and I could see him struggling with half-forgotten memories. "Do I really know you from somewhere?"

"No . . . I'm okay. I'll leave in a minute."

How could I tell him? What was I supposed to say?

130

Here, look at me, I'm Charlie, the son you wrote off the books? Not that I blame you for it, but here I am, all fixed up better than ever. Test me. Ask me questions. I speak twenty languages, living and dead; I'm a mathematical whiz, and I'm writing a piano concerto that will make them remember me long after I'm gone.

How could I tell him?

How absurd I was sitting in his shop, waiting for him to pat me on the head and say, "Good boy." I wanted his approval, the old glow of satisfaction that came to his face when I learned to tie my own shoelaces and button my sweater. I had come here for that look in his face, but I knew I wouldn't get it.

"You want me to call a doctor?"

I wasn't his son. That was another Charlie. Intelligence and knowledge had changed me, and he would resent me—as the others from the bakery resented me—because my growth diminished him. I didn't want that.

"I'm okay," I said. "Sorry to be a nuisance." I got up and tested my legs. "Something I ate. I'll let you close up now."

As I headed towards the door, his voice called after me sharply. "Hey, wait a minute!" His eyes met mine with suspicion. "What are you trying to pull?"

"I don't understand."

His hand was out, rubbing his thumb and forefinger together. "You owe me three-fifty."

I apologized as I paid him, but I could see that he didn't believe it. I gave him five, told him to keep the change, and hurried out of his barbershop without looking back.

June 21—I've added time sequences of increasing complexity to the three-dimensional maze, and Algernon learns them easily. There is no need to motivate him with food or water. He appears to learn for the sake of solving the problem—success appears to be its own reward.

But, as Burt pointed out at the convention, his behavior is erratic. Sometimes after, or even during a run, he will rage, throw himself against the walls of the maze, or curl up and refuse to work at all. Frustration? Or something deeper?

5:30 P.M.—That crazy Fay came in through the fire escape this afternoon with a female white mouse—about half Algernon's size—to keep him company, she said, on these lonely summer nights. She quickly overcame all my objections and convinced me that it would do Algernon good to have companionship. After I assured myself that little "Minnie" was of sound health and good moral character, I agreed. I was curious to see what he would do when confronted with a female. But once we had put Minnie into Algernon's cage, Fay grabbed my arm and pulled me out of the room.

"Where's your sense of romance?" she insisted. She turned on the radio, and advanced toward me menacingly. "I'm going to teach you the latest steps."

How can you get annoyed at a girl like Fay?

At any rate, I'm glad that Algernon is no longer alone.

June 23—Late last night the sound of laughter in the hallway and a tapping on my door. It was Fay and a man.

"Hi, Charlie," she giggled as she saw me. "Leroy, meet Charlie. He's my across-the-hall neighbor. A wonderful artist. He does sculpture with a living element."

Leroy caught hold of her and kept her from bumping into the wall. He looked at me nervously and mumbled a greeting.

"Met Leroy at the Stardust Ballroom," she explained. "He's a terrific dancer." She started into her apartment and then pulled him back. "Hey," she giggled, "why don't we invite Charlie over for a drink and make it a party?"

Leroy didn't think it was a good idea.

I managed an apology and pulled away. Behind my closed door, I heard them laughing their way into her apartment, and though I tried to read, the pictures kept forcing their way into my mind: a big white bed . . . white cool sheets and the two of them in each other's arms.

I wanted to phone Alice, but I didn't. Why torment myself? I couldn't even visualize Alice's face. I could picture Fay, dressed or undressed, at will, with her crisp blue eyes and her blonde hair braided and coiled around her head like a crown. Fay was clear, but Alice was wrapped in mist.

About an hour later I heard shouting from Fay's apartment, then her scream and the sound of things being thrown, but as I started out of bed to see if she needed help, I heard the door slam—Leroy cursing as he left. Then, a few minutes afterward, I heard a tapping on my living room window. It was open, and Fay slipped in and sat on the ledge, a black silk kimono revealing lovely legs.

"Hi," she whispered, "got a cigareet?"

I handed her one and she slipped down from the window ledge to the couch. "Whew!" she sighed, "I can usually take care of myself, but there's one type that's so hungry it's all you can do to hold them off."

"Oh," I said, "you brought him up here to hold him off."

She caught my tone and looked up sharply. "You don't approve?"

"Who am I to disapprove? But if you pick up a guy in a public dance hall you've got to expect advances. He had the right to make a pass at you."

She shook her head. "I go to the Stardust Ballroom because I like to dance, and I don't see that because I let a guy bring me home I've got to go to bed with him. You don't think I went to bed with him, do you?"

My image of the two of them in each other's arms popped like soap bubbles.

"Now if you were the guy," she said, "it would be different."

"What is that supposed to mean?"

"Just what it sounds like. If you asked me, I'd go to bed with you."

I tried to keep my composure. "Thanks," I said. "I'll keep that in mind. Can I get you a cup of coffee?"

"Charlie, I can't figure you out. Most men like me or not, and I know it right away. But you seem afraid of me. You're not a homosexual, are you?"

"Hell, no!"

"I mean you don't have to hide it from me if you are, because then we could be just good friends. But I'd have to know."

"I'm not a homosexual. Tonight, when you went into your place with that guy, I wished it was me."

She leaned forward and the kimono open at the neck revealed her bosom. She slipped her arms around me,

133

waiting for me to do something. I knew what was expected of me, and I told myself there was no reason not to. I had the feeling there would be no panic now—not with her. After all, I wasn't the one making the advances. And she was different from any woman I'd ever met before. Perhaps she was right for me at this emotional level.

I slipped my arms around her.

"That's different," she cooed. "I was beginning to think you didn't care."

"I care," I whispered, kissing her throat. But as I did it, I saw the two of us, as if I were a third person standing in the doorway. I was watching a man and woman in each other's arms. But seeing myself that way, from a distance, left me unresponsive. There was no panic, it was true, but there was also no excitement—no desire.

"Your place or mine?" she asked.

"Wait a minute."

"What's the matter?"

"Maybe we'd better not. I don't feel well this evening."

She looked at me wonderingly. "Is there anything else? . . . Anything you want me to do? . . . I don't mind . . ."

"No, that's not it," I said sharply. "I just don't feel well tonight." I was curious about the ways she had of getting a man excited, but this was no time to start experimenting. The solution to my problem lay elsewhere.

I didn't know what else to say to her. I wished she'd go away, but I didn't want to tell her to go. She was studying me, and then finally she said, "Look, do you mind if I spend the night here?"

"Why?"

She shrugged. "I like you. I don't know. Leroy might come back. Lots of reasons. If you don't want me to . . ."

She caught me off guard again. I might have found a dozen excuses to get rid of her, but I gave in.

"Got any gin?" she asked.

"No, I don't drink much."

"I've got some in my place. I'll bring it over." Before I could stop her she was out the window and a few minutes later she returned with a bottle about two-thirds full, and a lemon. She took two glasses from my kitchen and poured some gin into each. "Here," she said, "this'll make you feel better. It'll take the starch out of those straight lines. That's what's bugging you. Everything is too neat and straight and you're all boxed in. Like Algernon in his sculpture there."

I wasn't going to at first, but I felt so lousy that I figured why not. It couldn't make things any worse, and it might possibly dull the feeling that I was watching myself through eyes that didn't understand what I was doing.

She got me drunk.

I remember the first drink, and getting into bed, and her slipping in beside me with the bottle in her hand. And that was all until this afternoon when I got up with a hangover.

She was still asleep, face to the wall, her pillow bunched up under her neck. On the night table beside the ash tray overflowing with crushed butts stood the empty bottle, but the last thing I remembered before the curtain came down was watching myself take the second drink.

She stretched and rolled toward me—nude. I moved back and fell out of bed. I grabbed a blanket to wrap around myself.

"Hi," she yawned. "You know what I want to do one of these days?"

"What?"

"Paint you in the nude. Like Michelangelo's 'David.' You'd be beautiful. You okay?"

I nodded. "Except for a headache. Did I—uh—drink too much last night?"

She laughed and propped herself up on one elbow. "You were loaded. And boy did you act queer—I don't mean fairyish or anything like that but strange."

"What"—I said, struggling to work the blanket around so that I could walk—"is that supposed to mean? What did I do?"

"I've seen guys get happy, or sad, or sleepy, or sexy, but I never saw anyone act the way you did. It's a good thing you don't drink often. Oh, my God, I only wish I had a camera. What a short subject you'd have made."

"Well, for Christ's sake, what'd I do?"

"Not what I expected. No sex, or anything like that. But you were phenomenal. What an act! The weirdest. You'd be great on the stage. You'd wow them at the Palace. You went all confused and silly. You know, as if a grown man starts acting like a kid. Talking about how you wanted to go to school and learn to read and write so you could be smart like everyone else. Crazy stuff like that. You were a different person—like they do with method-acting—and you kept saying you couldn't play with me because your mother would take away your peanuts and put you in a cage."

"Peanuts?"

"Yeah! So help me!" she laughed, scratching her head. "And you kept saying I couldn't have your peanuts. The weirdest. But I tell you, the way you talked! Like those dimwits on street corners, who work themselves up by just *looking* at a girl. A different guy completely. At first I thought you were just kidding around, but now I think you're compulsive or something. All this neatness and worrying about everything."

It didn't upset me, although I would have expected it to. Somehow, getting drunk had momentarily broken down the conscious barriers that kept the old Charlie Gordon hidden deep in my mind. As I suspected all along, he was not really gone. Nothing in our minds is ever really gone. The operation had covered him over with a veneer of education and culture, but emotionally he was there—watching and waiting.

What was he waiting for?

"You okay now?"

I told her I was fine.

She grabbed the blanket I was wrapped in, and pulled me back into bed. Before I could stop her she slipped her arms around me and kissed me. "I was scared last night, Charlie. I thought you flipped. I've heard about guys who are impotent, how it suddenly gets them and they become maniacs."

"How come you stayed?"

She shrugged. "Well, you were like a scared little kid. I was sure you wouldn't hurt me, but I thought you might hurt yourself. So I figured I'd hang around. I felt so sorry. Anyway, I kept this handy, just in case . . ." She pulled out a heavy book end she had wedged between the bed and the wall.

"I guess you didn't have to use it."

She shook her head. "Boy, you must have liked peanuts when you were a kid."

136

She got out of bed and started to dress. I lay there for a while watching her. She moved in front of me with no shyness or inhibition. Her breasts were full as she had painted them in that self-portrait. I longed to reach out for her, but I knew it was futile. In spite of the operation Charlie was still with me.

And Charlie was afraid of losing his peanuts.

June 24—Today I went on a strange kind of anti-intellectual binge. If I had dared to, I would have gotten drunk, but after the experience with Fay, I knew it would be dangerous. So, instead, I went to Times Square, from movie house to movie house, immersing myself in westerns and horror movies—the way I used to. Each time, sitting through the picture, I would find myself whipped with guilt. I'd walk out in the middle of the picture and wander into another one. I told myself I was looking for something in the make-believe screen world that was missing from my new life.

Then, in a sudden intuition, right outside the Keno Amusement Center, I knew it wasn't the movies I wanted, but *the audiences*. I wanted to be with the people around me in the darkness.

The walls between people are thin here, and if I listen quietly, I hear what is going on. Greenwich Village is like that too. Not just being close—because I don't feel it in a crowded elevator or on the subway during the rush—but on a hot night when everyone is out walking, or sitting in the theater, there is a rustling, and for a moment I brush against someone and sense the connection between the branch and trunk and the deep root. At such moments my flesh is thin and tight, and the unbearable hunger to be part of it drives me out to search in the dark corners and blind alleys of the night.

Usually, when I'm exhausted from walking, I go back to the apartment and drop off into a deep sleep, but tonight instead of going up to my own place I went to the diner. There was a new dishwasher, a boy of about sixteen, and there was something familiar about him, his movements, the look in his eyes. And then, clearing away the table behind me, he dropped some dishes.

They crashed to the floor, shattering and sending bits of white china under the tables. He stood there, dazed and frightened, holding the empty tray in his hand. The whistles and catcalls from the customers (cries of "hey, there go the profits!" . . . *"Mazel tov!"* . . . and "well, *he* didn't work here very long . . ." which invariably seems to follow the breaking of dishware in a public restaurant) confused him.

When the owner came to see what the excitement was about, the boy cowered—threw up his arms as if to ward off a blow.

"All right! All right, you dope," shouted the man, "don't just stand there! Get the broom and sweep up that mess. A broom . . . a broom! you idiot! It's in the kitchen. Sweep up all the pieces."

When the boy saw that he was not going to be punished, his frightened expression disappeared, and he smiled and hummed as he came back with the broom. A few of the rowdier customers kept up the remarks, amusing themselves at his expense.

"Here, sonny, over here. There's a nice piece behind you . . ."

"C'mon, do it again . . ."

"He's not so dumb. It's easier to break 'em than to wash 'em . . ."

As the boy's vacant eyes moved across the crowd of amused onlookers, he slowly mirrored their smiles and finally broke into an uncertain grin at the joke which he did not understand.

I felt sick inside as I looked at his dull, vacuous smile—the wide, bright eyes of a child, uncertain but eager to please, and I realized what I had recognized in him. They were laughing at him because he was retarded.

And at first I had been amused along with the rest.

Suddenly, I was furious at myself and all those who were smirking at him. I wanted to pick up the dishes and throw them. I wanted to smash their laughing faces. I jumped up and shouted: "Shut up! Leave him alone! He can't understand. He can't help what he is . . . but for God's sake, have some respect! *He's a human being!*"

The restaurant grew silent. I cursed myself for losing control and creating a scene, and I tried not to look at the boy as I paid my check and walked out without touching my food. I felt ashamed for both of us.

How strange it is that people of honest feelings and

sensibility, who would not take advantage of a man born without arms or legs or eyes—how such people think nothing of abusing a man born with low intelligence. It infuriated me to remember that not too long ago I—like this boy—had foolishly played the clown.

And I had almost forgotten.

Only a short time ago, I learned that people laughed at me. Now I can see that unknowingly I joined them in laughing at myself. That hurts most of all.

I have often reread my early progress reports and seen the illiteracy, the childish naïveté, the mind of low intelligence peering from a dark room, through the keyhole, at the dazzling light outside. In my dreams and memories I've seen Charlie smiling happily and uncertainly at what people around him were saying. Even in my dullness I knew I was inferior. Other people had something I lacked—something denied me. In my mental blindness, I had believed it was somehow connected with the ability to read and write, and I was sure that if I could get those skills I would have intelligence too.

Even a feeble-minded man wants to be like other men.

A child may not know how to feed itself, or what to eat, yet it knows hunger.

This day was good for me. I've got to stop this childish worrying about myself—*my* past and *my* future. Let me give something of myself to others. I've got to use my knowledge and skills to work in the field of increasing human intelligence. Who is better equipped? Who else has lived in both worlds?

Tomorrow, I'm going to get in touch with the board of directors at the Welberg Foundation and ask for permission to do some independent work on the project. If they'll let me, I may be able to help them. I have some ideas.

There is so much that can be done with this technique, if it is perfected. If I could be made into a genius, what about the more than five million mentally retarded in the United States? What about the countless millions all over the world, and those yet unborn destined to be retarded? What fantastic levels might be achieved by using this technique on normal people. On geniuses?

There are so many doors to open I am impatient to apply my own knowledge and skills to the problem. I've got to make them all see that this is something important for me to do. I'm sure the Foundation will grant me permission.

But I can't be alone any more. I have to tell Alice about it.

June 25—I called Alice today. I was nervous, and I must have sounded incoherent, but it was good to hear her voice, and she sounded happy to hear from me. She agreed to see me, and I took a taxi uptown, impatient at the slowness with which we moved.

Before I could knock, she opened the door and threw her arms around me. "Charlie, we've been so worried about you. I had horrible visions of you dead in an alleyway, or wandering around skid row with amnesia. Why didn't you let us know you were all right? You could have done that."

"Don't scold me. I had to be alone for a while to find some answers."

"Come in the kitchen. I'll make some coffee. What have you been doing?"

"Days—I've been thinking, reading, and writing; and nights—wandering in search of myself. And I've discovered that Charlie is watching me."

"Don't talk like that," she shuddered. "This business about being watched isn't real. You've built it up in your mind."

"I can't help feeling that I'm not me. I've usurped his place and locked him out the way they locked me out of the bakery. What I mean to say is that Charlie Gordon exists in the past, and the past is real. You can't put up a new building on a site until you destroy the old one, and the old Charlie can't be destroyed. He exists. At first I was searching for him: I went to see his—my—father. All I wanted to do was prove that Charlie existed as a person in the past, so that I could justify my own existence. I was insulted when Nemur said he created me. But I've discovered that not only did Charlie exist in the past, he exists now. In me and around me. He's been coming between us all along. I thought my intelligence created the barrier—my pompous, foolish pride, the feeling we had nothing in common because I had gone beyond you.

You put that idea into my head. But that's not it. It's Charlie, the little boy who's afraid of women because of things his mother did to him. Don't you see? All these months while I've been growing up intellectually, I've still had the emotional wiring of the childlike Charlie. And every time I came close to you, or thought about making love to you, there was a short circuit."

I was excited, and my voice pounded at her until she began to quiver. Her face became flushed. "Charlie," she whispered, "can't I do anything? Can't I help?"

"I think I've changed during these weeks away from the lab," I said. "I couldn't see how to do it at first, but tonight, while I was wandering around the city, it came to me. The foolish thing was trying to solve the problem all by myself. But the deeper I get tangled up in this mass of dreams and memories the more I realize that emotional problems can't be solved as intellectual problems are. That's what I discovered about myself last night. I told myself I was wandering around like a lost soul, and then I saw that I *was* lost.

"Somehow I've become separated emotionally from everyone and everything. And what I was really searching for out there in the dark streets—the last damned place I could ever find it—was a way to make myself a part of people again emotionally, while still retaining my freedom intellectually. I've got to grow up. For me it means everything. . . ."

I talked on and on, spewing out of myself every doubt and fear that bubbled to the surface. She was my sounding board and she sat there hypnotized. I felt myself grow warm, feverish, until I thought my body was on fire. I was burning out the infection in front of someone I cared about, and that made all the difference.

But it was too much for her. What had started as trembling became tears. The picture over the couch caught my eye—the cringing, red-cheeked maiden—and I wondered what Alice was feeling just then. I knew she would give herself to me, and I wanted her, but what about Charlie?

Charlie might not interfere if I wanted to make love to Fay. He would probably just stand in the doorway and watch. But the moment I came close to Alice, he panicked. Why was he afraid to let me love Alice?

She sat on the couch, looking at me, waiting to see what I would do. And what could I do? I wanted to take her in my arms and . . .

As I began to think of it, the warning came.

"Are you all right, Charlie? You're so pale."

I sat down on the couch beside her. "Just a little dizzy. It'll pass." But I knew it would only get worse as long as Charlie felt there was danger I'd make love to her.

And then I got the idea. It disgusted me at first, but suddenly I realized the only way to overcome this paralysis was to outwit him. If for some reason Charlie was afraid of Alice but not of Fay, then I would turn out the lights, and pretend I was making love to Fay. He would never know the difference.

It was wrong—disgusting—but if it worked it would break Charlie's strangle hold on my emotions. I would know afterwards that I had loved Alice, and that this was the only way.

"I'm all right now. Let's sit in the dark for a while," I said, turning off the lights and waiting to collect myself. It wasn't going to be easy. I had to convince myself, visualize Fay, hypnotize myself into believing that the woman sitting beside me was Fay. And even if he separated himself from me to watch from outside my body, it would do him no good because the room would be dark.

I waited for some sign that he suspected—the warning symptoms of panic. But nothing. I felt alert and calm. I put my arm around her.

"Charlie, I—"

"Don't talk!" I snapped, and she shrank from me. "Please," I reassured her, "don't say anything. Just let me hold you quietly in the dark." I brought her close to me, and there under the darkness of my closed lids, I conjured up the picture of Fay—with her long blonde hair and fair skin. Fay, as I had seen her last beside me. I kissed Fay's hair, Fay's throat, and finally came to rest upon Fay's lips. I felt Fay's arms stroking the muscles on my back, my shoulders, and the tightness inside me built up as it had never before done for a woman. I caressed her slowly at first and then with impatient, mounting excitement that would soon tell.

The hairs on my neck began to tingle. Someone else was in the room, peering through the darkness, trying to see. And feverishly I thought the name over and over to myself. Fay! Fay! FAY! I imagined her face sharply and clearly so that nothing could come between us. And then, as she gripped me closer, I cried out and pushed her away.

"Charlie!" I couldn't see Alice's face, but her gasp mirrored the shock.

"No, Alice! I can't. You don't understand."

I jumped up from the couch and turned on the light. I almost expected to see him standing there. But of course not. We were alone. It was all in my mind. Alice was lying there, her blouse open where I had unbuttoned it, her face flushed, eyes wide in disbelief. "I love you . . ." the words choked out of me, "but I can't do it. Something I can't explain, but if I hadn't stopped, I would hate myself for the rest of my life. Don't ask me to explain, or you'll hate me too. It has to do with Charlie. For some reason, he won't let me make love to you."

She looked away and buttoned her blouse. "It was different tonight," she said. "You didn't get nausea or panic or anything like that. You wanted me."

"Yes, I wanted you, but I wasn't really making love to *you*. I was going to use you—in a way—but I can't explain. I don't understand it myself. Let's just say I'm not ready yet. And I can't fake it or cheat or pretend it's all right when it's not. It's just another blind alley."

I got up to go.

"Charlie, don't run away again."

"I'm through running. I've got work to do. Tell them I'll be back in the lab in a few days—as soon as I get control of myself."

I left the apartment in a frenzy. Downstairs, in front of the building, I stood, not knowing which way to go. No matter which path I took I got a shock that meant another mistake. Every path was blocked. But, God . . . everything I did, everywhere I turned, doors were closed to me.

There was no place to enter. No street, no room, no woman.

Finally, I stumbled down into the subway and took it down to Forty-ninth Street. Not many people, but there was a blonde with long hair who reminded me of Fay. Heading toward the crosstown bus, I passed a liquor store, and without thinking about it, I went in and bought a fifth of gin. While I waited for the bus, I opened the bottle in the bag as I had seen bums do, and I took a long, deep drink. It burned all the way down, but it felt good. I took another—just a sip—and by the time the bus came, I was bathed in a powerful tingling sensation. I didn't take any more. I didn't want to get drunk now.

When I got to the apartment, I knocked at Fay's door. There was no answer. I opened the door and looked in. She hadn't come in yet, but all the lights were on in the place. She didn't give a damn about anything. Why couldn't I be that way?

I went to my own place to wait. I undressed, took a shower and put on a robe. I prayed that this wouldn't be one of the nights that someone came home with her.

About two thirty in the morning I heard her coming up the steps. I took my bottle, climbed out onto the fire escape and slipped over to her window just as her front door opened. I hadn't intended to crouch there and watch. I was going to tap on the window. But as I raised my hand to make my presence known, I saw her kick her shoes off and twirl around happily. She went to the mirror, and slowly, piece by piece, began to pull off her clothes in a private strip tease. I took another drink. But I couldn't let her know I had been watching her.

I went through my own apartment without turning on the lights. At first I thought of inviting her over to my place, but everything was too neat and orderly—too many straight lines to erase—and I knew it wouldn't work here. So I went out into the hallway. I knocked at her door, softly at first and then louder.

"Door's open!" she shouted.

She was in her underwear, lying on the floor, arms outstretched and legs up against the couch. She tilted her head back and looked at me upside down. "Charlie, darling! Why are you standing on your head?"

"Never mind," I said, pulling the bottle out of the paper bag. "The lines and boxes are too straight, and I thought you'd join me in erasing some of them."

"Best stuff in the world for that," she said. "If you concentrate on the warm spot that starts in the pit of your stomach, all the lines begin to melt."

"That's what's happening."

"Wonderful!" She jumped to her feet. "Me too. I danced with too many squares tonight. Let's melt 'em all down." She picked up a glass and I filled it for her.

As she drank, I slipped my arm around her and toyed with the skin of her bare back.

"Hey, there, boy! Whoa! What's up?"

"Me. I was waiting for you to come home."

She backed away. "Oh, wait a minute, Charlie boy. We've been through all this before. You know it doesn't do any good. I mean, you know I think a lot of you, and I'd drag you into bed in a minute if I thought there was a chance. But I don't want to get all worked up for nothing. It's not fair, Charlie."

"It'll be different tonight. I swear it." Before she could protest, I had her in my arms, kissing her, caressing her, overwhelming her with all the built-up excitement that was ready to tear me apart. I tried to unhook her brassière, but I pulled too hard and the hook tore out.

"For God's sake, Charlie, my bra—"

"Don't worry about your bra . . ." I choked, helping her to take it off. "I'll buy you a new one. I'm going to make up for the other times. I'm going to make love to you all night long."

She pulled away from me. "Charlie, I've never heard you talk like that. And stop looking at me as if you want to swallow me whole." She swept up a blouse from one of the chairs, and held it in front of her. "Now you're making me feel undressed."

"I want to make love to you. Tonight I can do it. I know it . . . I feel it. Don't turn me away, Fay."

"Here," she whispered, "have another drink."

I took one and poured another for her, and while she drank it, I covered her shoulder and neck with kisses. She began to breathe heavily as my excitement communicated itself to her.

"God, Charlie, if you get me started and disappoint me again I don't know what I'll do. I'm human too, you know."

I pulled her down beside me on the couch, on top of the pile of her clothing and underthings.

"Not here on the couch, Charlie," she said, struggling to her feet. "Let's go to bed."

"Here," I insisted, pulling the blouse away from her.

She looked down at me, set her glass on the floor, and stepped out of her underwear. She stood there in front of me, nude. "I'll turn out the lights," she whispered.

"No," I said, pulling her down onto the couch again. "I want to look at you."

She kissed me deeply and held me tightly in her arms. "Just don't disappoint me this time, Charlie. You'd better not."

Her body moved slowly, reaching for me, and I knew that this time nothing would interfere. I knew what to do and how to do it. She gasped and sighed and called my name.

For one moment I had the cold feeling he was watching. Over the arm of the couch, I caught a glimpse of his face staring back at me through the dark beyond the window—where just a few minutes earlier I had been crouching. A switch in perception, and I was out on the fire escape again, watching a man and a woman inside, making love on the couch.

Then, with a violent effort of the will, I was back on the couch with her, aware of her body and my own urgency and potency, and I saw the face against the window, hungrily watching. And I thought to myself, go ahead, you poor bastard—watch. I don't give a damn any more.

And his eyes went wide as he watched.

June 29—Before I go back to the lab I'm going to finish the projects I've started since I left the convention. I phoned Landsdoff at the New Institute for Advanced Study, about the possibility of utilizing the pair-production nuclear photoeffect for exploratory work in biophysics. At first he thought I was a crackpot, but after I pointed out the flaws in his article in the *New Institute Journal* he kept me on the phone for nearly an hour. He wants me to come to the Institute to discuss my ideas with his group. I might take him up on it after I've finished my work at the lab—if there is time. That's the problem, of course. I don't know how much time I have. A month? A year? The rest of my life? That depends on what I find out about the psychophysical side-effects of the experiment.

June 30—I've stopped wandering the streets now that I have Fay. I've given her a key to my place. She kids me about my locking the door, and I kid her about the mess her place is in. She's warned me not to try to change her. Her husband divorced her five years ago because she couldn't be bothered about picking things up and taking care of her home.

That's the way she is about most things that seem unimportant to her. She just can't or won't bother. The other day I discovered a stack of parking tickets in a corner behind a chair—there must have been forty or fifty of them. When she came in with the beer, I asked her why she was collecting them.

"Those!" she laughed. "As soon as my ex-husband sends me my goddamned check, I've got to pay some of them. You have no idea how bad I feel about those tickets. I keep them behind that chair because otherwise I get an attack of guilt feelings every time I see them. But what is a girl supposed to do? Everywhere I go they've got signs all over the place—don't park here! don't park there!—I just can't be bothered stopping to read a sign every time I want to get out of the car."

So I've promised I won't try to change her. She's exciting to be with. A great sense of humor. But most of all she's a free and independent spirit. The only thing that may become wearing after a while is her craze for dancing. We've been out every night this week until two or three in the morning. I don't have that much energy left.

It's not love—but she's important to me. I find myself listening for her footsteps down the hallway whenever she's been out.

Charlie has stopped watching us.

July 5—I dedicated my first piano concerto to Fay. She was excited by the idea of having something dedicated to her, but I don't think she really liked it. Just goes to show that you can't have everything you want in one woman. One more argument for polygamy.

The important thing is that Fay is bright and good-hearted. I learned today why she ran out of money so early this month. The week before she met me, she had befriended a girl she'd met at the Stardust Ballroom. When the girl told Fay she had no family in the city, was broke, and had no place to sleep, Fay invited her to move in. Two days later the girl found the two hundred and thirty-two dollars that Fay kept in her dresser drawer, and disappeared with the money. Fay hadn't reported it to the police—and as it turned out, she didn't even know the girl's last name.

"What good would it do to notify the police?" she wanted to know. "I mean this poor bitch must have needed the money pretty badly to do it. I'm not going to ruin her life over a few hundred bucks. I'm not rich or anything, but I'm not going after her skin—if you know what I mean."

I knew what she meant.

I have never met anyone as open and trusting as Fay is. She's what I need most of all right now. I've been starved for simple human contact.

July 8—Not much time for work—between the nightly club-hopping and the morning hangovers. It was only with aspirin and something Fay concocted for me that I was able to finish my linguistic analysis of Urdu verb forms and send the paper to the *International Linguistics Bulletin*. It will send the linguists back to India with their tape recorders, because it undermines the critical super-structure of their methodology.

I can't help but admire the structural linguists who have carved out for themselves a linguistic discipline based on the deterioration of written communication. Another case of men devoting their lives to studying more and more about less and less—filling volumes and libraries with the subtle linguistic analysis of the *grunt*. Nothing wrong with that, but it should not be used as an excuse to destroy the stability of language.

Alice called today to find out when I am coming back to work at the lab. I told her I wanted to finish the projects I had started, and that I was hoping to get permission from the Welberg Foundation for my own special study. She's right though—I've got to take time into consideration.

Fay still wants to go out dancing all the time. Last night started out with us drinking and dancing at the White Horse Club, and from there to Benny's Hideaway, and then on to the Pink Slipper . . . and after that I don't remember many of the places, but we danced until I was ready to drop. My tolerance for liquor must have increased because I was pretty far gone before Charlie made his appearance. I can only recall him doing a silly tap dance on the stage of the Allakazam Club. He got a great hand before the manager threw us out, and Fay said everyone thought I was a wonderful comedian and everyone liked my moron act.

What the hell happened then? I know I strained my back. I thought it was from all the dancing, but Fay says I fell off the goddamned couch.

Algernon's behavior is becoming erratic again. Minnie seems to be afraid of him.

July 9—A terrible thing happened today. Algernon bit Fay. I had warned her against playing with him, but she always liked to feed him. Usually when she came into his room, he'd perk up and run to her. Today it was different. He was at the far side, curled up into a white puff. When she put her hand in through the top trap door, he cringed and forced himself back into the corner. She tried to coax him, by opening the barrier to the maze, and before I could tell her to leave him alone, she made the mistake of trying to pick him up. He bit her thumb. Then he glared at both of us and scurried back into the maze.

We found Minnie at the other end in the reward box. She was bleeding from a gash in her chest, but she was alive. As I reached in to take her out Algernon came into the reward box and snapped at me. His teeth caught my sleeve and he hung on until I shook him loose.

He calmed down after that. I observed him for more than an hour afterward. He seems listless and confused, and though he still learns new problems without external rewards, his performance is peculiar. Instead of the careful, determined movements down the maze corridors, his actions are rushed and out of control. Time and again he turns into a corner too quickly and crashes into a barrier. There is a strange sense of urgency in his behavior.

I hesitate to make a snap judgment. It could be many things. But now I've got to get him back to the lab. Whether or not I hear from the Foundation about my special grant, I'm going to call Nemur in the morning.

PROGRESS REPORT 15

July 12—Nemur, Strauss, Burt, and a few of the others on the project were waiting for me in the psych office. They tried to make me feel welcome but I could see how anxious Burt was to take Algernon, and I turned him over. No one said anything, but I knew that Nemur would not soon forgive me for going over his head and getting in touch with the Foundation. But it had been necessary. Before I returned to Beekman, I had to be assured they would permit me to begin an independent study of the project. Too much time would be wasted if I had to account to Nemur for everything I did.

He had been informed of the Foundation's decision, and my reception was a cold and formal one. He held out his hand, but there was no smile on his face. "Charlie," he said, "we're all glad you're back and going to work with us. Jayson called and told me the Foundation was putting you to work on the project. This staff and the lab are at your disposal. The computer center has assured us that your work will have priority—and of course if I can help in any way . . ."

He was doing his utmost to be cordial, but I could see by his face that he was skeptical. After all, what experience did I have with experimental psychology? What did I know about the techniques that he had spent so many years developing? Well, as I say, he appeared cordial, and willing to suspend judgment. There isn't much else he can do now. If I don't come up with an explanation for Algernon's behavior, all of his work goes down the drain, but if I solve the problem I bring in the whole crew with me.

I went into the lab where Burt was watching Algernon in one of the multiple problem boxes. He sighed and shook his head. "He's forgotten a lot. Most of his complex responses seem to have been wiped out. He's solving problems on a much more primitive level than I would have expected."

"In what way?" I asked.

"Well, in the past he was able to figure out simple patterns—in that blind-door run, for example: every other door, every third door, red doors only, or the green doors only—but now he's been through that run three times and he's still using trial and error."

"Could it be because he was away from the lab for so long?"

"Could be. We'll let him get used to things again and see how he works out tomorrow."

I had been in the lab many times before this, but now I was here to learn everything it had to offer. I had to absorb procedures in a few days that the others had taken years to learn. Burt and I spent four hours going through the lab section by section, as I tried to familiarize myself with the total picture. When we were all through I noticed one door we had not looked into.

"What's in there?"

"The freeze and the incinerator." He pushed open the heavy door and turned on the light. "We freeze our specimens before we dispose of them in the incinerator. It helps cut down the odors if we control decomposition." He turned to leave, but I stood there for a moment.

"Not Algernon," I said. "Look . . . if and . . . when . . . I mean I don't want him dumped in there. Give him to me. I'll take care of him myself." He didn't laugh. He just nodded. Nemur had told him that from now on I could have anything I wanted.

Time was the barrier. If I was going to find out the answers for myself I had to get to work immediately. I got lists of books from Burt, and notes from Strauss and Nemur. Then, on the way out, I got a strange notion.

"Tell me," I asked Nemur, "I just got a look at your incinerator for disposing of experimental animals. What plans have been made for me?"

My question stunned him. "What do you mean?"

"I'm sure that from the beginning you planned for all exigencies. So what happens to me?"

When he was silent I insisted: "I have a right to know everything that pertains to the experiment, and that includes my future."

"No reason why you shouldn't know." He paused and

151

lit an already lit cigarette. "You understand, of course, that from the beginning we had the highest hopes of permanence, and we still do . . . we definitely do—"

"I'm sure of that," I said.

"Of course, taking you on in this experiment was a serious responsibility. I don't know how much you remember or how much you've pieced together about things in the beginning of the project, but we tried to make it clear to you that there was a strong chance it might be only temporary."

"I had that written down in my progress reports, at the time," I agreed, "though I didn't understand at the time what you meant by it. But that's beside the point because I'm aware of it now."

"Well, we decided to risk it with you," he went on, "because we felt there was very little chance of doing you any serious harm, and we were sure there was a great chance of doing you some good."

"You don't have to justify that."

"But you realize we had to get permission from someone in your immediate family. You were incompetent to agree to this yourself."

"I know all about that. You're talking about my sister, Norma. I read about it in the papers. From what I remember of her, I imagine she'd have given you approval for my execution."

He raised his eyebrows, but let it pass. "Well, as we told her, in the event that the experiment failed, we couldn't send you back to the bakery or to that room where you came from."

"Why not?"

"For one thing, you might not be the same. Surgery and injections of hormones might have had effects not immediately evident. Experiences since the operation might have left their mark on you. I mean, possibly emotional disturbances to complicate the retardation; you couldn't possibly be the same kind of person—"

"That's great. As if one cross weren't enough to bear."

"And for another thing there's no way of knowing if you would go back to the same mental level. There might be regression to an even more primitive level of functioning."

He was letting me have the worst of it—getting the

weight off his mind. "I might as well know everything," I said, "while I'm still in a position to have some say about it. What plans have you made for me?"

He shrugged. "The Foundation has arranged to send you to the Warren State Home and Training School."

"What the hell!"

"Part of the agreement with your sister was that all the home's fees would be assumed by the Foundation, and you would receive a regular monthly income to be used for your personal needs for the rest of your life."

"But why there? I was always able to manage on my own on the outside, even when they committed me there, after Uncle Herman died. Donner was able to get me out right away, to work and live on the outside. Why do I have to go back?"

"If you can take care of yourself on the outside, you won't have to stay in Warren. The less severe cases are permitted to live off the grounds. But we had to make provision for you—just in case."

He was right. There was nothing for me to complain about. They had thought of everything. Warren was the logical place—the deep freeze where I could be put away for the rest of my days.

"At least it's not the incinerator," I said.

"What?"

"Never mind. A private joke." Then I thought of something. "Tell me, is it possible to visit Warren, I mean go through the place and look it over as a visitor?"

"Yes, I think they have people coming down all the time—regular tours through the home as a kind of public relations thing. But why?"

"Because I want to see. I've got to know what's going to happen while I'm still enough in control to be able to do something about it. See if you can arrange it—as soon as possible."

I could see he was upset about the idea of my visiting Warren. As if I were ordering my coffin to sit in before I died. But then, I can't blame him because he doesn't realize that finding out who I really am—the meaning of my total existence involves knowing the possibilities of my future as well as my past, where I'm going as well as where I've been. Although we know the end of the maze holds death (and it is something I have not always known—not long ago the adolescent in me thought death could happen only to other people), I see now that the path I choose through that maze makes me what I am. I am not only a thing, but also a way of being—one of many ways—and knowing the paths I have followed and the ones left to take will help me understand what I am becoming.

That evening and for the next few days I immersed myself in psychology texts: clinical, personality, psychometrics, learning, experimental psychology, animal psychology, physiological psychology, behaviorist, gestalt, analytical, functional, dynamic, organismic, and all the rest of the ancient and modern factions, schools, and systems of thought. The depressing thing is that so many of the ideas on which our psychologists base their beliefs about human intelligence, memory, and learning are all wishful thinking.

Fay wants to come down and visit the lab, but I've told her not to. All I need now is for Alice and Fay to run into each other. I've enough to worry about without that.

PROGRESS REPORT 16

July 14—It was a bad day to go out to Warren—gray and drizzly—and that may account for the depression that grips me when I think about it. Or perhaps I'm kidding myself and it was the idea of possibly being sent there that bothered me. I borrowed Burt's car. Alice wanted to come along, but I had to see it alone. I didn't tell Fay I was going.

It was an hour-and-a-half drive out to the farmland community of Warren, Long Island, and I had no trouble finding the place: a sprawling gray estate revealed to the world only by an entrance of two concrete pillars flanking a narrow side-road and a well-polished brass plate with the name *Warren State Home and Training School*.

The roadside sign said 15 MPH, so I drove slowly past the blocks of buildings looking for the administrative offices.

A tractor came across the meadow in my direction,

and in addition to the man at the wheel there were two others hanging on the rear. I stuck out my head and called: "Can you tell me where Mr. Winslow's office is?"

The driver stopped the tractor and pointed to the left and ahead. "Main Hospital. Turn left and bear to your right."

I couldn't help noticing the staring young man riding at the rear of the tractor, hanging on to a handrail. He was unshaven, and there was the trace of an empty smile. He had on a sailor's hat with the brim pulled down childishly to shield his eyes, although there was no sun out. I caught his glance for a moment—his eyes wide, inquiring—but I had to look away. When the tractor started forward again, I could see in the rear view mirror that he was looking after me, curiously. It upset me . . . because he reminded me of Charlie.

I was startled to find the head psychologist so young, a tall, lean man with a tired look on his face. But his steady blue eyes suggested a strength behind the youthful expression.

He drove me around the grounds in his own car, and pointed out the recreation hall, hospital, school, administrative offices, and the two-story brick buildings he called *cottages* where the patients lived.

"I didn't notice a fence around Warren," I said.

"No, only a gate at the entrance and hedges to keep out curiosity seekers."

"But how do you keep . . . them . . . from wandering off . . . from leaving the grounds?"

He shrugged and smiled. "We can't, really. Some of them do wander off, but most of them return."

"Don't you go after them?"

He looked at me as if trying to guess what was behind my question. "No. If they get into trouble, we soon know about it from the people in town—or the police bring them back."

"And if not?"

"If we don't hear about them, or from them, we assume they've made some satisfactory adjustment on the outside. You've got to understand, Mr. Gordon, this isn't a prison. We are required by the state to make all reasonable efforts to get our patients back, but we're not equipped to closely supervise four thousand people at all times. The ones who manage to leave are all high-moron types—not that we're getting many of those any more. Now we get more of the brain-damaged cases who require constant custodial care—but the high-morons can move around more freely, and after a week or so on the outside most of them come back when they find there's nothing for them out there. The world doesn't want them and they soon know it."

We got out of the car and walked over to one of the *cottages*. Inside, the walls were white tile, and the building had a disinfectant smell to it. The first-floor lobby opened up to a recreation room filled with some seventy-five boys sitting around waiting for the lunch bell to be sounded. What caught my eye immediately was one of the bigger boys on a chair in the corner, cradling one of the other boys—fourteen or fifteen years old— cuddling him in his arms. They all turned to look as we entered, and some of the bolder ones came over and stared at me.

"Don't mind them," he said, seeing my expression. "They won't hurt you."

The woman in charge of the floor, a large-boned, handsome woman, with rolled up shirt sleeves and a denim apron over her starched white skirt, came up to us. At her belt was a ring of keys that jangled as she moved, and only when she turned did I see that the left side of her face was covered by a large, wine-colored birthmark.

"Didn't expect any company today, Ray," she said. "You usually bring your visitors on Thursdays."

'This is Mr. Gordon, Thelma, from Beekman University. He just wants to look around and get an idea of the work we're doing here. I knew it wouldn't make any difference with you, Thelma. Any day is all right with you."

"Yeah," she laughed strongly, "but Wednesday we turn the mattresses. It smells a lot better here on Thursday."

I noticed that she kept to my left so that the blotch on her face was hidden. She took me through the dormitory, the laundry, the supply rooms, and the dining hall—now set and waiting for the food to be delivered from the central commissary. She smiled as she talked, and her expression and the hair piled in a bun high on her head made her

156

look like a Lautrec dancer but she never looked straight at me. I wondered what it would be like living here with her to watch over me.

"They're pretty good here in this building," she said. "But you know what it is. Three hundred boys—seventy-five on a floor—and only five of us to look after them. It's not easy to keep them under control. But it's a lot better than the *untidy* cottages. The staff *there* doesn't last very long. With babies you don't mind so much, but when they get to be adults and still can't care for themselves, it can be a nasty mess."

"You seem to be a very nice person," I said. "The boys are fortunate to have you as their house-supervisor."

She laughed heartily still looking straight ahead, and showed her white teeth. "No better or worse than the rest. I'm very fond of my boys. It's not easy work, but it's rewarding when you think how much they need you." The smile left her for a moment. "Normal kids grow up too soon, stop needing you . . . go off on their own . . . forget who loved them and took care of them. But these children need all you can give—all of their lives." She laughed again, embarrassed at her seriousness. "It's hard work here, but worth it."

Back downstairs, where Winslow was waiting for us, the dinner bell sounded, and the boys filed into the dining room. I noticed that the big boy who had held the smaller one in his lap was now leading him to the table by the hand.

"Quite a thing," I said, nodding in that direction.

Winslow nodded too. "Jerry's the big one, and that's Dusty. We see that sort of thing often here. When there's no one else who has time for them, sometimes they know enough to seek human contact and affection from each other."

As we passed one of the other cottages on our way to the school, I heard a shriek followed by a wailing, picked up and echoed by two or three other voices. There were bars on the windows.

Winslow looked uncomfortable for the first time that morning. "Special security cottage," he explained. "Emotionally disturbed retardates. When there's a chance they'll harm themselves or others, we put them in Cottage K. Locked up at all times."

"Emotionally disturbed patients here? Don't they belong in psychiatric hospitals?"

"Oh, sure," he said, "but it's a difficult thing to control. Some, the borderline emotionally disturbed, don't break down until after they've been here for a while. Others were committed by the courts, and we had no choice but to admit them even though there's really no room for them. The real problem is that there's no room for anyone anywhere. Do you know how long our own waiting list is? Fourteen hundred. And we *may* have room for twenty-five or thirty of them by the end of the year."

"Where are those fourteen hundred now?"

"Home. On the outside, waiting for an opening here or in some other institution. You see, our space problem is not like the usual hospital overcrowding. Our patients usually come here to stay for the rest of their lives."

As we arrived at the new school building, a one-story glass-and-concrete structure with large picture windows, I tried to imagine what it would be like walking through these corridors as a patient. I visualized myself in the middle of a line of men and boys waiting to enter a classroom. Perhaps I'd be one of those pushing another boy in a wheelchair, or guiding someone else by the hand, or cuddling a smaller boy in my arms.

In one of the woodworking classrooms, where a group of older boys were making benches under a teacher's supervision, they clustered around us, eyeing me curiously. The teacher put down the saw and came towards us.

"This is Mr. Gordon from Beekman University," said Winslow. "Wants to look over some of our patients. He's thinking of buying the place."

The teacher laughed and waved at his pupils. "Well, if he b-buys it, he's g-got to t-take us with it. And he's g-got to get us some more w-wood to w-work with."

As he showed me around the shop, I noticed how strangely quiet the boys were. They went on with their work of sanding or varnishing the newly finished benches, but they didn't talk.

"These are my s-silent b-boys, you know," he said, as if he sensed my unspoken question. "D-deaf m-mutes."

"We have a hundred and six of them here," explained Winslow, "as a special study sponsored by the federal government."

What an incredible thing! How much less they had than other human beings. Mentally retarded, deaf, mute—and still eagerly sanding benches.

One of the boys who had been tightening a block of wood in a vise, stopped what he was doing, tapped Winslow on the arm, and pointed to the corner where a number of finished objects were drying on display shelves. The boy pointed to a lamp base on the second shelf, and then to himself. It was a poor job, unsteady, the patches of wood-filler showing through, and the varnish heavy and uneven. Winslow and the teacher praised it enthusiastically, and the boy smiled proudly and looked at me, waiting for my praise too.

"Yes," I nodded, mouthing the words exaggeratedly, "very good . . . very nice." I said it because he needed it, but I felt hollow. The boy smiled at me, and when we turned to leave he came over and touched my arm as a way of saying good-bye. It choked me up, and I had a great deal of difficulty controlling my emotions until we were out in the corridor again.

The principal of the school was a short, plump, motherly lady who sat me down in front of a neatly lettered chart, showing the various types of patients, the number of faculty assigned to each category, and the subjects they studied.

"Of course," she explained, "we don't get many of the upper I.Q.'s any more. They're taken care of—the sixty and seventy I.Q.'s—more and more in the city schools in special classes, or else there are community facilities for caring for them. Most of the ones we get are able to live out, in foster homes, boarding houses, and do simple work on the farms or in a menial capacity in factories or laundries—"

"Or bakeries," I suggested.

She frowned. "Yes, I guess they might be able to do that. Now, we also classify our children (I call them all children, no matter what their ages are, they're all children here), we classify them as *tidy* or *untidy*. It makes the administration of their cottages a lot easier if they can be kept with their own levels. Some of the *untidies* are severely brain-damaged cases, kept in cribs, and they will be cared for that way for the rest of their lives . . ."

"Or until science finds a way to help them."

"Oh," she smiled, explaining to me carefully, "I'm afraid these are beyond help."

"No one is beyond help."

She peered at me, uncertainly now. "Yes, yes, of course, you're right. We must have hope."

I made her nervous. I smiled to myself at the thought of how it would be if they brought me back here as one of her children. Would I be *tidy* or not?

Back at Winslow's office, we had coffee as he talked about his work. "It's a good place," he said. "We have no psychiatrists on our staff—only an outside consulting man who comes in once every two weeks. But it's just as well. Every one of the psych staff is dedicated to his work. I could have hired a psychiatrist, but at the price I'd have to pay I'm able to hire two psychologists—men who aren't afraid to give away a part of themselves to these people."

"What do you mean by 'a part of themselves'?"

He studied me for a moment, and then through the tiredness flashed an anger. "There are a lot of people who will give money or materials, but very few who will give time and affection. That's what I mean." His voice grew harsh, and he pointed to an empty baby bottle on the bookshelf across the room.

"You see that bottle?"

I told him I had wondered about it when we came into his office.

"Well, how many people do you know who are prepared to take a grown man into his arms and let him nurse with the bottle? And take the chance of having the patient urinate or defecate all over him? You look surprised. You can't understand it, can you, from way up there in your research ivory tower? What do you know about being shut out from every human experience as our patients have been?"

I couldn't restrain a smile, and he apparently misunderstood, because he stood up and ended the conversation abruptly. If I come back here to stay, and he finds out the whole story, I'm sure he'll understand. He's the kind of man who would.

As I drove out of Warren, I didn't know what to think. The feeling of cold grayness was everywhere around me—a sense of resignation. There had been no talk of rehabilitation, of cure, of someday sending these people out into the world again. No one had spoken of hope. The feeling was of living death—or worse, of never having been fully alive and knowing. Souls withered from the beginning, and doomed to stare into the time and space of every day.

I wondered about the house-mother with her redblotched face, and the stuttering shop teacher, and the motherly principal, and youthful tired-looking psychologist, and wished I knew how they had found their way here to work and dedicate themselves to these silent minds. Like the boy who held the younger one in his arms, each had found a fulfillment in giving away a part of himself to those who had less.

And what about the things I wasn't shown?

I may soon be coming to Warren, to spend the rest of my life with the others . . . waiting.

July 15—I've been putting off a visit to my mother. I want to see her and I don't. Not until I'm sure what is going to happen to me. Let's see first how the work goes and what I discover.

Algernon refuses to run the maze any more; general motivation has decreased. I stopped off again today to see him, and this time Strauss was there too. Both he and Nemur looked disturbed as they watched Burt force-feed him. Strange to see the little puff of white clamped down on the worktable and Burt forcing the food down his throat with an eye-dropper.

If it keeps up this way, they'll have to start feeding him by injection. Watching Algernon squirm under those tiny bands this afternoon, I felt them around my own arms and legs. I started to gag and choke, and I had to get out of the lab for fresh air. I've got to stop identifying with him.

I went down to Murray's Bar and had a few drinks. And then I called Fay and we made the rounds. Fay is annoyed that I've stopped taking her out dancing, and she got angry and walked out on me last night. She has no idea of my work and no interest in it, and when I do try to talk to her about it she makes no attempt to hide her boredom. She just can't be bothered, and I can't blame her. She's interested in only three things that I can see: dancing, painting, and sex. And the only thing we really have in common is sex. It's foolish of me to try to interest her in my work. So she goes dancing without me. She told me that the other night she dreamed she had come into the apartment and set fire to all my books and notes, and that we went off dancing around the flames. I've got to watch out. She's becoming possessive. I just realized tonight that my own place is starting to resemble her apartment—a mess. I've got to cut down on the drinking.

July 16—Alice met Fay last night. I'd been concerned about what would happen if they came face to face. Alice came to see me after she found out about Algernon from Burt. She knows what it may mean, and she still feels responsible for having encouraged me in the first place.

We had coffee and we talked late. I knew that Fay had gone out dancing at the Stardust Ballroom, so I didn't expect her home so early. But at about one forty-five in the morning we were startled by Fay's sudden appearance on the fire-escape. She tapped, pushed open the half-open window and came waltzing into the room with a bottle in her hand.

"Crashing the party," she said. "Brought my own refreshments."

I had told her about Alice working on the project at the university, and I had mentioned Fay to Alice earlier—so they weren't surprised to meet. But after a few seconds of sizing each other up, they started talking about art and me, and for all they cared I could have been anywhere else in the world. They liked each other.

"I'll get the coffee," I said, and wandered out to the kitchen to leave them alone.

When I came back, Fay had taken off her shoes and was sitting on the floor, sipping gin out of the bottle. She was explaining to Alice that as far as she was concerned there was nothing more valuable to the human body than sunbathing, and that nudist colonies were the answer to the world's moral problems.

Alice was laughing hysterically at Fay's suggestion that we all join a nudist colony, and she leaned over and accepted a drink that Fay poured for her.

We sat and talked until dawn, and I insisted on seeing

Alice home. When she protested that it wasn't necessary, Fay insisted that she would be a fool to go out alone in the city at this hour. So I went down and hailed a cab.

"There's something about her," said Alice on the way home. "I don't know what it is. Her frankness, her open trust, her unselfishness . . ."

I agreed.

"And she loves you," said Alice.

"No. She loves everyone," I insisted. "I'm just the neighbor across the hall."

"Aren't you in love with her?"

I shook my head. "You're the only woman I've ever loved."

"Let's not talk about that."

"Then you've cut me off from an important source of conversation."

"Only one thing I'm worried about, Charlie. The drinking. I've heard about some of those hangovers."

"Tell Burt to confine his observations and reports to the experimental data. I won't have him poisoning you against me. I can handle the drinks."

"I've heard that one before."

"But never from me."

"That's the only thing I have against her," she said. "She's got you drinking and she's interfering with your work."

"I can handle that too."

"This work is important now, Charlie. Not only to the world and millions of unknown people, but to you. Charlie, you've got to solve this thing for yourself as well. Don't let anyone tie your hands."

"So, now the truth comes out," I teased. "You'd like me to see less of her."

"That's not what I said."

"It's what you meant. If she's interfering with my work we both know I've got to cut her out of my life."

"No, I don't think you should cut her out of your life. She's good for you. You need a woman who's been around as she has."

"You would be good for me."

She turned her face away. "Not in the same way she is." She looked back at me. "I came here tonight prepared to hate her. I wanted to see her as a vile, stupid

163

whore you'd gotten mixed up with, and I had big plans about coming between you and saving you from her in spite of yourself. But now that I've met her, I realize I have no right to judge her behavior. I think she's good for you. So that really lets the air out of me. I like her even if I disapprove. But in spite of that, if you've got to drink with her and spend all of your time with her in night clubs and cabarets dancing, then she's in your way. And that's a problem only you can solve."

"Another one of those?" I laughed.

"Are you up to this one? You're deeply involved with her. I can tell."

"Not all that deep."

"Have you told her about yourself?"

"No."

Imperceptibly, I could see her relax. By keeping the secret about myself, I had somehow not committed myself to Fay completely. We both knew that, wonderful as she was, Fay would never understand.

"I needed her," I said, "and in a way she needed me, and living right across from each other, well it was just handy, that's all. But I wouldn't call it love—not the same thing that exists between us."

She looked down at her hands and frowned. "I'm not sure I know what does exist between us."

"Something so deep and significant that Charlie inside me is terrified whenever there seems to be any chance of my making love to you."

"And not with her?"

I shrugged. "That's how I know it's not important with her. It doesn't mean enough for Charlie to panic."

"Great!" she laughed. "And ironic as hell. When you talk about him that way, I hate him for coming between us. Do you think he'll ever let you . . . let us . . ."

"I don't know. I hope so."

I left her at the door. We shook hands, and yet, strangely, it was much closer and more intimate than an embrace would have been.

I went home and made love to Fay, but kept thinking of Alice.

July 27—Working around the clock. Over Fay's protests, I've had a cot moved into the lab. She's become too possessive and resentful of my work. I think she could tolerate another woman, but not this complete absorption in something she can't follow. I was afraid it would come to this, but I have no patience with her now. I'm jealous of every moment away from the work—impatient with anyone who tries to steal my time.

Though most of my writing time is spent on notes which I keep in a separate folder, from time to time I have to put down my moods and thoughts out of sheer habit.

The calculus of intelligence is a fascinating study. In a sense this is the problem I've been concerned with all my life. Here is the place for the application of all the knowledge I have acquired.

Time assumes another dimension now—work and absorption in the search for an answer. The world around me and my past seem far away and distorted, as if time and space were taffy being stretched and looped and twisted out of shape. The only real things are the cages and the mice and the lab equipment here on the fourth floor of the main building.

There is no night or day. I've got to cram a lifetime of research into a few weeks. I know I should rest, but I can't until I know the truth about what is happening.

Alice is a great help to me now. She brings me sandwiches and coffee, but she makes no demands.

About my perception: everything is sharp and clear, each sensation heightened and illuminated so that reds and yellows and blues glow. Sleeping here has a strange effect. The odors of the laboratory animals, dogs, monkeys, mice, spin me back into memories, and it is difficult to know whether I am experiencing a new sensation or recalling the past. It is impossible to tell what proportion is memory and what exists here and now—so that a strange compound is formed of memory and reality; past and present; response to stimuli stored in my brain centers, and response to stimuli in this room. It's as if all the things I've learned have fused into a crystal universe spinning before me so that I can see all the facets of it reflected in gorgeous bursts of light. . . .

A monkey sitting in the center of his cage, staring at me out of sleepy eyes, rubbing his cheeks with little old-man shriveled hands . . . *chee* . . . *cheee* . . . *cheeeee* . . . and bouncing off the cage wire, up to the swing overhead where the other monkey sits staring dumbly into space. Urinating, defecating, passing wind, staring at me and laughing . . . *cheeee* . . . *cheeeee* . . . *cheeeee.* . . .

And bouncing around, leap, hop, up around and down, he swings and tries to grab the other monkey's tail, but the one on the bar keeps swishing it away, without fuss, out of his grasp. Nice monkey . . . pretty monkey . . . with big eyes and swishy tail. Can I feed him a peanut? . . . No, the man'll holler. That sign says do not feed the animals. That's a chimpanzee. Can I pet him? No. I want to pet the chip-a-zee. Never mind, come and look at the elephants.

Outside, crowds of bright sunshiny people are dressed in spring.

Algernon lies in his own dirt, unmoving, and the odors are stronger than ever before. And what about me?

July 28—Fay has a new boy friend. I went home last night to be with her. I went to my room first to get a bottle and then headed over on the fire escape. But fortunately I looked before going in. They were together on the couch. Strange, I don't really care. It's almost a relief.

I went back to the lab to work with Algernon. He has moments out of his lethargy. Periodically, he will run a shifting maze, but when he fails and finds himself in a dead-end, he reacts violently. When I got down to the lab, I looked in. He was alert and came up to me as if he knew me. He was eager to work, and when I set him down through the trap door in the wire mesh of the maze, he moved swiftly along the pathways to the reward box. Twice he ran the maze successfully. The third time, he got halfway through, paused at an intersection, and then with a twitching movement took the wrong turn. I could see what was going to happen, and I wanted to reach down and take him out before he ended up in a blind alley. But I restrained myself and watched.

When he found himself moving along the unfamiliar path, he slowed down, and his actions became erratic: start, pause, double back, turn around and then forward again, until finally he was in the cul-de-sac that informed him with a mild shock that he had made a mistake. At this point, instead of turning back to find an alternate route, he began to move in circles, squeaking like a phonograph needle scratched across the grooves. He threw himself against the walls of the maze, again and again, leaping up, twisting over backwards and falling, and throwing himself again. Twice he caught his claws in the overhead wire mesh, screeching wildly, letting go, and trying hopelessly again. Then he stopped and curled himself up into a small, tight ball.

When I picked him up, he made no attempt to uncurl, but remained in that state much like a catatonic stupor. When I moved his head or limbs, they stayed like wax. I put him back into his cage and watched him until the stupor wore off and he began to move around normally.

What eludes me is the reason for his regression—is it a special case? An isolated reaction? Or is there some general principle of failure basic to the whole procedure? I've got to work out the rule.

If I can find that out, and if it adds even one jot of information to whatever else has been discovered about mental retardation and the possibility of helping others like myself, I will be satisfied. Whatever happens to me, I will have lived a thousand normal lives by what I might add to others not yet born.

That's enough.

July 31—I'm on the edge of it. I sense it. They all think I'm killing myself at this pace, but what they don't understand is that I'm living at a peak of clarity and beauty I never knew existed. Every part of me is attuned to the work. I soak it up into my pores during the day, and at night—in the moments before I pass off into sleep—ideas explode into my head like fireworks. There is no greater joy than the burst of solution to a problem.

Incredible that anything could happen to take away this bubbling energy, the zest that fills everything I do. It's as if all the knowledge I've soaked in during the past months has coalesced and lifted me to a peak of light and understanding. This is beauty, love, and truth all rolled into one. This is joy. And now that I've found it, how can I give it up? Life and work are the most wonderful things a man can have. I am in love with what I am doing, because the answer to this problem is right here in my mind, and soon—very soon—it will burst into consciousness. Let me solve this one problem. I pray God it is the answer I want, but if not I will accept any answer at all and try to be grateful for what I had.

Fay's new boy friend is a dance instructor from the Stardust Ballroom. I can't really blame her since I have so little time to be with her.

August 11—Blind alley for the past two days. Nothing. I've taken a wrong turn somewhere, because I get answers to a lot of questions, but not to the most important question of all: How does Algernon's regression affect the basic hypothesis of the experiment?

Fortunately, I know enough about the processes of the mind not to let this block worry me too much. Instead of panicking and giving up (or what's even worse, pushing hard for answers that won't come) I've got to take my mind off the problem for a while and let it stew. I've gone as far as I can on a conscious level, and now it's up to those mysterious operations below the level of awareness. It's one of those inexplicable things, how everything I've learned and experienced is brought to bear on the problem. Pushing too hard will only make things freeze up. How many great problems have gone unsolved because men didn't know enough, or have enough faith in the creative process and in themselves, to let go for the *whole* mind to work at it?

So I decided yesterday afternoon to put the work aside for a while and go to Mrs. Nemur's cocktail party. It was in honor of the two men on the board of the Welberg Foundation who had been instrumental in getting her husband the grant. I planned to take Fay, but she said she had a date and she'd rather go dancing.

I started out the evening with every intention of being pleasant and making friends. But these days I have trouble getting through to people. I don't know if it's me or them, but any attempt at conversation usually fades away in a minute or two, and the barriers go up. Is it because they are afraid of me? Or is it that deep down they don't care and feel the same about them?

I took a drink and wandered around the big room. There were little knots of people sitting in conversation groups, the kind I find it impossible to join. Finally, Mrs. Nemur cornered me and introduced me to Hyram Harvey, one of the board members. Mrs. Nemur is an attractive woman, early forties, blonde hair, lots of make-up and long red nails. She had her arm through Harvey's. "How is the research coming?" She wanted to know.

"As well as can be expected. I'm trying to solve a tough problem right now."

She lit a cigarette and smiled at me. "I know that everyone on the project is grateful that you've decided to pitch in and help out. But I imagine you'd much rather be working on something of your own. It must be rather dull taking up someone else's work rather than something you've conceived and created yourself."

She was sharp, all right. She didn't want Hyram Harvey to forget that her husband had the credit coming. I couldn't resist tossing it back at her. "No one really starts anything new, Mrs. Nemur. Everyone builds on other men's failures. There is nothing really original in science. What each man contributes to the sum of knowledge is what counts."

"Of course," she said, talking to her elderly guest rather than to me. "It's a shame Mr. Gordon wasn't around earlier to help solve these little final problems." She laughed. "But then—oh, I forgot, you weren't in any position to do psychological experimentation."

Harvey laughed, and I thought I'd better keep quiet. Bertha Nemur was not going to let me get the last word in, and if things went any further it would really get nasty.

I saw Dr. Strauss and Burt talking to the other man from the Welberg Foundation—George Raynor. Strauss was saying: "The problem, Mr. Raynor, is getting sufficient funds to work on projects like these, without having strings tied to the money. When amounts are earmarked for specific purposes, we can't really operate."

Raynor shook his head and waved a big cigar at the small group around him. "The real problem is convincing the board that this kind of research has practical value."

Strauss shook his head. "The point I've been trying to make is that this money is intended for research. No one can ever know in advance if a project is going to result in

169

something useful. Results are often negative. We learn what something is not—and that is as important as a positive discovery to the man who is going to pick up from there. At least he knows what not to do."

As I approached the group, I noticed Raynor's wife, to whom I had been introduced earlier. She was a beautiful, dark-haired woman of thirty or so. She was staring at me, or rather at the top of my head—as if she expected something to sprout. I stared back, and she got uncomfortable and turned back to Dr. Strauss. "But what about the present project? Do you anticipate being able to use these techniques on other retardates? Is this something the world will be able to use?"

Strauss shrugged and nodded towards me. "Still too early to tell. Your husband helped us put Charlie to work on the project, and a great deal depends on what he comes up with."

"Of course," Mr. Raynor put in, "we all understand the necessity for *pure* research in fields like yours. But it would be such a boon to our image if we could produce a really workable method for achieving permanent results outside the laboratory, if we could show the world that there is some tangible good coming out of it."

I started to speak, but Strauss, who must have sensed what I was going to say, stood up and put his arm on my shoulder. "All of us at Beekman feel that the work Charlie is doing is of the utmost importance. His job now is to find the truth wherever it leads. We leave it to your foundations to handle the public, to educate society."

He smiled at the Raynors and steered me away from them.

"That," I said, "is not at all what I was going to say."

"I didn't think you were," he whispered, holding onto my elbow. "But I could see by that gleam in your eye you were ready to cut them to pieces. And I couldn't allow that, could I?"

"Guess not," I agreed, helping myself to another martini.

"Is it wise of you to drink so heavily?"

"No, but I'm trying to relax and I seem to have come to the wrong place."

"Well, take it easy," he said, "and keep out of trouble

tonight. These people are not fools. They know the way you feel about them, and even if you don't need them, we do."

I waved a salute at him. "I'll try, but you'd better keep Mrs. Raynor away from me. I'm going to goose her if she wiggles her fanny at me again."

"Shhhh!" he hissed. "She'll hear you."

"Shhhh!" I echoed. "Sorry. I'll just sit here in the corner and keep out of everyone's way."

The haze was coming over me, but through it I could see people staring at me. I guess I was muttering to myself—too audibly. I don't remember what I said. A little while later I had the feeling that people were leaving unusually early, but I didn't pay much attention until Nemur came up and stood in front of me.

"Just who the hell do you think you are, that you can behave that way? I have never seen such insufferable rudeness in my life."

I struggled to my feet. "Now, what makes you say that?"

Strauss tried to restrain him, but he spluttered and gasped out: "I say it, because you have no gratitude or understanding of the situation. After all, you are indebted to these people if not to us—in more ways than one."

"Since when is a guinea pig supposed to be grateful?" I shouted. "I've served your purposes, and now I'm trying to work out your mistakes, so how the hell does that make me indebted to anyone?"

Strauss started to move in to break it up, but Nemur stopped him. "Just a minute. I want to hear this. I think it's time we had this out."

"He's had too much to drink," said his wife.

"Not that much," snorted Nemur. "He's speaking pretty clearly. I've put up with a lot from him. He's endangered—if not actually destroyed—our work, and now I want to hear from his own mouth what he thinks his justification is."

"Oh, forget it," I said. "You don't really want to hear the truth."

"But I do, Charlie. At least your version of the truth. I want to know if you feel any gratitude for all the things that have been done for you—the abilities you've developed, the things you've learned, the experiences you've had. Or do you think possibly you were better off before?"

"In some ways, yes."

That shocked them.

"I've learned a lot in the past few months," I said. "Not only about Charlie Gordon, but about life and people, and I've discovered that nobody really cares about Charlie Gordon, whether he's a moron or a genius. So what difference does it make?"

"Oh," laughed Nemur. "You're feeling sorry for yourself. What did you expect? This experiment was calculated to raise your intelligence, not to make you popular. We had no control over what happened to your personality, and you've developed from a likeable, retarded young man into an arrogant, self-centered, antisocial bastard."

"The problem, dear professor, is that you wanted someone who could be made intelligent but still be kept in a cage and displayed when necessary to reap the honors you seek. The hitch is that I'm a person."

He was angry, and I could see he was torn between ending the fight and trying once more to beat me down. "You're being unfair, as usual. You know we've always treated you well—done everything we could for you."

"Everything but treat me as a human being. You've boasted time and again that I was nothing before the experiment, and I know why. Because if I was nothing, then you were responsible for creating me, and that makes you my lord and master. You resent the fact that I don't show my gratitude every hour of the day. Well, believe it or not, I am grateful. But what you did for me—wonderful as it is—doesn't give you the right to treat me like an experimental animal. I'm an individual now, and so was Charlie before he ever walked into that lab. You look shocked! Yes, suddenly we discover that I was always a person—even before—and that challenges your belief that someone with an I.Q. of less than 100 doesn't deserve consideration. Professor Nemur, I think when you look at me your conscience bothers you."

"I've heard enough," he snapped. "You're drunk."

"Ah, no," I assured him. "Because if I get drunk, you'll see a different Charlie Gordon from the one you've

172

come to know. Yes, the other Charlie who walked in the darkness is still here with us. Inside me."

"He's gone out of his head," said Mrs. Nemur. "He's talking as if there were two Charlie Gordons. You'd better look after him, doctor."

Dr. Strauss shook his head. "No. I know what he means. It's come up recently in therapy sessions. A peculiar dissociation has taken place in the past month or so. He's had several experiences of perceiving himself as he was before the experiment—as a separate and distinct individual still functioning in his consciousness—as if the old Charlie were struggling for control of the body—"

"No! I never said that! Not struggling for control. Charlie is there, all right, but not struggling with me. Just waiting. He has never tried to take over or tried to prevent me from doing anything I wanted to do." Then, remembering about Alice, I modified it. "Well, almost never. The humble, self-effacing Charlie you were all talking about a while ago is just waiting patiently. I'll admit I'm like him in a number of ways, but humility and self-effacement are not among them. I've learned how little they get a person in this world.

"You've become cynical," said Nemur. "That's all this opportunity has meant to you. Your genius has destroyed your faith in the world and in your fellow men."

"That's not completely true," I said softly. "But I've learned that intelligence alone doesn't mean a damned thing. Here in your university, intelligence, education, knowledge, have all become great idols. But I know now there's one thing you've all overlooked: intelligence and education that hasn't been tempered by human affection isn't worth a damn."

I helped myself to another martini from the nearby sideboard and continued my sermon.

"Don't misunderstand me," I said. "Intelligence is one of the greatest human gifts. But all too often a search for knowledge drives out the search for love. This is something else I've discovered for myself very recently. I present it to you as a hypothesis: Intelligence without the ability to give and receive affection leads to mental and moral breakdown, to neurosis, and possibly even psychosis. And I say that the mind absorbed in and involved in itself as a self-centered end, to the exclusion of human relationships, can only lead to violence and pain.

"When I was retarded I had lots of friends. Now I have no one. Oh, I know lots of people. Lots and lots of people. But I don't have any real friends. Not like I used to have in the bakery. Not a friend in the world who means anything to me, and no one I mean anything to." I discovered that my speech was becoming slurred, and there was a lightness in my head. "That can't be right, can it?" I insisted. "I mean, what do you think? Do you think that's . . . that's right?"

Strauss came over and took my arm.

"Charlie, maybe you'd better lie down a while. You've had too much to drink."

"Why y'all looking at me like that? What did I say wrong? Did I say something wrong? I din't mean to say anything that wasn't right."

I heard the words thick in my mouth, as if my face had been shot full of novocaine. I was drunk—completely out of control. At that moment, almost with the flick of a switch, I was watching the scene from the dining room doorway, and I could see myself as the other Charlie— there near the sideboard, drink in hand, eyes wide and frightened.

"I always try to do the right things. My mother always taught me to be nice to people because she said that way you won't get into trouble and you'll always have lots of friends."

I could see by the way he was twitching and writhing that he had to get to the bathroom. Oh, my God, not there in front of them. "Excuse me, please," he said, "I got to go . . ." Somehow, in that drunken stupor, I managed to turn him away from them and head him toward the bathroom.

He made it in time, and after a few seconds I was again in control. I rested my cheek against the wall, and then washed my face with cool water. Still groggy, but I knew I was going to be all right.

That's when I saw Charlie watching me from the mirror behind the washbasin. I don't know how I knew it was Charlie and not me. Something about the dull, questioning look in his face. His eyes, wide and frightened, as if at one word from me he would turn and run deep into the dimension of the mirrored world. But he didn't run. He just stared back at me, mouth open, jaw hanging loosely.

"Hello," I said, "so you've finally come face to face with me."

He frowned, just a bit, as if he didn't understand what I meant, as if he wanted an explanation but didn't know how to ask for it. Then, giving it up, he smiled wryly from the corner of his mouth.

"Stay there right in front of me," I shouted. "I'm sick and tired of your spying on me from doorways and dark places where I can't catch up with you."

He stared.

"Who are you, Charlie?"

Nothing but the smile.

I nodded and he nodded back.

"Then what do you want?" I asked.

He shrugged.

"Oh, come now," I said, "you must want something. You've been following me—"

He looked down and I looked at my hands to see what he was looking at. "You want these back, don't you? You want me out of here so you can come back and take over where you left off. I don't blame you. It's your body and your brain—and your life, even though you weren't able to make much use of it. I don't have the right to take it away from you. Nobody does. Who's to say that my light is better than your darkness? Who's to say death is better than your darkness? Who am I to say? . . .

"But I'll tell you something else, Charlie." I stood up and backed away from the mirror. "I'm not your friend. I'm your enemy. I'm not going to give up my intelligence without a struggle. I can't go back down into that cave. There's no place for *me* to go now, Charlie. So you've got to stay away. Stay inside my unconscious where you belong, and stop following me around. I'm not going to give up—no matter what they all think. No matter how lonely it is. I'm going to keep what they've given me and do great things for the world and for other people like you."

As I turned toward the door, I had the impression he

was reaching out his hand toward me. But the whole damned thing was foolish. I was just drunk and that was my own reflection in the mirror.

When I came out, Strauss wanted to put me into a taxi, but I insisted I could get home all right. All I needed was a little fresh air, and I didn't want anyone to come with me. I wanted to walk by myself.

I was seeing myself as I really had become: Nemur had said it. I was an arrogant, self-centered bastard. Unlike Charlie, I was incapable of making friends or thinking about other people and their problems. I was interested in myself, and myself only. For one long moment in that mirror I had seen myself through Charlie's eyes— looked down at myself and saw what I had really become. And I was ashamed.

Hours later I found myself in front of the apartment house, and made my way upstairs and through the dimly lit hallway. Passing Fay's room, I could see there was a light on, and I started toward her door. But just as I was about to knock I heard her giggling, and a man's answering laugh.

It was too late for that.

I let myself into my apartment quietly and stood there for a while in the dark, not daring to move, not daring to turn on the light. Just stood there and felt the whirlpool in my eyes.

What has happened to me? Why am I so alone in the world?

4:30 A.M.—The solution came to me, just as I was dozing off. Illuminated! Everything fits together, and I see what I should have known from the beginning. No more sleep. I've got to get back to the lab and test this against the results from the computer. This, finally, is the flaw in the experiment. I've found it.

Now what becomes of me?

August 26—LETTER TO PROFESSOR NEMUR (COPY)
Dear Professor Nemur:
Under separate cover I am sending you a copy of my report entitled: "The Algernon-Gordon Effect: A Study of Structure and Function of Increased Intelligence," which may be published if you see fit.

As you know, my experiments are completed. I have included in my report all of my formulas, as well as mathematical analyses of the data in the appendix. Of course, these should be verified.

The results are clear. The more sensational aspects of my rapid climb cannot obscure the facts. The surgery-and-injection techniques developed by you and Dr. Strauss must be viewed as having little or no practical applicability, at the present time, to the increase of human intelligence.

Reviewing the data on Algernon: although he is still in his physical youth, he has regressed mentally. Motor activity impaired; general reduction of glandular functioning; accelerated loss of coordination; and strong indications of progressive amnesia.

As I show in my report, these and other physical and mental deterioration syndromes can be predicted with statistically significant results by the application of my new formula. Although the surgical stimulus to which we were both subjected resulted in an intensification and acceleration of all mental processes, the flaw, which I have taken the liberty of calling the "Algernon-Gordon Effect," is the logical extension of the entire intelligence speed-up. The hypothesis here proved may be described most simply in the following terms:

ARTIFICIALLY-INDUCED INTELLIGENCE DETERIORATES AT A RATE OF TIME DIRECTLY PROPORTIONAL TO THE QUANTITY OF THE INCREASE.

As long as I am able to write, I will continue to put down my thoughts and ideas in these progress reports. It is one of my few solitary pleasures and is certainly necessary to the completion of this research. However, by all indications, my own mental deterioration will be quite rapid.

I have checked and rechecked my data a dozen times in hope of finding an error, but I am sorry to say the results must stand. Yet, I am grateful for the little bit that I here add to the knowledge of the function of the human mind and of the laws governing the artificial increase of human intelligence.

The other night Dr. Strauss was saying that an experimental failure, the disproving of a theory, was as important to the advancement of learning as a success would be. I know now that this is true. I am sorry, however, that my own contribution to the field must rest upon the ashes of the work of this staff, and especially those who have done so much for me.

Yours truly,
Charles Gordon

encl: report
copy: Dr. Strauss
     The Welberg Foundation

September 1—I must not panic. Soon there will be signs of emotional instability and forgetfulness, the first symptoms of the burnout. Will I recognize these in myself? All I can do now is keep recording my mental state as objectively as possible, remembering that this psychological journal will be the first of its kind, and possibly the last.

This morning Nemur had Burt take my report and the statistical data down to Hallston University to have some of the top men in the field verify my results and the application of my formulas. All last week they had Burt going over my experiments and methodological charts. I shouldn't really be annoyed by their precautions. After all, I'm just a Charlie-come-lately, and it is difficult for Nemur to accept the fact that my work might be beyond him. He had come to believe in the myth of his own authority, and after all I am an outsider.

I don't really care any more what he thinks, or what any of them think for that matter. There isn't time. The work is done, the data is in, and all that remains is to see whether I have accurately projected the curve on the Algernon figures as a prediction of what will happen to me.

Alice cried when I told her the news. Then she ran out. I've got to impress on her that there is no reason for her to feel guilty about this.

September 2—Nothing definite yet. I move in a silence of clear white light. Everything around me is waiting. I dream of being alone on the top of a mountain, surveying the land around me, greens and yellows—and the sun directly above, pressing my shadow into a tight ball around my legs. As the sun drops into the afternoon sky, the shadow undrapes itself and stretches out toward the horizon, long and thin, and far behind me. . . .

I want to say here again what I've said already to Dr. Strauss. No one is in any way to blame for what has happened. This experiment was carefully prepared, extensively tested on animals, and statistically validated. When they decided to use me as the first human test, they were reasonably certain that there was no physical danger involved. There was no way to foresee the psychological pitfalls. I don't want anyone to suffer because of what happens to me.

The only question now is: How much can I hang on to?

September 15—Nemur says my results have been confirmed. It means that the flaw is central and brings the entire hypothesis into question. Someday there might be a way to overcome this problem, but that time is not yet. I have recommended that no further tests be made on human beings until these things are clarified by additional research on animals.

It is my own feeling that the most successful line of research will be that taken by the men studying enzyme imbalances. As with so many other things, time is the key factor—speed in discovering the deficiency, and speed in administering hormonal substitutes. I would like to help in that area of research, and in the search for radioisotopes that may be used in local cortical control, but I know now that I won't have the time.

September 17—Becoming absent minded. Put things away on my desk or in the drawers of the lab tables, and when I can't find them I lose my temper and flare up at everyone. First signs?

Algernon died two days ago. I found him at four thirty in the morning when I came back to the lab after wandering around down at the waterfront—on his side, stretched out in the corner of his cage. As if he were running in his sleep.

Dissection shows that my predictions were right. Compared to the normal brain, Algernon's had decreased in

weight and there was a general smoothing out of the cere-
bral convolutions as well as a deepening and broadening
of brain fissures.

It's frightening to think that the same thing might be
happening to me right now. Seeing it happen to Algernon
makes it real. For the first time, I'm afraid of the future.

I put Algernon's body into a small metal container and
took him home with me. I wasn't going to let them dump
him into the incinerator. It's foolish and sentimental, but
late last night I buried him in the back yard. I wept as I
put a bunch of wild flowers on the grave.

September 21—I'm going to Marks Street to visit my
mother tomorrow. A dream last night triggered off a se-
quence of memories, lit up a whole slice of the past and
the important thing is to get it down on paper quickly before I forget it because I seem to forget things sooner
now. It has to do with my mother, and now—more than
ever—I want to understand her, to know what she was
like and why she acted the way she did. I mustn't hate
her.

I've got to come to terms with her *before* I see her so
that I won't act harshly or foolishly.

September 27—I should have written this down right
away, because it's important to make this record complete.

I went to see Rose three days ago. Finally, I forced
myself to borrow Burt's car again. I was afraid, and yet I
knew I had to go.

At first when I got to Marks Street I thought I had
made a mistake. It wasn't the way I remembered it at all.
It was a filthy street. Vacant lots where many of the
houses had been torn down. On the sidewalk, a discarded
refrigerator with its face ripped off, and on the curb an
old mattress with wire intestines hanging out of its belly.
Some houses had boarded up windows, and others looked
more like patched-up shanties than homes. I parked the
car a block away fom the house and walked.

There were no children playing on Marks Street—not
at all like the mental picture I had brought with me of
children everywhere, and Charlie watching them through

the front window (strange that most of my memories of the street are framed by the window, with me always inside watching the children play). Now there were only old people standing in the shade of tired porches.

As I approached the house, I had a second shock. My mother was on the front stoop, in an old brown sweater, washing the ground floor windows from the outside even though it was cold and windy. Always working to show the neighbors what a good wife and mother she was.

The most important thing had always been what other people thought—appearances before herself or her family. And righteous about it. Time and again Matt had insisted that what others thought about you wasn't the only thing in life. But it did no good. Norma had to dress well; the house had to have fine furniture; Charlie had to be kept inside so that other people wouldn't know anything was wrong.

At the gate, I paused to watch as she straightened up to catch her breath. Seeing her face made me tremble, but it was not the face I had struggled so hard to recall. Her hair had become white and streaked with iron, and the flesh of her thin cheeks was wrinkled. Perspiration made her forehead glisten. She caught sight of me and stared back.

I wanted to look away, to turn back down the street, but I couldn't—not after having come so far. I would just ask directions, pretending I was lost in a strange neighborhood. Seeing her had been enough. But all I did was stand there waiting for her to do something first. And all she did was stand there and look at me.

"Do you want something?" Her voice, hoarse, was an unmistakable echo down the corridors of memory.

I opened my mouth, but nothing came out. My mouth worked, I know, and I struggled to speak to her, to get something out, because in that moment I could see recognition in her eyes. This was not at all the way I wanted her to see me. Not standing there in front of her, dumbly, unable to make myself understood. But my tongue kept getting in the way, like a huge obstruction, and my mouth was dry.

Finally, something came out. Not what I had intended (I had planned something soothing and encouraging, to take control of the situation and wipe out all the past and pain with a few words) but all that came out of my cracked throat was: "Maaa . . ."

With all the things I had learned—in all the languages I had mastered—all I could say to her, standing on the porch staring at me, was, *"Maaaa."* Like a dry-mouthed lamb at the udder.

She wiped her forehead with the back of her arm and frowned at me, as if she could not see me clearly. I stepped forward, past the gate to the walk, and then toward the steps. She drew back.

At first, I wasn't sure whether or not she really recognized me, but then she gasped: *"Charlie! . . ."* She didn't scream it or whisper it. She just gasped it as one might do coming out of a dream.

"Ma . . ." I started up the steps. "It's me . . ."

My movement startled her, and she stepped backwards, kicking over the bucket of soapy water, and the dirty suds rushed down the steps. "What are you doing here?"

"I just wanted to see you . . . talk to you . . ."

Because my tongue kept getting in my way, my voice came out of my throat differently, with a thick whining tone, as I might have spoken a long time ago. "Don't go away," I begged. "Don't run away from me."

But she had gone inside the vestibule and locked the door. A moment later I could see her peering at me from behind the sheer white curtain of the door window, her eyes terrified. Behind the window her lips moved soundlessly. "Go away! Leave me alone!"

Why? Who was she to deny me this way? By what right did she turn away from me?

"Let me in! I want to talk to you! Let me in!" I banged on the door against the glass so hard it cracked, and the crack spread a web that caught my skin for a moment and held it fast. She must have thought I was out of my mind and had come to harm her. She let go of the outer door and fled down the hallway that led into the apartment.

I pushed again. The hook gave way and, unprepared for the sudden yielding, I fell into the vestibule, off balance. My hand was bleeding from the glass I had broken, and not knowing what else to do, I put my hand into my pocket to prevent the blood from staining her freshly scrubbed linoleum.

I started in, past the stairs I had seen so often in my nightmares. I had often been pursued up that long, narrow staircase by demons who grabbed at my legs and pulled me down into the cellar below, while I tried to scream without voice, strangling on my tongue and gagging in silence. Like the silent boys at Warren.

The people who lived on the second floor—our landlord and landlady, the Meyers—had always been kind to me. They gave me sweets and let me come to sit in their kitchen and play with their dog. I wanted to see them, but without being told I knew they were gone and dead and that strangers lived upstairs. That path was now closed to me forever.

At the end of the hallway, the door through which Rose had fled was locked, and for a moment I stood—undecided.

"Open the door."

The answer was the high-pitched yapping of a small dog. It took me by surprise.

"All right," I said. "I don't intend to hurt you or anything, but I've come a long way, and I'm not leaving without talking to you. If you don't open the door, I'm going to break it down."

I heard her saying: "Shhhh, Nappie . . . Here, into the bedroom you go." A moment later I heard the click of the lock. The door opened and she stood there staring at me.

"Ma," I whispered, "I'm not going to do anything. I just want to talk to you. You've got to understand, I'm not the same as I was. I've changed. I'm normal now. Don't you understand? I'm not retarded any more. I'm not a moron. I'm just like anyone else. I'm normal—just like you and Matt and Norma."

I tried to keep talking, babbling so she wouldn't close the door. I tried to tell her the whole thing, all at once. "They changed me, performed an operation on me and made me different, the way you always wanted me to be. Didn't you read about it in the newspapers? A new scientific experiment that changes your capacity for intelligence, and I'm the first one they tried it on. Can't you understand? Why are you looking at me that way? I'm smart now, smarter than Norma, or Uncle Herman, or Matt. I know things even college professors don't know. Talk to me! You can be proud of me now and tell all the neighbors. You don't have to hide me in the cellar when company comes. Just talk to me. Tell me about things, the way it was when I was a little boy, that's all I want. I won't hurt you. I don't hate you. But I've got to know about myself, to understand myself before it's too late. Don't you see, I can't be a complete person unless I can understand myself, and you're the only one in the world who can help me now. Let me come in and sit down for a little while."

It was the way I spoke rather than what I said that hypnotized her. She stood there in the doorway and stared at me. Without thinking, I pulled my bloody hand out of my pocket and clenched it in my pleading. When she saw it her expression softened.

"You hurt yourself . . ." She didn't necessarily feel sorry for me. It was the sort of thing she might have felt for a dog that had torn its paw, or a cat that had been gashed in a fight. It wasn't because I was her Charlie, but in spite of it.

"Come in and wash it. I've got some bandage and iodine."

I followed her to the cracked sink with the corrugated drainboard at which she had so often washed my face and hands after I came in from the back yard, or when I was ready to eat or go to sleep. She watched me roll up my sleeves. "You shouldn't have broke the window. The landlord's gonna be sore, and I don't have enough money to pay for it." Then, as if impatient with the way I was doing it, she took the soap from me and washed my hand. As she did it, she concentrated so hard that I kept silent, afraid of breaking the spell. Occasionally she clucked her tongue, or sighed, "Charlie, Charlie, always getting yourself into a mess. When are you going to learn to take care of yourself?" She was back twenty-five years earlier when I was her little Charlie and she was willing to fight for my place in the world.

When the blood was washed off and she had dried my hands with paper toweling, she looked up into my face and her eyes went round with fright. "Oh, my God!" she gasped, and backed away.

I started talking again, softly, persuasively to convince her that nothing was wrong and I meant no harm. But as I spoke I could tell her mind was wandering. She looked around vaguely, put her hand to her mouth and groaned as she looked at me again. "The house is such a mess," she said. "I wasn't expecting company. Look at those windows, and that woodwork over there."

"That's all right, Ma. Don't worry about it."

"I've got to wax those floors again. It's got to be clean." She noticed some fingermarks on the door and taking up her washrag she scrubbed them away. When she looked up and saw me watching her, she frowned. "Have you come about the electric bill?"

Before I could say no, she wagged her finger, scolding, "I intend to send a check out the first of the month, but my husband is out of town on business. I told them all they don't have to worry about the money, because my daughter gets paid this week, and we'll be able to take care of all our bills. So there's no need bothering me for money."

"Is she your only child? Don't you have any other children?"

She started, and then her eyes looked far away. "I had a boy. So brilliant that all the other mothers were jealous of him. And they put the evil eye on him. They called it the *I.Q.* but it was the *evil-I.Q.* He would have been a great man, if not for that. He was really very bright— *exceptional,* they said. He could have been a genius . . ."

She picked up a scrub brush. "Excuse me now. I've got to get things ready. My daughter has a young man coming for dinner, and I've got to get this place clean." She got down on her knees and started to scrub the already shining floor. She didn't look up again.

She was muttering to herself now, and I sat down at the kitchen table. I would wait until she came out of it, until she recognized me and understood who I was. I couldn't leave until she knew that I was her Charlie. Somebody had to understand.

She had started humming sadly to herself, but she stopped, her rag poised midway between the bucket and the floor, as if suddenly aware of my presence behind her.

She turned, her face tired and her eyes glistening, and

cocked her head. "How could it be? I don't understand. They told me you could never be changed."

"They performed an operation on me, and that changed me. I'm famous now. They've heard of me all over the world. I'm intelligent now, Mom. I can read and write, and I can—"

"Thank God," she whispered. "My prayers—all these years I thought He didn't hear me, but He was listening all the time, just waiting His own good time to do His will."

She wiped her face in her apron, and when I put my arm around her, she wept freely on my shoulder. All the pain was washed away, and I was glad I had come.

"I've got to tell everyone," she said, smiling, "all those teachers at the school. Oh, wait till you see their faces when I tell them. And the neighbors. And Uncle Herman—I've got to tell Uncle Herman. He'll be so pleased. And wait until your father comes home, and your sister! Oh, she'll be so happy to see you. You have no idea."

She hugged me, talking excitedly, making plans for the new life we were going to have together. I hadn't the heart to remind her that most of my childhood teachers were gone from this school, that the neighbors had long moved away, that Uncle Herman had died many years ago, and that my father had left her. The nightmare of all those years had been pain enough. I wanted to see her smiling and know I had been the one to make her happy. For the first time in my life, I had brought a smile to her lips.

Then after a while, she paused thoughtfully as if remembering something. I had the feeling her mind was going to wander. "No!" I shouted, startling her back to reality, "Wait, Ma! There's something else. Something I want you to have before I go."

"Go? You can't go away now."

"I have to go, Ma. I have things to do. But I'll write to you, and I'll send you money."

"But when will you come back?"

"I don't know—yet. But before I go, I want you to have this."

"A magazine?"

"Not exactly. It's a scientific report I wrote. Very technical. Look, it's called *The Algernon-Gordon Effect.* Something I discovered, and it's named partly after me. I want you to keep a copy of the report so that you can show people that your son turned out to be more than a dummy after all."

She took it and looked at it in awe. "It's . . . it's your name. I knew it would happen. I always said it would happen someday. I tried everything I could. You were too young to remember, but I tried. I told them all that you'd go to college and become a professional man and make your mark in the world. They laughed, but I told them."

She smiled at me through tears, and then a moment later she wasn't looking at me any more. She picked up her rag and began to wash the woodwork around the kitchen door, humming—more happily, I thought—as if in a dream.

The dog started barking again. The front door opened and closed and a voice called: "Okay, Nappie. Okay, it's me." The dog was jumping excitedly against the bedroom door.

I was furious at being trapped here. I didn't want to see Norma. We had nothing to say to each other, and I didn't want my visit spoiled. There was no back door. The only way would be to climb out the window into the back yard and go over the fence. But someone might mistake me for a burglar.

As I heard her key in the door, I whispered to my mother—I don't know why—"Norma's home." I touched her arm, but she didn't hear me. She was too busy humming to herself as she washed the woodwork.

The door opened. Norma saw me and frowned. She didn't recognize me at first—it was dim, the lights hadn't been turned on. Putting down the shopping bag she was carrying, she switched on the light. "Who are you? . . ." But before I could answer, her hand went over her mouth, and she slumped back against the door.

"Charlie!" She said it the same way my mother had, gasping. And she looked the way my mother used to look—thin, sharp features, birdlike, pretty. "Charlie! My God, what a shock! You might have gotten in touch and warned me. You should have called. I don't know what to say . . ." She looked at my mother, sitting on the floor near the sink. "Is she all right? You didn't shock her or anything . . ."

"She came out of it for a while. We had a little talk."

"I'm glad. She doesn't remember much these days. It's old age—senility. Dr. Portman wants me to put her into a nursing home, but I can't do it. I can't stand to think of her in one of those institutions." She opened the bedroom door to let the dog out, and when he jumped and whined joyously, she picked him up and hugged him. "I just can't do that to my own mother." Then she smiled at me uncertainly. "Well, what a surprise. I never dreamed. Let me look at you. I never would have recognized you. I'd have passed you by in the street. So different." She sighed. "I'm glad to see you, Charlie."

"Are you? I didn't think you'd want to see me again."

"Oh, Charlie!" She took my hands in hers. "Don't say that. I *am* glad to see you. I've been expecting you. I didn't know when, but I knew someday you'd come back. Ever since I read that you had run away in Chicago." She pulled back to look up at me. "You don't know how I've thought about you and wondered where you were and what you were doing. Until that professor came here last—when was it? last March? just seven months ago?—I had no idea you were still alive. She told me you died in Warren. I believed it all these years. When they told me you were alive and they needed you for the experiment, I didn't know what to do. Professor . . . Nemur?—is that his name?—wouldn't let me see you. He was afraid to upset you before the operation. But when I saw in the papers that it worked and you had become a *genius*—oh, my!—you don't know what it felt like to read about that.

"I told all the people in my office, and the girls at my bridge club. I showed them your picture in the paper, and I told them you'd be coming back here to see us one day. And you have. You really have. You didn't forget us."

She hugged me again. "Oh, Charlie. Charlie . . . it's so wonderful to find all of a sudden I've got a big brother. You have no idea. Sit down—let me make you something to eat. You've got to tell me all about it and what your plans are. I . . . I don't know where to start asking questions. I must sound ridiculous—like a girl who has just found out her brother is a hero, or a movie star, or something."

I was confused. I had not expected a greeting like this from Norma. It had never occurred to me that all these years alone with my mother might change her. And yet it was inevitable. She was no longer the spoiled brat of my memories. She had grown up, had become warm and sympathetic and affectionate.

We talked. Ironic to sit there with my sister, the two of us talking about my mother—right there in the room with us—as if she wasn't there. Whenever Norma would refer to their life together, I'd look to see if Rose was listening, but she was deep in her own world, as if she didn't understand our language, as if none of it concerned her any more. She drifted around the kitchen like a ghost, picking things up, putting things away, without ever getting in the way. It was frightening.

I watched Norma feed her dog. "So you finally got him. Nappie—short for Napoleon, isn't it?"

She straightened up and frowned. "How did you know?"

I explained about my memory: the time she had brought home her test paper hoping to get the dog, and how Matt had forbidden it. As I told it, the frown became deeper.

"I don't remember any of it. Oh, Charlie, was I so mean to you?"

"There's one memory I'm curious about. I'm not really sure if it's a memory, or a dream, or if I just made it all up. It was the last time we played together as friends. We were in the basement, and we were playing a game with the lamp shades on our heads, pretending we were Chinese coolies—jumping up and down on an old mattress. You were seven or eight, I think, and I was about thirteen. And, as I recall, you bounced off the mattress and hit your head against the wall. It wasn't very hard—just a bump—but Mom and Dad came running down because you were screaming, and you said I was trying to kill you.

"She blamed Matt for not watching me, for leaving us alone together, and she beat me with a strap until I was nearly unconscious. Do you remember it? Did it really happen that way?"

Norma was fascinated by my description of the memory, as if it awakened sleeping images. "It's all so vague. You know, I thought that was my dream. I remember us wearing the lampshades, and jumping up and down on the mattresses." She stared out of the window. "I hated you because they fussed over *you* all the time. They never spanked you for not doing your homework right, or for not bringing home the best marks. You skipped classes most of the time and played games, and I had to go to the hard classes in school. Oh, how I hated you. In school the other children scribbled pictures on the blackboard, a boy with a duncecap on his head, and they wrote *Norma's Brother* under it. And they scribbled things on the sidewalk in the schoolyard—*Moron's Sister* and *Dummy Gordon Family*. And then one day when I wasn't invited to Emily Raskin's birthday party, I knew it was because of you. And when we were playing there in the basement with those lampshades on our heads, I had to get even." She started to cry. "So I lied and said you hurt me. Oh, Charlie, what a fool I was—what a spoiled brat. I'm so ashamed—"

"Don't blame yourself. It must have been hard to face the other kids. For me, this kitchen was my world—and that room there. The rest of it didn't matter as long as this was safe. You had to face the rest of the world."

"Why did they send you away, Charlie? Why couldn't you have stayed here and lived with us? I always wondered about that. Every time I asked her, she always said it was for your own good."

"In a way she was right."

She shook her head. "She sent you away because of *me*, didn't she? Oh, Charlie, why did it have to be? Why did all this happen to us?"

I didn't know what to tell her. I wished I could say that like the House of Atreus or Cadmus we were suffering for the sins of our forefathers, or fulfilling an ancient Greek oracle. But I had no answers for her, or for myself.

"It's past," I said. "I'm glad I met you again. It makes it a little easier."

She grabbed my arm suddenly. "Charlie, you don't know what I've been through all these years with her. The apartment, this street, my job. It's all been a nightmare, coming home each day, wondering if she's still here, if she's harmed herself, guilty for thinking about things like that."

I stood up and let her rest against my shoulder, and she wept. "Oh, Charlie. I'm glad you're back now. We've needed someone. I'm so tired. . . ."

I had dreamed of a time like this, but now that it was here, what good was it? I couldn't tell her what was going to happen to me. And yet, could I accept her affection on false pretenses? Why kid myself? If I had still been the old, feeble-minded, dependent Charlie, she wouldn't have spoken to me the same way. So what right did I have to it now? My mask would soon be ripped away.

"Don't cry, Norma. Everything will work out all right." I heard myself speaking in reassuring platitudes. "I'll try to take care of you both. I have a little money saved, and with what the Foundation has been paying me, I'll be able to send you some money regularly—for a while anyway."

"But you're not going away! You've got to stay with us now—"

"I've got to do some traveling, some research, make a few speeches, but I'll try to come back to visit you. Take care of her. She's been through a lot. I'll help you for as long as I can."

"Charlie! No, don't go!" She clung to me. "I'm frightened!"

The role I had always wanted to play—the big brother.

At that moment, I sensed that Rose, who had been sitting in the corner quietly, was staring at us. Something in her face had changed. Her eyes were wide, and she leaned forward on the edge of her seat. All I could think of was a hawk ready to swoop down.

I pushed Norma away from me, but before I could say anything, Rose was on her feet. She had taken the kitchen knife from the table and was pointing at me.

"What are you doing to her? Get away from her! I told you what I'd do to you if I ever caught you touching your sister again! Dirty mind! You don't belong with normal people!"

We both jumped back, and for some insane reason, I felt guilty, as if I had been caught doing something wrong, and I knew Norma felt the same way. It was as if my mother's accusation had made it true, that we were doing something obscene.

Norma screamed at her: "Mother! Put down that knife!"

Seeing Rose standing there with the knife brought back the picture of that night she had forced Matt to take me away. She was reliving that now. I couldn't speak or move. The nausea swept over me, the choking tension, the buzzing in my ears, my stomach knotting and stretching as if it wanted to tear itself out of my body.

She had a knife, and Alice had a knife, and my father had a knife, and Dr. Strauss had a knife. . . .

Fortunately, Norma had the presence of mind to take it away from her, but she couldn't erase the fear in Rose's eyes as she screamed at me. "Get him out of here! He's got no right to look at his sister with sex in his mind!"

Rose screamed and sank back into the chair, weeping.

I didn't know what to say, and neither did Norma. We were both embarrassed. Now she knew why I had been sent away.

I wondered if I had ever done anything to justify my mother's fear. There were no such memories, but how could I be sure there weren't horrible thoughts repressed behind the barriers of my tortured conscience? In the sealed-off passageways, beyond blind alleys, that I would never see. Possibly I will never know. Whatever the truth is, I must not hate Rose for protecting Norma. I must understand the way she saw it. Unless I forgive her, I will have nothing.

Norma was trembling.

"Take it easy," I said. "She doesn't know what she's doing. It wasn't me she was raving at. It was the old Charlie. She was afraid of what *he* might do to you. I can't blame her for wanting to protect you. But we don't have to think about it now, because he's gone forever, isn't he?"

She wasn't listening to me. There was a dreamy expression on her face. "I've just had one of those strange experiences where something happens, and you have the feeling you know it's going to happen, as if it all took place before, the exact same way, and you watch it unfold again. . . ."

"A very common experience."

She shook her head. "Just now, when I saw her with that knife, it was like a dream I had a long time ago."

What was the use of telling her she had undoubtedly been awake that night as a child, and had seen the whole thing from her room—that it had been repressed and twisted until she imagined it as a fantasy. No reason for burdening her with the truth. She would have enough sadness with my mother in the days to come. I would gladly have taken the burden and the pain off her hands, but there was no sense in starting something I couldn't finish. I would have my own suffering to live with. There was no way to stop the sands of knowledge from slipping through the hourglass of my mind.

"I've got to go now," I said. "Take care of yourself, and of her." I squeezed her hand. As I went out, Napoleon barked at me.

I held it in for as long as I could, but when I reached the street it was impossible. It's hard to write it down, but people turned to look at me as I walked back to the car, crying like a child. I couldn't help myself, and I didn't care.

As I walked, the ridiculous words drummed themselves into my head over and over again, rising to the rhythm of a buzzing noise:

> Three blind mice . . . three blind mice,
> See how they run! See how they run!
> They all run after the farmer's wife,
> She cut off their tails with a carving knife,
> Did you ever see such a sight in your life,
> As three . . . blind . . . mice?

I tried to shut it out of my ears, but I couldn't, and once when I turned to look back at the house and the porch, I saw the face of a boy, staring at me, his cheek pressed against the window pane.

PROGRESS REPORT 17

October 3—Downhill. Thoughts of suicide to stop it all now while I am still in control and aware of the world around me. But then I think of Charlie waiting at the window. His life is not mine to throw away. I've just borrowed it for a while, and now I'm being asked to return it.

I must remember I'm the only person this ever happened to. As long as I can, I've got to keep putting down my thoughts and feelings. These progress reports are Charlie Gordon's contribution to mankind.

I have become edgy and irritable. Having fights with people in the building about playing the hi-fi set late at night. I've been doing that a lot since I've stopped playing the piano. It isn't right to keep it going all hours, but I do it to keep myself awake. I know I should sleep, but I begrudge every second of waking time. It's not just because of the nightmares; it's because I'm afraid of letting go.

I tell myself there'll be time enough to sleep later, when it's dark.

Mr. Vernor in the apartment below never used to complain, but now he's always banging on the pipes or on the ceiling of his apartment so that I hear the pounding beneath my feet. I ignored it at first, but last night he came up in his bathrobe. We quarreled, and I slammed the door in his face. An hour later he was back with a policeman who told me I couldn't play records that loudly at 4 A.M. The smile on Vernor's face so enraged me that it was all I could do to keep from hitting him. When they left I smashed all the records and the machine. I've been kidding myself anyway. I don't really like that kind of music any more.

October 4—Strangest therapy session I ever had. Strauss was upset. It was something he hadn't expected either.

What happened—I don't dare call it a memory—was a psychic experience or a hallucination. I won't attempt to explain or interpret it, but will only record what happened.

I was touchy when I came into his office, but he pretended not to notice. I lay down on the couch immediately, and he, as usual, took his seat to one side and a little behind me—just out of sight—and waited for me to begin the ritual of pouring out all the accumulated poisons of the mind.

I peered back at him over my head. He looked tired, and flabby, and somehow he reminded me of Matt sitting on his barber's chair waiting for customers. I told Strauss of the association and he nodded and waited.

"*Are* you waiting for customers?" I asked. "You ought to have this couch designed like a barber's chair. Then when you want free association, you could stretch your patient out the way the barber does to lather up his customer, and when the fifty minutes are up, you could tilt the chair forward again and hand him a mirror so he can see what he looks like on the outside after you've shaved his ego."

He said nothing, and while I felt ashamed at the way I was abusing him, I couldn't stop. "Then your patient could come in at each session and say, 'A little off the top of my anxiety, please,' or 'Don't trim the super-ego too close, if you don't mind,' or he might even come in for an egg shampoo—I mean, *ego shampoo*. Aha! Did you notice that slip of the tongue, doctor? Make a note of it. I said I wanted an *egg shampoo* instead of an *ego shampoo*. Egg . . . ego . . . close, aren't they? Does that mean I want to be washed clean of my sins? Reborn? Is it baptism symbolism? Or are we shaving too close? Does an *idiot* have an *id*?"

I waited for a reaction, but he just shifted in his chair.

"Are you awake?" I asked.

"I'm listening, Charlie."

"Only listening? Don't you ever get angry?"

"Why do you want me to be angry with you?"

I sighed. "Stolid Strauss—unmovable. I'll tell you something. I'm sick and tired of coming here. What's the sense of therapy any more? You know as well as I do what's going to happen."

"But I think you don't want to stop," he said. "You want to go on with it, don't you?"

"It's stupid. A waste of my time and yours."

I lay there in the dim light and stared at the pattern of squares on the ceiling . . . noise-absorbing tiles with thousands of tiny holes soaking up every word. Sound buried alive in little holes in the ceiling.

I found myself becoming lightheaded. My mind was a blank, and that was unusual because during therapy sessions I always had a great deal of material to bring out

and talk about. Dreams . . . memories . . . associations
. . . problems . . . But now I felt isolated and empty.

Only Stolid Strauss breathing behind me.

"I feel strange," I said.

"You want to talk about it?"

Oh, how brilliant, how subtle he was! What the hell
was I doing there anyway, having my associations absorbed by little holes in the ceiling and big holes in my
therapist?

"I don't know if I want to talk about it," I said. "I feel
unusually hostile toward you today." And then I told him
what I had been thinking.

Without seeing him, I could tell he was nodding to
himself.

"It's hard to explain," I said. "A feeling I've had once
or twice before, just before I fainted. A lightheadedness
. . . everything intense . . . but my body feels cold and
numb . . ."

"Go on." His voice had an edge of excitement. "What
else?"

"I can't feel my body any more. I'm numb. I have the
feeling that Charlie is close by. My eyes are open—I'm
sure of that—are they?"

"Yes, wide open."

"And yet I see a blue-white glow from the walls and
the ceiling gathering into a shimmering ball. Now it's
suspended in midair. Light . . . forcing itself into my eyes
. . . and my brain . . . Everything in the room is aglow
. . . I have the feeling of floating . . . or rather *expanding* up and out . . . and yet without looking down I
know my body is still here on the couch. . . ."

Is this a hallucination?

"Charlie, are you all right?"

Or the things described by the mystics?

I hear his voice but I don't want to answer him. It annoys me that he is there. I've got to ignore him. Be passive and let this—whatever it is—fill me with the light
and absorb me into itself.

"What do you see, Charlie? What's the matter?"

* * *

Upward, moving, like a leaf in an upcurrent of warm
196

air. Speeding, the atoms of my body hurtling away from each other. I grow lighter, less dense, and larger . . . larger . . . exploding outward into the sun. I am an expanding universe swimming upward in a silent sea. Small at first, encompassing with my body, the room, the building, the city, the country, until I know that if I look down I will see my shadow blotting out the earth.

Light and unfeeling. Drifting and expanding through time and space.

And then, as I know I am about to pierce the crust of existence, like a flying fish leaping out of the sea, I feel the pull from below.

It annoys me. I want to shake it off. On the verge of blending with the universe I hear the whispers around the ridges of consciousness. And that ever-so-slight tug holds me to the finite and mortal world below.

Slowly, as waves recede, my expanding spirit shrinks back into earthly dimensions—not voluntarily, because I would prefer to lose myself, but I am pulled from below, back to myself, into myself, so that for just one moment I am on the couch again, fitting the fingers of my awareness into the glove of my flesh. And I know I can move this finger or wink that eye—if I want to. But I don't want to move. I will not move!

I wait, and leave myself open, passive, to whatever this experience means. Charlie doesn't want me to pierce the upper curtain of the mind. Charlie doesn't want to know what lies beyond.

Does he fear seeing God?

Or seeing nothing?

As I lie here waiting, the moment passes during which I *am* myself *in* myself, and again I lose all feeling of body or sensation. Charlie is drawing me down into myself. I stare inward in the center of my unseeing eye at the red spot that transforms itself into a multipetaled flower—the shimmering, swirling, luminescent flower that lies deep in the core of my unconscious.

I am shrinking. Not in the sense of the atoms of my body becoming closer and more dense, but a fusion—as the atoms of my-*self* merge into microcosm. There will be great heat and unbearable light—the hell within hell—but I don't look at the light, only at the flower, *un*multiplying, *un*dividing itself back from the many toward one. And for an instant the shimmering flower turns into the golden disk twirling on a string, and then to the bubble of swirling rainbows, and finally I am back in the cave where everything is quiet and dark and I swim the wet labyrinth searching for one to receive me . . . embrace me . . . absorb me . . . into *it*self.

That I may begin.

In the core I see the light again, an opening in the darkest of caves, now tiny and far away—through the wrong end of a telescope—brilliant, blinding, shimmering, and once again the multipetaled flower (swirling lotus—that floats near the entrance of the unconscious). At the entrance of that cave I will find the answer, if I dare go back and plunge through it into the grotto of light beyond.

Not yet!

I am afraid. Not of life, or death, or nothingness, but of wasting it as if I had never been. And as I start through the opening, I feel the pressure around me, propelling me in violent wavelike motions toward the mouth of the cave.

It's too small! I can't get through!

And suddenly I am hurled against the walls, again and again, and forced through the opening where the light threatens to burst my eyes. Again, I know I will pierce the crust into that holy light. More than I can bear. Pain as I have never known, and coldness, and nausea, and the great buzzing over my head flapping like a thousand wings. I open my eyes, blinded by the intense light. And flail the air and tremble and scream.

* * *

I came out of it at the insistence of a hand shaking me roughly. Dr. Strauss.

"Thank God," he said, when I looked into his eyes. "You had me worried."

I shook my head. "I'm all right."

"I think maybe that's all for today."

I got up and swayed as I regained my perspective. The room seemed very small. "Not only for today," I said. "I don't think I should have any more sessions. I don't want to see any more."

He was upset, but he didn't try to talk me out of it. I took my hat and coat and left.

And now—Plato's words mock me in the shadows on the ledge behind the flames:

". . . the men of the cave would say of him that up he went and down he came without his eyes. . . ."

October 5—Sitting down to type these reports is difficult, and I can't think with the tape recorder going. I keep putting it off for most of the day, but I know how important it is, and I've got to do it. I've told myself I won't have dinner until I sit down and write something—anything.

Professor Nemur sent for me again this morning. He wanted me at the lab for some tests, the kind I used to do. At first I figured it was only right, because they're still paying me, and it's important to have the record complete, but when I got down to Beekman and went through it all with Burt, I knew it would be too much for me.

First it was the paper and pencil maze. I remembered how it was before when I learned to do it quickly, and when I raced against Algernon. I could tell it was taking me a lot longer to solve the maze now. Burt had his hand out to take the paper, but I tore it up instead and threw the pieces into the waste basket.

"No more. I'm through running the maze. I'm in a blind alley now, and that's all there is to it."

He was afraid I'd run out, so he calmed me down. "That's all right, Charlie. Just take it easy."

"What do you mean 'take it easy'? You don't know what it's like."

"No, but I can imagine. We all feel pretty sick about it."

"Keep your sympathy. Just leave me alone."

He was embarrassed, and then I realized it wasn't his fault, and I was being lousy toward him. "Sorry I blew up," I said. "How's everything going? Got your thesis finished yet?"

He nodded. "Having it retyped now. I'll get my Ph.D. in February."

"Good boy." I slapped him on the shoulder to show him I wasn't angry with him. "Keep plugging. Nothing like an education. Look, forget what I said before. I'll do anything else you want. Just no more mazes—that's all."

"Well, Nemur wants a Rorschach check."

"To see what's happening down deep? What does he expect to find?"

I must have looked upset, because he started to back off. "We don't have to. You're here voluntarily. If you don't want to—"

"That's all right. Go ahead. Deal out the cards. But don't tell me what you find out."

He didn't have to.

I knew enough about the Rorschach to know that it wasn't what you saw in the cards that counted, but how you reacted to them. As wholes, or parts, with movement or just motionless figures, with special attention to the color spots or ignoring them, with lots of ideas or just a few stereotyped responses.

"It's not valid," I said. "I know what you're looking for. I know the kind of responses I'm supposed to have, to create a certain picture of what my mind is like. All I've got to do is . . ."

He looked up at me, waiting.

"All I've got to do is . . ."

But then it hit me like a fist against the side of my head that I didn't remember what I had to do. It was as if I had been looking at the whole thing clearly on the blackboard of my mind, but when I turned to read it, part of it had been erased and the rest didn't make sense.

At first, I refused to believe it. I went through the cards in a panic, so fast that I was choking on my words. I wanted to tear the inkblots apart to make them reveal themselves. Somewhere in those inkblots there were answers I had known just a little while ago. Not really in the inkblots, but in the part of my mind that would give form and meaning to them and project my imprint on them.

And I couldn't do it. I couldn't remember what I had to say. All missing.

"That's a woman . . ." I said, ". . . on her knees washing the floors. I mean—no—it's a man holding a knife." And even as I said it, I knew what I was saying and I switched away and started off in another direction. "Two figures tugging at something . . . like a doll . . . and each one is pulling so it looks as if they're going to

200

tear it apart and—no!— I mean it's two faces staring at each other through the window, and—"

I swept the cards off the table and got up.

"No more tests. I don't want to take any more tests."

"All right, Charlie. We'll stop for today."

"Not just for today. I'm not coming back here any more. Whatever there is left in me that you need, you can get from the progress reports. I'm through running the maze. I'm not a guinea pig any more. I've done enough. I want to be left alone now."

"All right, Charlie. I understand."

"No, you don't understand because it isn't happening to you, and no one can understand but me. I don't blame you. You've got your job to do, and your Ph.D. to get, and—oh, yes, don't tell me, I know you're in this largely out of love of humanity, but still you've got your life to live and we don't happen to belong on the same level. I passed your floor on the way up, and now I'm passing it on the way down, and I don't think I'll be taking this elevator again. So let's just say good-bye here and now."

"Don't you think you should talk to Dr.—"

"Say good-bye to everyone for me, will you? I don't feel like facing any of them again."

Before he could say any more or try to stop me, I was out of the lab, and I caught the elevator down and out of Beekman for the last time.

October 7—Strauss tried to see me again this morning, but I wouldn't open the door. I want to be left to myself now.

It's a strange sensation to pick up a book you read and enjoyed just a few months ago and discover you don't remember it. I recall how wonderful I thought Milton was. When I picked up *Paradise Lost* I could only remember it was about Adam and Eve and the Tree of Knowledge, but now I couldn't make sense of it.

I stood up and closed my eyes and saw Charlie—myself—six or seven years old, sitting at the dinner table with a schoolbook, learning to read, saying the words over and over with my mother sitting beside him, beside me . . .

"Try it again."

"See Jack. See Jack run. See Jack see."

"No! Not *See* Jack *see!* It's *Run* Jack *run!*" Pointing with her rough-scrubbed finger.

"See Jack. See Jack run. Run Jack see."

"No! You're not trying. Do it again!"

Do it again . . . do it again . . . do it again . . .

"Leave the boy alone. You've got him terrified."

"He's got to learn. He's too lazy to concentrate."

*Run Jack run . . . run Jack run . . . run Jack run
. . . run Jack run . . .*

"He's slower than the other children. Give him time."

"He's normal. There's nothing wrong with him. Just lazy. I'll beat it into him until he learns."

*Run Jack run . . . run Jack run . . . run Jack run
. . . run Jack run . . .*

And then looking up from the table, it seems to me I saw myself, through Charlie's eyes, holding *Paradise Lost,* and I realized I was breaking the binding with the pressure of both hands as if I wanted to tear the book in half. I broke the back of it, ripped out a handful of pages, and flung them and the book across the room to the corner where the broken records were. I let it lay there and its torn white tongues were laughing because I couldn't understand what they were saying.

I've got to try to hold onto some of the things I've learned. Please, God, don't take it all away.

October 10—Usually at night I go out for walks, wander around the city. I don't know why. To see faces, I guess. Last night I couldn't remember where I lived. A policeman took me home. I have the strange feeling that this has all happened to me before—a long time ago. I don't want to write it down, but I keep reminding myself that I'm the only one in the world who can describe what happens when it goes this way.

Instead of walking I was floating through space, not clear and sharp, but with a gray film over everything. I know what's happening to me, but there is nothing I can do about it. I walk, or just stand on the sidewalk and watch people go by. Some of them look at me, and some of them don't but nobody says anything to me—except one night a man came up and asked if I wanted a girl. He

202

took me to a place. He wanted ten dollars first and I gave it to him, but he never came back.

And then I remembered what a fool I was.

October 11—When I came into my apartment this morning, I found Alice there, asleep on the couch. Everything was cleaned up, and at first I thought I was in the wrong apartment, but then I saw she hadn't touched the smashed records or the torn books or the sheet music in the corner of the room. The floor creaked and she woke up and looked at me.

"Hi," she laughed. "Some night owl."

"Not an owl. More of a dodo. A dumb dodo. How'd you get in here?"

"Through the fire escape. Fay's place. I called her to find out about you and she said she was worried. She says you've been acting strangely—causing disturbances. So, I decided it was time for me to put in an appearance. I straightened up a bit. I didn't think you'd mind."

"I do mind . . . very much. I don't want anybody coming around feeling sorry for me."

She went to the mirror to comb her hair. "I'm not here because I feel sorry for you. It's because I feel sorry for me."

"What's that supposed to mean?"

"It doesn't mean," she shrugged. "It just is—like a poem. I wanted to see you."

"What's wrong with the zoo?"

"Oh, come off it, Charlie. Don't fence with me. I waited long enough for you to come and get me. I decided to come to you."

"Why?"

"Because there's still time. And I want to spend it with you."

"Is that a song?"

"Charlie, don't laugh at me."

"I'm not laughing. But I can't afford to spend my time with anyone—there's only enough left for myself."

"I can't believe you want to be completely alone."

"I do."

"We had a little time together before we got out of touch. We had things to talk about, and things to do together. It didn't last very long but it was something. Look, we've known this might happen. It was no secret. I didn't go away, Charlie, I've just been waiting. You're about at my level again, aren't you?"

I stormed around the apartment. "But that's crazy. There's nothing to look forward to. I don't dare let myself think ahead—only back. In a few months, weeks, days—who the hell knows?—I'll go back to Warren. You can't follow me there."

"No," she admitted, "and I probably won't even visit you there. Once you're in Warren I'll do my best to forget you. I'm not going to pretend otherwise. But until you go, there's no reason for either of us to be alone."

Before I could say anything, she kissed me. I waited, as she sat beside me on the couch, resting her head against my chest, but the panic didn't come. Alice was a woman, but perhaps now Charlie would understand that she wasn't his mother or his sister.

With the relief of knowing I had passed through a crisis, I sighed because there was nothing to hold me back. It was no time for fear or pretense, because it could never be this way with anyone else. All the barriers were gone. I had unwound the string she had given me, and found my way out of the labyrinth to where she was waiting. I loved her with more than my body.

I don't pretend to understand the mystery of love, but this time it was more than sex, more than using a woman's body. It was being lifted off the earth, outside fear and torment, being part of something greater than myself. I was lifted out of the dark cell of my own mind, to become part of someone else—just as I had experienced it that day on the couch in therapy. It was the first step outward to the universe—beyond the universe—because in it and with it we merged to recreate and perpetuate the human spirit. Expanding and bursting outward, and contracting and forming inward, it was the rhythm of being—of breathing, of heartbeat, of day and night—and the rhythm of our bodies set off an echo in my mind. It was the way it had been back there in that strange vision. The gray murk lifted from my mind, and through it the light pierced into my brain (how strange that light should blind!), and my body was absorbed back into a great sea of space, washed under in a strange baptism. My body shuddered with giving, and her body shuddered its acceptance.

This was the way we loved, until the night became a silent day. And as I lay there with her I could see how important physical love was, how necessary it was for us to be in each other's arms, giving and taking. The universe was exploding, each particle away from the next, hurtling us into dark and lonely space, eternally tearing us away from each other—child out of the womb, friend away from friend, moving from each other, each through his own pathway toward the goal-box of solitary death.

But this was the counterweight, the act of binding and holding. As when men to keep from being swept overboard in the storm clutch at each other's hands to resist being torn apart, so our bodies fused a link in the human chain that kept us from being swept into nothing.

And in the moment before I fell off into sleep, I remembered the way it had been between Fay and myself, and I smiled. No wonder that had been easy. It had been only physical. This with Alice was a mystery.

I leaned over and kissed her eyes.

Alice knows everything about me now, and accepts the fact that we can be together for only a short while. She has agreed to go away when I tell her to go. It's painful to think about that, but what we have, I suspect, is more than most people find in a lifetime.

October 14—I wake up in the morning and don't know where I am or what I'm doing here, and then I see her beside me and I remember. She senses when something is happening to me, and she moves quietly around the apartment, making breakfast, cleaning up the place, or going out and leaving me to myself, without any questions.

We went to a concert this evening, but I got bored and we left in the middle. Can't seem to pay much attention any more. I went because I know I used to like Stravinsky but somehow I no longer have the patience for it.

The only bad thing about having Alice here with me is that now I feel I should fight this thing. I want to stop time, freeze myself at this level and never let go of her.

October 17—Why can't I remember? I've got to try to

resist this slackness. Alice tells me I lie in bed for days and don't seem to know who or where I am. Then it all comes back and I recognize her and remember what's happening. Fugues of amnesia. Symptoms of second childhood—what do they call it?—senility? I can watch it coming on.

All so cruelly logical, the result of speeding up all the processes of the mind. I learned so much so fast, and now my mind is deteriorating rapidly. What if I won't let it happen? What if I fight it? Think of those people at Warren, the empty smiles, the blank expressions, everyone laughing at them.

Little Charlie Gordon staring at me through the window—waiting. Please, not that again.

October 18—I'm forgetting things I learned recently. It seems to be following the classic pattern, the last things learned are first things forgotten. Or is that the pattern? Better look it up again.

Reread my paper on the *Algernon-Gordon Effect* and even though I know I wrote it, I keep feeling it was written by someone else. Most of it I don't even understand.

But why am I so irritable? Especially when Alice is so good to me? She keeps the place neat and clean, always putting my things away and washing dishes and scrubbing floors. I shouldn't have shouted at her the way I did this morning because it made her cry, and I didn't want that to happen. But she shouldn't have picked up the broken records and the music and the book and put them all neatly into a box. That made me furious. I don't want anyone to touch any of those things. I want to see them pile up. I want them to remind me of what I'm leaving behind. I kicked the box and scattered the stuff all over the floor and told her to leave them just where they were.

Foolish. No reason for it. I guess I got sore because I knew she thought it was silly to keep those things, and she didn't tell me she thought it was silly. She just pretended it was perfectly normal. She's humoring me. And when I saw that box I remembered the boy at Warren and the lousy lamp he made and the way we were all humoring him, pretending he had done something wonderful when he hadn't.

That was what she was doing to me, and I couldn't stand it.

When she went to the bedroom and cried I felt bad about it and I told her it was all my fault. I don't deserve someone as good as her. Why can't I control myself just enough to keep on loving her? Just enough.

October 19—Motor activity impaired. I keep tripping and dropping things. At first I didn't think it was me. I thought she was changing things around. The wastebasket was in my way, and so were the chairs, and I thought she had moved them.

Now I realize my coordination is bad. I have to move slowly to get things right. And it's increasingly difficult to type. Why do I keep blaming Alice? And why doesn't she argue? That irritates me even more because I see the pity in her face.

My only pleasure now is the TV set. I spend most of the day watching the quiz programs, the old movies, the soap operas, and even the kiddie shows and cartoons. And then I can't bring myself to turn it off. Late at night there are the old movies, the horror pictures, the late show, and the late-late show, and even the little sermon before the channel signs off for the night, and the "Star-Spangled Banner" with the flag waving in the background, and finally the channel test pattern that stares back at me through the little square window with its unclosing eye. . . .

Why am I always looking at life through a window?

And after it's all over I'm sick with myself because there is so little time left for me to read and write and think, and because I should know better than to drug my mind with this dishonest stuff that's aimed at the child in me. Especially me, because the child in me is reclaiming my mind.

I know all this, but when Alice tells me I shouldn't waste my time, I get angry and tell her to leave me alone.

I have a feeling I'm watching because it's important for me not to think, not to remember about the bakery, and my mother and father, and Norma. I don't want to remember any more of the past.

I had a terrible shock today. Picked up a copy of an article I had used in my research, Krueger's *Über Psy-*

chische Ganzheit, to see if it would help me understand the paper I wrote and what I had done in it. First I thought there was something wrong with my eyes. Then I realized I could no longer read German. Tested myself in other languages. All gone.

October 21—Alice is gone. Let's see if I can remember. It started when she said we couldn't live like this with the torn books and papers and records all over the floor and the place in such a mess.

"Leave everything the way it is," I warned her.

"Why do you want to live this way?"

"I want everything where I put it. I want to see it all out here. You don't know what it's like to have something happening inside you, that you can't see and can't control, and know it's all slipping through your fingers."

"You're right. I never said I could understand the things that were happening to you. Not when you became too intelligent for me, and not now. But I'll tell you one thing. Before you had the operation, you weren't like this. You didn't wallow in your own filth and self-pity, you didn't pollute your own mind by sitting in front of the TV set all day and night, you didn't snarl and snap at people. There was something about you that made us respect you—yes, even as you were. You had something I had never seen in a retarded person before."

"I don't regret the experiment."

"Neither do I, but you've lost something you had before. You had a smile . . ."

"An empty, stupid smile."

"No, a warm, real smile, because you wanted people to like you."

"And they played tricks on me, and laughed at me."

"Yes, but even though you didn't understand why they were laughing, you sensed that if they could laugh at you they would like you. And you wanted them to like you. You acted like a child and you even laughed at yourself along with them."

"I don't feel like laughing at myself right now, if you don't mind."

She was trying to keep from crying. I think I wanted to make her cry. "Maybe that's why it was so important for me to learn. I thought it would make people like me. I thought I would have friends. That's something to laugh at, isn't it?"

"There's more to it than just having a high I.Q."

That made me angry. Probably because I didn't really understand what she was driving at. More and more these days she didn't come right out and say what she meant. She hinted at things. She talked around them and expected me to know what she was thinking. And I listened, pretending I understood but inside I was afraid she would see that I missed the point completely."

"I think it's time for you to leave."

Her face turned red. "Not yet, Charlie. It's not time yet. Don't send me away."

"You're making it harder for me. You keep pretending I can do things and understand things that are far beyond me now. You're pushing me. Just like my mother . . ."

"That's not true!"

"Everything you do says it. The way you pick up and clean up after me, the way you leave books around that you think will get me interested in reading again, the way you talk to me about the news to get me thinking. You say it doesn't matter, but everything you do shows how much it matters. Always the schoolteacher. I don't want to go to concerts or museums or foreign films or do anything that's going to make me struggle to think about life or about myself."

"Charlie—"

"Just leave me alone. I'm not myself. I'm falling apart, and I don't want you here."

That made her cry. This afternoon she packed her bags and left. The apartment feels quiet and empty now.

October 25—Deterioration progressing. I've given up using the typewriter. Coordination is too bad. From now on I'll have to write out these reports in longhand.

I thought a lot about the things Alice said, and then it hit me that if I kept on reading and learning *new* things, even while I was forgetting the old ones, I would be able to keep some of my intelligence. I was on a down escalator now. If I stood still I'd go all the way to the bottom, but if I started to run up maybe I could at least stay in the same place. The important thing was to keep moving upward no matter what happened.

So I went to the library and got out a lot of books to read. I've been reading a lot now. Most of the books are too hard for me, but I don't care. As long as I keep reading I'll learn new things and I won't forget how to read. That's the most important thing. If I keep reading, maybe I can hold my own.

Dr. Strauss came around the day after Alice left, so I guess she told him about me. He pretended all he wanted was the progress reports but I told him I would send them. I don't want him coming around here. I told him he doesn't have to be worried about me because when I think I won't be able to take care of myself any more I'll get on a train and go to Warren.

I told him I'd rather just go by myself when the time comes.

I tried to talk to Fay, but I can see she's afraid of me. I guess she figures I've gone out of my mind. Last night she came home with somebody—he looked very young.

This morning the landlady, Mrs. Mooney, came up with a bowl of hot chicken soup and some chicken. She said she just thought she would look in on me to see if I was doing all right. I told her I had lots of food to eat but she left it anyway and it was good. She pretended she was doing it on her own but I'm not that stupid yet. Alice or Strauss must have told her to look in on me and make sure I was all right. Well, that's okay. She's a nice old lady with an Irish accent and she likes to talk all about the people in the building. When she saw the mess on the floor inside my apartment she didn't say anything about it. I guess she's all right.

November 1—A week since I dared to write again. I don't know where the time goes. Todays Sunday I know because I can see through my window the people going into the church across the street. I think I laid in bed all week but I remember Mrs. Mooney bringing me food a few times and asking if I was sick.

What am I going to do with myself? I cant just hang around here all alone and look out the window. Ive got to get hold of myself. I keep saying over and over that Ive got to do something but then I forget or maybe its just easier not to do what I say Im going to do.

I still have some books from the library but a lot of

them are too hard for me. I read a lot of mystery stories now and books about kings and queens from old times. I read a book about a man who thought he was a knight and went out on an old horse with his friend. But no matter what he did he always ended up getting beaten and hurt. Like when he thought the windmills were dragons. At first I thought it was a silly book because if he wasnt crazy he could see that windmills werent dragons and there is no such thing as sorcerers and enchanted castles but then I rememberd that there was something else it was all supposed to mean—something the story didnt say but only hinted at. Like there was other meanings. But I dont know what. That made me angry because I think I used to know. But Im keeping up with my reading and learning new things every day and I know its going to help me.

I know I should have written some progress reports before this so they will know whats happening to me. But writing is harder. I have to look up even simple words in the dictionary now and it makes me angry with myself.

November 2—I forgot to write in yesterdays report about the woman from the building across the alley one floor down. I saw her through my kitchen window last week. I dont know her name, or even what her top part looks like but every night about eleven oclock she goes into her bathroom to take a bath. She never pulls her shade down and thru my window when I put out my lights I can see her from the neck down when she comes out of the bath to dry herself.

It makes me excited, but when the lady turns out the light I feel let down and lonely. I wish I could see what she looks like sometimes, whether shes pretty or what. I know its not nice to watch a woman when shes like that but I cant help it. Anyway what difference does it make to her if she doesnt know Im watching.

Its nearly eleven oclock now. Time for her bath. So Id better go see . . .

Nov 5—Mrs Mooney is very worried about me. She says the way I lay around all day and dont do anything I remind her of her son before she threw him out of the house. She said she dont like loafters. If Im sick its one thing but if Im a loafter thats another thing and she has no use for me. I told her I think Im sick.

I try to read a little bit every day mostly stories but sometimes I have to read the same thing over and over again because I dont know what it means. And its hard to write. I know I should look up all the words in the dictionary but Im so tired all the time.

Then I got the idea that I would only use the easy words instead of the long hard ones. That saves time. Its getting chilly out but I still put flowers on Algernons grave. Mrs Mooney thinks Im silly to put flowers on a mouses grave but I told her that Algernon was a special mouse.

I went over to visit Fay across the hall. But she told me to go away and not come back. She put a new lock on her door.

Nov 9—Sunday again. I dont have anything to do to keep me busy now because the TV is broke and I keep forgetting to get it fixed. I think I lost this months check from the college. I dont remember.

I get awful headaches and asperin doesnt help much. Mrs. Mooney believes now that Im really sick and she feels very sory for me. She's a wonderful woman whenever someone is sick. Its getting so cold out now that Ive got to wear two sweaters.

The lady across the way pulls down her windowshade now, so I can't watch any more. My lousy luck.

Nov 10—Mrs Mooney called a strange doctor to see me. She was afraid I was going to die. I told the doctor I wasnt to sick and that I only forget sometimes. He asked me did I have any friends or relatives and I said no I dont have any. I told him I had a friend called Algernon once but he was a mouse and we use to run races together. He looked at me kind of funny like he thot I was crazy.

He smiled when I told him I use to be a genius. He talked to me like I was a baby and he winked at Mrs Mooney. I got mad because he was making fun of me and laughing and I chased him out and locked the door.

I think I know why I been haveing bad luck. Because I

lost my rabits foot and my horshoe. I got to get another rabits foot fast.

Nov 11—Dr Strauss came to the door today and Alice to but I didnt let them come in. I told them I didnt want anyone to see me. I want to be left alone. Later Mrs Mooney came up with some food and she told me they paid the rent and left money for her to buy food and anything I need. I told her I dont want to use there money any more. She said moneys money and someone has to pay or I have to put you out. Then she said why dont I get some job instead of just hanging around.

I dont know any work but the job I use to do at the bakery. I dont want to go back their because they all knew me when I was smart and maybe theyll laff at me. But I dont know what else to do to get money. And I want to pay for everything myself. I am strong and I can werk. If I cant take care of myself Ill go to Warren. I wont take charety from anybody.

Nov 15—I was looking at some of my old progress reports and its very strange but I cant read what I wrote. I can make out some of the words but they dont make sense. I think I wrote them but I dont remember so good. I get tired very fast when I try to read some of the books I baught in the drugstore. Exept the ones with the picturs of the pretty girls. I like to look at them but I have funny dreams about them. Its not nice. I wont buy them any more. I saw in one of those books they got magic powder that can make you strong and smart and do lots of things. I think mayby Ill send away and by some for myself.

Nov 16—Alice came to the door again but I said go away I dont want to see you. She cryed and I cryed to but I woudnt let her in because I didnt want her to laff at me. I told her I didnt like her any more and I didnt want to be smart any more either. Thats not true but. I still love her and I still want to be smart but I had to say that so she woud go away. Mrs Mooney told me Alice brout some more money to look after me and for the rent. I dont want that. I got to get a job.

Please . . . please . . . dont let me forget how to reed and rite . . .

Nov 18—Mr Donner was very nice when I came back and askd him for my old job at the bakery. Frist he was very suspicius but I told him what happened to me and then he looked very sad and put his hand on my shoulder and said Charlie you got guts.

Evrybody looked at me when I came downstairs and started working in the toilet sweeping it out like I use to do. I said to myself Charlie if they make fun of you dont get sore because you remember their not so smart like you once thot they were. And besides they were once your frends and if they laffed at you that dont mean anything because they liked you to.

One of the new men who came to werk their after I went away his name is Meyer Klaus did a bad thing to me. He came up to me when I was loading the sacks of flower and he said hey Charlie I hear your a very smart fella—a real quiz kid. Say something inteligent. I felt bad because I could tell by the way he said it he was making fun of me. So I kept on with my werk. But then he came over and grabed me by the arm real hard and shouted at me. When I talk to you boy you better listen to me. Or I coud brake your arm for you. He twisted my arm so it hurt and I got scared he was going to brake it like he said. And he was laffing and twisting it, and I didnt know what to do. I got so afraid I felt like I was gonna cry but I didnt and then I had to go to the bathroom something awful. My stomack was all twisting inside like I was gonna bust open if I didnt go right away . . . because I couldnt hold it back.

I told him please let me go because I got to go to the toilet but he was just laffing at me and I dint know what to do. So I started crying. Let me go. Let me go. And then I made. It went in my pants and it smelled bad and I was crying. He let go of me then and made a sick face and he looked scared then. He said For gods sake I didnt mean anything Charlie.

But then Joe Carp came in and grabbed Klaus by the shirt and said leave him alone you lousy bastard or Ill brake your neck. Charlie is a good guy and nobodys gonna start up with him without answering for it. I felt ashamed and I ran to the toilet to clean myself and change my cloths.

When I got back Frank was there to and Joe was telling him about it and then Gimpy came in and they told him about it and he said theyd get rid of Klaus. They were gonna tell Mr Donner to fire him. I told them I dint think he should be fired and have to find another job because he had a wife and a kid. And besides he said he was sorry for what he did to me. And I remember how sad I was when I had to get fired from the bakery and go away. I said Klaus shoud get a second chance because now he wouldnt do anything bad to me anymore.

Later Gimpy came over limping on his bad foot and he said Charlie if anyone bothers you or trys to take advantage you call me or Joe or Frank and we will set him strait. We all want you to remember that you got frends here and dont you ever forget it. I said thanks Gimpy. That makes me feel good.

Its good to have frends . . .

nov 21—I did a dumb thing today I forgot I wasnt in Miss Kinnians class at the adult center any more like I use to be. I went in and sat down in my old seat in the back of the room and she lookd at me funny and she said Charlie where have you been. So I said hello Miss Kinnian Im redy for my lessen today only I lossed the book we was using.

She started to cry and run out of the room and everbody looked at me and I saw alot of them wasnt the same pepul who use to be in my class.

Then all of a suddin I remembered some things about the operashun and me getting smart and I said holy smoke I reely pulled a Charlie Gordon that time. I went away before she came back to the room.

Thats why Im going away from here for good to the Warren Home school. I dont want to do nothing like that agen. I dont want Miss Kinnian to feel sorry for me. I know evrybody feels sorry for me at the bakery and I dont want that eather so Im going someplace where they are a lot of other pepul like me and nobody cares that Charlie Gordon was once a genus and now he cant even reed a book or rite good.

Im taking a cuple of books along and even if I cant reed them Ill practise hard and mabye Ill even get a littel bit smarter then I was before the operashun without an operashun. I got a new rabits foot and a luky penny and even a littel bit of that majic powder left and mabye they will help me.

If you ever reed this Miss Kinnian dont be sorry for me. Im glad I got a second chanse in life like you said to be smart because I lerned alot of things that I never even new were in this werld and Im grateful I saw it all even for a littel bit. And Im glad I found out all about my family and me. It was like I never had a family til I remembird about them and saw them and now I know I had a family and I was a person just like evryone.

I dont no why Im dumb agen or what I did rong. Mabye its because I dint try hard enuf or just some body put the evel eye on me. But if I try and practis very hard mabye Ill get a littel smarter and no what all the words are. I remembir a littel bit how nice I had a feeling with the blue book that I red with the toren cover. And when I close my eyes I think about the man who tored the book and he looks like me only he looks different and he talks different but I dont think its me because its like I see him from the window.

Anyway thats why Im gone to keep trying to get smart so I can have that feeling agen. Its good to no things and be smart and I wish I new evrything in the hole world. I wish I coud be smart agen rite now. If I coud I woud sit down and reed all the time.

Anyway I bet Im the frist dumb persen in the world who found out some thing inportent for sience. I did somthing but I dont remembir what. So I gess its like I did it for all the dumb pepul like me in Warren and all over the world.

Goodby Miss Kinnian and dr Strauss and evrybody . . .

P.S. please tel prof Nemur not to be such a grouch when pepul laff at him and he woud have more frends. Its easy to have frends if you let pepul laff at you. Im going to have lots of frends where I go.

P.S. please if you get a chanse put some flowrs on Algernons grave in the bak yard.

ABOUT THE AUTHOR

DANIEL KEYES was born in Brooklyn and received his B.A. and M.A. degrees from Brooklyn College. He has been a merchant seaman, ship's purser, fiction editor and high school teacher. At the present time, Mr. Keyes is on the English faculty at Ohio University in Athens, Ohio.

Flowers for Algernon made its first appearance as a magazine story in 1960 and won the Hugo award that year for the best science novelette. It was then a television drama, is here enlarged to novel length, and is also the basis for a motion picture.

Mr. Keyes is the author of a second novel, *The Touch*, and of the nonfiction book, *The Minds of Billy Milligan.*

BANTAM
SHOP·AT·HOME
C·A·T·A·L·O·G

Special Offer
Buy a Bantam Book
for only 50¢.

Now you can have Bantam's catalog filled with hundreds of titles plus take advantage of our unique and exciting bonus book offer. A special offer which gives you the opportunity to purchase a Bantam book for only 50¢. Here's how!

By ordering any five books at the regular price per order, you can also choose any other single book listed (up to a $4.95 value) for just 50¢. Some restrictions do apply, but for further details why not send for Bantam's catalog of titles today!

Just send us your name and address and we will send you a catalog!